Sometimes the Darkness

Will Campbell

Clink
Street

London | New York

This book is dedicated to my wife Tresa Davis-Weir

I would like to thank the author Kathie Giorgio, founder of the All Writer's Workplace & Workshop for her help in the development of my book. Without her guidance, this work would not have happened.

After Kosti

Her prayer was answered, but the language of answered prayers is God's language. The nun had failed to understand God's message. Much had been gained, but much had been lost.

The plane, the tool she had hoped God would send, shook relentlessly, the children screamed and cried as the nun's shoes slid off the pedals. Sister Marie Claire brought them back to the worn metal once more. Pushing as hard as she could, the nun applied the brakes while Hanley kept the plane on the roadway. Thirty seconds after touchdown the plane rolled to a stop. Hanley cut the ignition, silencing the roar and thrum of the big engines and slumped over, his wounded body failing faster now. Struggling out of her seat, the nun slowly pulled him upright. Taking water from a bottle, she splashed his face and patted it while saying, "Hanley, wake up. I'm going to check on the children and go for help." She called out, "Aisha, are the children safe? Aisha?"

Appearing behind the nun, carrying the smallest child in her arms, Aisha told her the children were frightened, but all right. Leaving Hanley, the nun turned and led Aisha and the children from the plane, sitting all of them on the ground beneath the Beech. The morning air was now warm and the shade comfortable.

"I will go into Shambe for help. You will stay with the children right here. Do not leave or let any of the children leave.

If someone comes near you, put the children back on the plane and close the door. Wait here until I return. Do you understand?"

Aisha nodded and the nun immediately turned toward the village and started off at a trot. The girl watched until the nun was perhaps three hundred yards down the dirt track, then turned, counted the children, told them to stay where they were and entered the plane.

Moving to the cockpit, she looked at Hanley, who was unconscious, his head again resting against the window frame, his mouth open, his breathing a shallow wheeze, his body shivering. A thin line of blood dripped from his brow staining his shirt sleeve. Turning, she took a blanket from the floor of the cargo hold, placed it over the American, tucking it around his shoulders and arms. Putting her lips to his ear, Aisha whispered, "You did it," then returned to the children.

1

For Hanley Martin, time had become an obsession. The effect of time on his existence was maddening. An uncle, his mentor, told him years ago he would need, if he was lucky, to balance the scales, to account for any good fortune that came his way. It had and he hadn't, and now he felt time was running out.

He was fifty-one years old, felt older, was successful at business but not life. He tried to understand where that life had taken him. By all accounts he was lucky, but it was not the kind of luck that made him feel good, in fact it made him feel bad, especially of late. Years ago this feeling began to press against him, made him uncomfortable with himself. His twice daily walks with his old dog turned into self-analysis sessions used to deal with these feelings of guilt and inadequacy.

His head seemed to always ache, the strain of trying to sleep wearing on him, the pain always dull, a hammer face pressed to his forehead. The Jack and water was not helping. The effects of his drinking and thinking made his nights sleepless. It's not what he wanted, but is what he got.

He sometimes felt poor, ridiculous for a wealthy man, the founder of three aircraft industries all bearing the name Martin. He owned airplanes. But this was not about money; he was poor of spirit, an empty soul, as empty and dark as his house.

Hanley and his old Airedale Weed tried walking out his issues but only gained the exercise. He was unlucky with answers he sought, not knowing why fate had picked him and not someone else. Now he thought he knew what to do. He must take his search elsewhere.

Fate stepped in to make him believe someone actually had the answer. Chance meetings over the past year revealed a woman, a Catholic nun, who might help him. She was good at it her friends said. Hanley could use the change and the opportunity to give to others through helping a charity in need. A new acquaintance, another nun, had given him her name. He now believed this woman of God could tell him what he needed to know about his fated life. Friends and family thought he had gone over the edge, but *he* believed it. It is the answer he needed to a question he chased around for years, and that answer is with her in Africa. Now he knew where to go and how to get there. It wouldn't be easy but he welcomed it.

There was now this belief, a correctness to what he was thinking, to his plan. The indecisiveness, the concern, the weight of not knowing, had been lifted from his shoulders. Things had fallen into place. He knew who to ask. He knew where to look. She was what he needed. When he was a child, he loved to dig to the bottom of a box of cereal searching for the toy buried there. She was the prize he hoped to find.

***

Hanley fiddled with the cargo net, the fiddling a balm, a necessity, like an old woman in church working beads, keeping his mind focused on something other than the conversation he was having and his trip across the Atlantic next week. The trip would be arduous, even dangerous, but so was the conversation he was having that moment. Rocky looked good, he thought, smelled good too. Damn her, she's not playing fair; women, by nature, he believed, never played fair, but, then, how could they?

Rocky said, "I think you've become infatuated with her or fixated, whatever. You see her as your savior, almost mythical.

The mythical Sister Marie Claire. You think she'll tell you what you need to know, answer the big question. She doesn't have the answer. For years you've wondered how to pay this great, cosmic debt you owe for your luck. You don't owe anyone anything; you've earned your success. You've worked hard. There is no answer. She certainly doesn't have it. She's just a nun, that's all she is, you know. A lonely old woman living in the bush In southern Sudan. I wish you had never heard of her."

Rocky Vicenti, Hanley's next door neighbor, his widowed lover, sat on a folding chair in his large, dimly lit hanger facing him as he sat on the steps that formed the interior wall of the plane's cargo door. It was March of 2001 and unusually cold in north-central Indiana. The hanger was built to house two planes and had, before Hanley crashed one when landing at the Russiaville Airport outside of Kokomo almost six months earlier.

"She's not that old," Hanley said, trying to not so gently correct her. "She's younger than me."

With a coarse black thread as heavy as a strand of dental floss, Hanley mended a weak spot on the border of the netting, which, once fixed, would stretch across the cargo hold of his old, meticulously restore Beech C-45, the plane he would hopscotch across the Atlantic to Europe and then on to Africa.

"Elizabeth called me again yesterday, the third call this week. She's desperate you know. She thinks I have more control over you than she has. She's begging me to make you change your mind. She cries every time we talk," Rocky said, rubbing her left index finger with her right thumb. Hanley watched her as he passed the curved needle back and forth through the fabric, his finger sliding dangerously along the metal toward the point when the needle met resistance. "What did you tell her?" he asked.

"I said what I always say, 'Your father has made up his mind and no one can change it, not you or me,' that's what I told her. I wish I had something else to say to her but I don't. I wish I had something else to say to you. I've run out of things to say. Obviously 'I love you' isn't good enough," she said.

"You don't need to say that. Listen, we've been through this enough. Elizabeth think's I've lost my mind. I'm sure her mother has helped her with that decision," he said.

"I don't know what to say anymore, really I don't. You're going to go no matter what anyone says. If your uncle were still alive I'd call him to talk you out of this but he isn't and he'd probably support you in this decision. He's the one that told you to always pay your debts in this life anyway. Did he use the word karma when he told you this?"

"Please don't."

"Really? It doesn't matter. You're leaving to find another woman to help you understand life. I'm afraid you'll travel ten thousand miles to learn she can't tell you any more than I can. The trouble is, to sit at her knee or where ever you'll be sitting, it will still be in a place that can kill you. Maybe that will be enough payment for you. I'll be left to try to explain that to your daughter and granddaughter. Thanks for that." Rocky said.

***

Rocky left and now Hanley sat alone, watching an odd cocked rectangle of fall's sunlight slide across the cement, a bright oddly shaped clock, pushed by the sun's burning time, admitted through a high window to educate him-about what he wasn't sure. The window was next to the large hanger door he used to take his plane to the tarmac, then the runway, then into the sky and to wherever he wanted. Flying was an expensive hobby, the plane an expensive toy. He love things of beauty, whether a meticulously restored airplane, a finely crafted table or a watch. He love to look at his plane, the shiny skin of the Beech, polished, reflective of both his money and his love of beautiful things, a mirror of this time of his life, the image there, distinguishable but flawed, no straight lines, no hard information, connected shapes, colors, post-modernistic life imagery that everyone saw differently. But the smooth skin of a woman reflected nothing back at him. A woman was that mirror he must now look to, knowing he would never see himself looking back, his image lost time and again. Hanley considered the conversation the past few minutes, the time spent with Rocky. It had told him nothing.

***

After flying for three weeks, Hanley finally saw Africa in the distance. He could see a deeper haze, gray melting to brown, beneath which lay Egypt. The land before him was the vision he had in his head for two years. That vision would certainly not be the reality. Leaning forward, he stared hard at what he hoped would soon become familiar and yet believed would remain a mystery to him. He had given up much to be here at this moment and he still wasn't certain why.

He would enter Africa through Egypt, but his destination was Sudan.

The plane, the noise, the squawk of the air traffic controller in his ear, the vibration of two four-hundred-and-fifty horsepower Pratt and Whitney R-985 engines coming through the steering pushed their way back into his head. The big engines thrummed, pulsing, grabbing air, pulling the old Beech C-45 Expeditor toward the coast. Hanley Martin thought about what he was about to get into. He smiled slightly and said aloud, "What have you done?"

Ground haze obscured the coastline as Hanley approached Northern Africa. He began searching the coasts for landmarks. The late morning sun reflected off the blindingly polished aluminum skin of the plane's engine housings, causing glints of light to bounce around the cockpit, off the crystal of his sport wristwatch, up to the surface of his sunglasses causing him some momentary visual disorientation. The nose of plane was painted a flat black, extending up to the cockpit windows, reducing the glare of the bright sun at altitude.

The Beech cruised at one-hundred-and-seventy-five miles per hour. At eight thousand feet, Hanley could fly with his cabin unpressurized for hours at a time; enough to hop between Crete and Egypt. When distances permitted, he'd been doing that since leaving Kokomo, Indiana three weeks earlier. Hanley found flying in an unpressurized cabin less tiring, keeping him more alert.

Turbulence bounced him off the seat. He tightened his grip on the old black bowtie-shaped yoke. The Beech maintained its trim through the mild turbulent air over the Mediterranean Sea. Checking his fuel, then his manifold pressure and his air speed, he reached for the red-knobbed throttle levers and pushed them forward, reducing his speed, adjusted his flaps and started a slow descent.

Seeing the continent for the first time thrilled him more than he expected. He was in it now, he thought, pumped-up and scared at the same time. It caused his gut to tighten a bit just thinking about it. Before leaving Kokomo, Hanley spent some time talking to people who had business dealings in Africa, one man in particular that Sister Mary Kathleen put him in touch with. His name was Bobby Stein. He supplied oil companies with replacement valves and seals. Dealing primarily in Ethiopia and the Mideast, business was good for a while, but local politics caused too many problems. Bobby Stein switched his focus to the countries of the former Soviet Union. While certainly no picnic, dealing with the local Russian criminal element beat dealing with radical Muslims by a mile, he told Hanley. He rated doing business internationally at a three or four out of ten, he said. Doing some business outside America allowed him to keep his contacts in place and active. He explained that he at least hoped to create some balance as a hedge against the ever-increasing ups and downs of the American business cycle.

Hanley remembered the one point that Stein kept coming back to; that no matter what Hanley's experience had been in dealing with European-based businesses, nothing would prepare him for being in Africa. "It's like nothing you've ever experienced or will ever experience," Stein said. "I'm from northern New Jersey and thought I was tough, at least I would never allow anyone to get the best of me. But Africa, it's something else entirely. It's not really being tough or even shrewd. It's not even that the rules are different. It's that there aren't any rules. I don't know you, Mr Martin. Our mutual friend tells me you're really successful. I hope you are good at covering your back or have someone around that will. It's not just a requirement, it's closer to survival. Being an American outside of America is becoming a risky business."

Hanley thought of explaining what he would be doing there, but skipped it. It did not matter, at least not in this conversation. He was tired of explaining anyway. It was time to get on with it, he told himself.

Flying alone gave Hanley time to reflect on his recent decision. As he aged, he realized choices were accompanied by a certain finality or at least a limited amount of time to correct them if the decisions were bad. His accumulated decisions began to haunt him. His financial success was not a comfort, but only added to the doubt he had about what he had become. Success was not really success, he believed. Conversations he had with his uncle when he was young began to come back to him as he shaved or lay in bed, unable to sleep. He even began to drift away during telephone conversations, back to when he spent his summers on his uncle's farm, listening to the lessons being taught. Not lessons, at least they weren't meant to be lessons, more like advice. They were lessons nonetheless.

To Hanley, time became a package with a bomb inside. The package always had to be opened, but at what cost? Control of his life was lost. His daughter's marriage and move to another state, his divorce, his loneliness, the creases and blotches on his skin. He came to see the wastefulness of the life he was leading and was ashamed. That vision became a burden he carried, the many minutes, hours, days, months and years he wasted piled on his back. Family and friends defended him from himself. He would not accept their support. Soon, events began pointing him toward change and the decisions made to make that change. He thought he saw a design to the events, maybe looked too hard, thought fate played a hand. Again thought himself foolish.

After landing in Heraklion on the island of Crete, he filed a flight plan that designated Cairo International Airport as his first stop after entering Africa. At every stop since leaving the US, he dealt with local customs officials, inspections and fees for landing, and parking while his plane was inspected. Most were polite or at least as polite as seemed reasonable in today's world, Hanley thought. The farther south he went after leaving Greenland, the more difficult and time-consuming became the process. Apparently, the Beech C-45 was the type of plane every customs inspector south of France imagined a drug smuggler might use. So thorough and long was the inspection process in Crete that Hanley checked the inspection form for a section specifying a cavity search. Not finding it mentioned in English did not mean it was not covered in the Greek sections, he reminded himself. He was very relieved when asked to sign the form and saw it stamped several times by the inspector. Leaving Crete for Africa and Cairo brought a mixture of joy and apprehension.

The coast of Egypt was flat and brown from an altitude of eight thousand feet. The green of the Mediterranean Sea turned to white as the sea ran to the land.

The fastest route, the straightest, would take Hanley over the city of Baltim. Touching the coast at that point, he planned to turn south, from there to Cairo was approximately one hundred miles. That Cairo would be the first city in Africa he reached would be a blessing, he believed, being something close to normal. Some English would be spoken; customs would be similar, perhaps tougher, at least no worse than Crete had been. No coercion or overt extortion. The plane might not draw as much attention as it did in Crete. His papers were in order. The one thing that worried him was that, now that he was in Africa, in the Mideast region, how would officials react to the letter of employment he carried from a Catholic charity? Any customs agent he met from here on would probably be Muslim. He knew an American working for a Christian order would generate little enthusiasm from the locals.

Approaching the coast, Baltim spread out before him. From altitude, the buildings appeared to be similar, various-sized boxes, some white, some gray, some beige, tattered, some supporting water tanks, electrical wires stretched like threads spun by blind spiders, stretched everywhere, a shimmer of heat above everything. The lives of thousands of people passed beneath him in seconds, a curious feeling as he thought about it. The city stopped at the ocean, a sudden change, the buildings seemingly tied in a bundle by a thin ribbon of beach. He watched as Baltim and its unseen people passed by. Did they hear him and wonder who he was? Would a child look up at the old plane and become fascinated, learn to love flying as he once did?

Since college, he had flown airplanes, loved flying, the accomplishment, the skill it required. Airplanes made him fairly wealthy, would keep his daughter and granddaughter comfortable all their lives. Growing his businesses had not been a difficult task.

Hanley decided to continue south–southeast to find a landmark he wanted to see. After another thirty minutes, a green fan appeared ahead to the right of the plane, its presence in the middle of the arid land a thrilling surprise. Somewhere within the fan was a river. No ordinary river, Hanley thought, but a myth. It was water of legend, bringing life to a place where none should exist, a heaven where a hell would be if not for it. Stories passed from generations for thousands of years mentioned the beauty of life carried by its currents and sometimes taken by them too. He knew he would see the Nile soon after making the coast, but was not prepared for the impact it would have once he saw it.

The green of the fan deepened, indicating the lushness of a delta. Dipping his right wing, he tracked a slow smooth arc in the hot Egyptian sky while he searched for the larger flow of water. The Beech was at five thousand feet. Hanley believed, at his current heading, he would cross the Nile soon. He could see the activity along the streams, the small boats, people living their lives, tied to the water that gave life to everything.

And then he saw it, the spot where the river divided itself, creating the streams and the delta, flowing to the Mediterranean.

Moving south, he watched the river grow, widening, showing its strength, the water occasionally reflecting the sunlight in glowing arcs. Thousands and thousands of years this river flowed, giving its gifts to kings and beggars, prophets and paupers, the lost and the found. It didn't matter, the river cared for all the same and took life with the same care. Love and indifference, perhaps all the same. Hanley, thrilled with it all, flew on.

***

As he neared Cairo, the air around the city grew brown, with a red tint toward the south. Cairo was a very polluted city, its air stifled and burdened with the exhalations of old buses and taxis and the breath of six million souls. Hanley reached air traffic control in Cairo at seventy-five miles and again at fifty. He was on approach, sandwiched in between two 747s. He would touch down and leave the runway at the first possible ramp, an arrangement agreeable to both he and approach control. Lowering his landing gear, Hanley concentrated on the task of landing the Beech, while a tiny signal continued to sound in the back of his mind; this was Africa and there were no rules.

Cairo was a pleasant surprise. The customs people were all efficient and courteous, English was spoken and he was finished with his inspection and paperwork in under two hours. Hanley also suspected he arrived at the right time of day to facilitate the process. Seeing he carried virtually nothing in his cargo hold, the inspectors checked in all the obvious areas, examined his paperwork, and questioned him about his destination, registering mild surprise at his answer of southwestern Sudan and the Catholic outpost. The young customs inspector, Riyhad, looked hard at Hanley and asked, "Mr Martin, what brings you to the desert?"

Hanley looked at the sky, removed his old, black baseball cap with the emblem of the Pittsburgh Steelers on it, swiped his forehead with the back of his hand and said, "A woman." Riyadh smiled and nodded.

After completing his inspection of Hanley's plane and paperwork in Cairo, the young Egyptian said, "May I suggest something to you, Mr Martin? As I know you are going to Sudan, and will enter at Port Sudan, I will offer you some advice. Things will not be what you are used to when dealing with customs. There, they expect you to behave in a certain manner; to know what the customary behavior is when processing through their customs area. In an odd way, because you are an American, they will expect more of you while expecting less."

Hanley thought, perhaps, his expression caused the young man to pause and smile. The inspector looked to Hanley to be about thirty years old, was slim and fastidious in his dress and grooming. The young customs agent continued, "I don't mean to confuse you. They know, as an American, you will be unfamiliar with how their system works, but, as an American, they will expect you to be capable of paying more respect to them and their position; more than others. And, I am ashamed to say, because you are American, they may want to punish you in some manner. I am not that way. As one man to another, I will allow you the benefit of already knowing what type of respect you should give these men. My wife's cousin, an older cousin, works for the customs inspection unit in Port Sudan."

Hanley explained that he was unaccustomed to such matters and asked the young man just how much respect a Sudanese customs inspector deserves. The young customs inspector said he was not certain, but once had been told one hundred thousand dinars was customary. Hanley was stunned. Riyadh reminded Hanley these would be Sudanese dinars. The young man appeared to be uncomfortable discussing money.

The American turned and went to the general aviation terminal where he exchanged all his dollars and euros for Sudanese dinars. Afterward, he completed filing a flight plan for Port Sudan and returned to his plane.

He looked at the young Egyptian customs inspector and said, "I will carry one hundred thousand dinars with me to Port Sudan."

"Good," the young man said. "Everyone needs companions when they travel."

2

The stench of the open sewer sat in his nose all morning. Hanley thought it smelled like cabbage and carrion, stewed together in the sewer by the brutal Sudanese sun. He now faced the smell *and* the heat. It was a bad cycle, the smell seemingly making the day hotter, the heat making the smell worse. The sewer, with its brackish water, looked oil-slicked, trickling some thirty feet behind the low building that served as the general aviation terminal in Port Sudan. A cloud of flies hovered over the stream, their buzz like heavy traffic in the distance.

The terminal, an aging pen of cement blocks, was painted desert tan, sloppily trimmed in red along the top and over the doorframes and the doors themselves. One story high, it was sixty feet long, maybe thirty deep. The terminal could have been one hundred feet high and a mile wide and still not kept the horrid odor of the sewer from reaching his nostrils. With no breeze and that smell making every minute torturous, Hanley wished he had chosen Khartoum as his point of entry and not Port Sudan.

The Beech was parked to the right and slightly behind the terminal, with the American sitting against the frame of its open door, its aluminum skin reflecting the burnt brown of the earth and the brilliant blue of the Sudanese sky.

After his arrival and check-in, Hanley sat for ten minutes in the terminal lounge, then returned to the plane. The odor of sweat, onions and dirty feet, mixed with the stares of the others, drove him back to the heat and the sewer. He found the sounds of the lounge maddening, the voices like that of a tightly packed, foul-smelling sports bar, people talking to each other, to themselves, often over their companions, always, it seemed, while staring at him. So, he left. He realized the comments of the others were probably about the weather, jobs, children and all the same inane subjects he would hear in a terminal lounge back in America. Hanley could not get out of his head the idea they weren't. He was tired. The weeks of flying wore him down. He waited in the plane, the heat and the smell preferable to his imagination in the terminal.

Hanley left behind a daughter and granddaughter, Elizabeth and Carrie, left good friends, and Rocky. Rocky was keeping Weed. Hanley Martin left his life, left everything behind, sold his businesses, boarded his old plane and set off for Africa. It wasn't as simple as that, but not far from it.

When he thought about his past good fortune, the only word that explained it was luck. The word hung suspended inside his head like a seed glued to a string. It was in there for years. He thought it haunted him, but that sounded too dramatic. Thirty years went by, he was very successful and he was damned if he really knew why. Certainly he worked hard, but so did others. The want of an explanation nagged him for years. Luck and fate were too simple. Life was too complex. Why the millions upon millions of daily occurrences surrounding each of us come together to push one life toward success and one to ruin. This was the question. Why Hanley Martin and not someone sleeping on the street? Hanley needed to find an answer, but thought the only real answer was to find a way to give back what he owed for his luck. How exactly to make the payment had been the real question. That was driving him crazy, had been driving him crazy for many years. Then, when attending the Paris Air Show, a chance meeting with a French priest who mentioned the need for pilots to aid mission work in Sudan, it felt right. He had no idea why, but it did.

The trip went smoothly, for the most part. There were some annoyances and a great deal of satisfaction. He was flying. Flying the Beech around the world was a trip he dreamt of for years. He was halfway there. Four more hours, if he was lucky, and he would be in Mapuordit. Desperate for something to take his mind off his miserable surroundings, he shaded his eyes to watch a small lizard moving slowly along the bottom of the terminal wall nearest the plane. The red and brown of the lizard's skin made it difficult to see as it moved onto the dirt. I wonder if it's poisonous, he asked himself. It probably is, he thought, everything here is probably poisonous. "At least it smells poisonous," he said aloud.

The wait was now into its fourth hour. Port Sudan was the nightmare Hanley had been waiting for. When flight-planning, he decided to skip Khartoum and chose Port Sudan as his next stop after Cairo. The choice was made for two reasons; he assumed a port city would offer a more experienced general aviation and customs service. Port Sudan was also a bit closer to Mapuordit. Since this would be his last stop before reaching the mission station, he chose the closer of the two, allowing him a bit more fuel upon arriving at the Catholic outpost. He was wrong about the customs part.

The heat of a Sudanese noon was more than oppressive; it was intruding, insistent. It made the tires on the plane dull and soft. Hanley could smell them. He could not recall ever having smelled the tires on his plane without handling them. He thought the heat crazy. It was only the beginning of March.

The noonday sun was on the other side of the Beech and that afforded Hanley some shade. The inside of the plane was a cooker, even with every window and door that would open, open. He was soaked with his own sweat, and dreaming of a shower, when a short, stocky man came around the corner of the building, a clipboard in his hand. He was dark, almost native African dark, but he had the features of an Arab. His hair was short, his face displaying a large crooked nose riding on a thick, seldom-trimmed mustache. He limped. Two more men followed, walked around the corner and stopped, squinting at Hanley and his plane. Both were wearing holsters with semiautomatic pistols in them. Hanley climbed down from the plane and stood, waiting for the man with the clipboard. He saw the lizard stop its crawl along the building's edge, watching the two men near the corner, its tongue flicking in the air.

"Mr Martin, I have some bad news to report," the man said in barely understandable English. "The chief customs inspector cannot review your documents at this time and I am powerless to provide such a review myself. As I am only an assistant, I cannot provide you with the necessary approvals that will allow you to leave this impounding area and continue on your journey to Mapuordit. Therefore, you must leave your plane here until the chief inspector can examine your papers. He is a busy man, you must see, huh? These men will guard your plane for you for a small fee. I think it wise to use them. People here are desperate for gasoline and tires and wood such as on the floor of your plane, a beautiful plane, I would like to say. Sudan has become a dangerous place; not the place of my grandfathers. Please, I can help you find a place to sleep tonight and maybe the inspector will see your papers tomorrow or the next day."

Well, shit, Hanley thought; there it is. The custom inspector in Cairo had been right. This is probably the cousin of his wife.

Now Hanley looked hard at the Sudan customs agent and said, "I know the chief customs inspector is a very busy man and I am certain tomorrow will be an even busier day than today. If there was a way I might alleviate the burden he faces of having to deal with a small man such as myself and my plane, I would certainly like to do so." Hanley kept his voice low and his expression blank. The two men near the corner of the building looked bored and began to bicker while squinting into the sun, trying to follow the conversation. Hanley had the impression they did not speak English and were following on tone alone. The custom agent turned and said something to the men and they fell silent. He turned back to Hanley and blinked, staring hard at the face of the American. Decision time, Hanley thought. The man cleared his throat and said, "Please wait here while I speak to my superior. These men will wait with you to insure you and your magnificent plane come to no harm."

He turned and walked away, stopping for an instant to say something to the two men and then disappeared around the corner of the building. Hanley saw that the lizard had not moved.

Trying to show little or no emotion, Hanley returned to the doorway of the Beech and sat down, leaving the men to squint in the sunlight. The day grew hotter. Hanley Martin hoped his guardians would grow tired of waiting in the heat and seek shade around the corner of the building. He'd drank four bottles of water since landing that morning. Last night in Cairo, he ate in a small dining area in the airport and had nothing since. Eating on a regular basis in Sudan would be a rarity, he expected. He needed to leave Port Sudan today. To his surprise, the two men sat down against the wall and continued to watch the plane while continuing to bicker.

Hanley knew that once he was free to depart, the flight to Mapuordit would be around three-and-a-half to four hours. There was a landing strip about ten miles northwest of the mission with a telephone there. Hanley had the number for the mission station. A ride could be at the airfield within thirty minutes of the call if all went well. Big if, he thought.

Hanley now believed he would be spending the night in Port Sudan. He would not abandon the plane and resigned himself to paying the chief customs inspector and these men to insure that he could leave first thing in the morning. He toyed with the idea of just taxiing out and departing, but then every son-of-a-bitch in the area probably had a handheld missile in his tent or truck and he would be down before he climbed to five hundred feet.

Hanley watched as the larger of the two men took the pistol from its holster and began pointing it at the plane, first at the tires and then other parts; the nose, the engine, the tip of the wing. As he worked his way toward the rear of the plane, he stopped for a millisecond at the doorway and Hanley and then moved to the tail. At each stop, the muzzle of the gun rose almost imperceptibly. Hanley knew little about guns, but recognized this gun to be an old 45-caliber Colt 911, once the sidearm of the American military. It looked barely functional to Hanley and, should the Sudanese guard pull the trigger, there was a greater chance it would fail than work, he thought. The second man sat and grinned at his partner's antics. Hanley suspected the smaller man hoped his companion would shoot this American fool.

Hanley did not wait for the thug to accidentally shoot him as he worked the gun back to the plane's nose. Getting his right foot under him, he pushed himself up, pulled the hatch shut, turned and walked to the cockpit. He began the startup procedure for the left engine; the side where the two Sudanese watchdogs were sitting. When Hanley hit the engine boost, the left engine kicked over and started immediately. Grit and dust filled the space between the plane and the building, swirling clockwise, enveloping the two men in a choking and blinding grit-fog. Hanley watched as the man with the gun tried covering his nose and mouth with his right hand, then dropped the gun while pushing the other toward the corner of the building and away from the swirl. Standing on the brakes, Hanley revved the left engine enough to insure dust would surround that side of the plane. Dropping the engine to an idle, Hanley set the brakes and got out of the seat. From a metal chest located at the bottom of the bulkhead, he took goggles and put them on as he exited the rear cargo door. He walked straight to the wall of the terminal and began searching. He saw the lizard just to his right, about a foot from the wall. Resting under the left front paw of the lizard was the old 45. He took the gun and walked back to the plane. I hope this thing is ready to fire, he thought.

Back in the pilot's seat, he shut the engine down and was surprised at how quickly the dust settled and how quickly the two men returned. Hanley watched as they began searching for the gun then, failing to find it, begin shouting at each other, with fingers pointing and soon each shoving the other. The larger of the two was the one who dropped the gun and was now the angriest and most animated. Soon, he was kicking dust at his companion, shouting so violently that spit flew everywhere, creating little round welts on the ground that he then blew to oblivion as he kicked the dirt. The second man, smaller and a little older, began retreating when the assistant customs inspector rounded the corner and received a face full of dust. The shouting stopped so suddenly, Hanley thought he heard its remnants carried off by the wind. The customs inspector was stunned for a second and then marched over and hit the dust kicker across the face with his clipboard. Then the assistant customs inspector unleashed his fury, letting it stream over the man like a bucket of scalding water. The second man disappeared around the corner. After a minute, the thug was ordered away and the assistant customs inspector approached the plane, knocking at the rear hatch as if he were a meter-reader back in Kokomo. Hanley walked to the back of the plane, opened the hatch, knelt and peered out at the customs inspector.

"What did your boss say about my inspection?" Hanley asked. The bureaucrat's face now resembled a tribal mask, painted on before battle. The red dust and perspiration together created twisted brown lines that ran down his face, surrounding his eyes, lips and exaggerated a nose that did not need the help.

"The chief customs inspector sends his regrets. Tomorrow will be the soonest he can attend to this matter. You must realize he is an important man and his time has a certain value. To inspect your plane now means his time is diminished and he would be forced to work longer today to make up for dealing with you. It not that you're an American, that has no bearing on this. It must be said that what you are doing is considered irregular. Where you are going and what you are doing are seen as a problem by some. The chief customs inspector is aware of this. However, that is not really the problem in this case. It is simply the value of time. You must understand."

Finally, there it is, Hanley thought. He considered bringing the gun into the bargaining that was about to start, but decided against that, at least until he saw how it went.

"Yes, I understand and appreciate the value of your time and of the chief inspector's time. Really, I do. I'm sorry to have caused you such trouble. I know you must think of the Sudanese people first and I appreciate that. I must be leaving soon, at least first thing in the morning. If there was a way that I might express my understanding of the value of both your time and that of the chief inspector, an expression that would allow me to depart in the morning, I would appreciate being allowed to demonstrate that understanding." Hanley said.

"It is rare to find a foreigner, and forgive me for saying so, an American, that understands the complexities of dealing with such a situation. Time is so valuable in a place such as this. One never knows when time will stop being a friend. We have a saying here, in Sudan, that a hundred thousand candles cannot find time when time is lost. With that many candles, the search is sometimes worthwhile."

Staring at the man for a moment longer, Hanley turned, entered the plane and walked to the same chest that he had taken the goggles from. He removed a large plastic box marked as a first-aid kit. Inside were an assortment of bandages and ointments found in kits of this nature anywhere in the world. Underneath the medical supplies, Hanley fitted a piece of white cardboard, beneath which he stored the Sudanese dinars he had acquired at the airport in Cairo. He counted out one-hundred-and-twenty-five thousand and rolled them up in a wad. He put the kit back and walked back to the door. The assistant custom inspector was standing with his back to the plane. Hanley said, "Here, I hope there are enough candles here to help you find the time you need."

The man turned and eyed the money in Hanley's hand. He smiled slightly and said, "Time is elusive, but can sometimes be found." He moved closer and took the money, opened the roll and quickly counted the bills. His smile broadened when he realized there was an additional twenty-five thousand Dinars in the roll.

"Please wait here for a few minutes more. I will return soon with the necessary papers." As he walked away, Hanley stepped from the plane and walked over to the building. Taking the gun from his pants pocket, he dropped it to the ground, covering it with some loose dirt and dust. Looking around, he no longer saw the lizard. Probably booted away during all the commotion, Hanley thought.

He returned to the plane to wait in the heat, aware that he may have given the money away with no assurances he would be allowed to leave Port Sudan.

Hanley just sat down when the assistant customs inspector came storming back with the two guards trailing behind. He looked distressed and the two men were sullen. The larger of the two was still without a gun.

"I'm sorry, but we must clear up a matter of importance. My men say you started your plane in an attempt to leave and they were forced to stop you. This man, Abdul Essam, says he dropped his gun and you now have it. This is very serious and we will be forced to detain you now."

Hanley held up his hand and said, "I did not try to escape. I started the left engine to insure that dust had not clogged…"

"What is clogged?" the assistant customs inspector interrupted.

"…that dust had not blocked the exhaust. Your man dropped his gun, which he was pointing at my plane at the time, and I believe it's still where he dropped it. Here, I'll help you look."

Hanley jumped from the plane and walked over to the building before his hosts could react. They turned and followed. Hanley stood, pretending to look around for a moment and then bent down and retrieved the gun. He blew the dust off it. Holding it by the barrel, he turned and offered it to the customs inspector. The man's look of concern instantly turned to anger. He whirled to face the two men and began yelling at them. Both trotted off and disappeared around the corner of the building. The assistant customs inspector turned to Hanley, placed the gun under his left arm, looked at his clipboard, signed a form, flipped over two pages and signed a second form. Taking copies from beneath both, he handed the copies to Hanley and said, "This was an unfortunate incident; very unusual. You are free to depart at any time. If I were you, I would not wait until morning."

He offered Hanley a grim smile, turned and walked away quickly. Not about to wait another moment, Hanley entered the plane, shut and locked the rear door, made his way to his seat and began the process to depart. He radioed the tower, and with some difficulty notified them of his plans to leave Port Sudan. With a blast of smoke, the big engines of the Beech turned over. Taxiing out and onto the departure area, Hanley waited a bit until he was cleared to depart. Hanley Martin taxied to the runway. It was now three-thirty. No matter, he was leaving and would land in Mapuordit at about seven o'clock. One way or another, he would be in Mapuordit.

3

The bottom of the Beech's windshield was aligned with the horizon. The setting sun, low in the sky to his right was enlarged by the denseness of the atmosphere, bright but not glaring, a perfect glowing orb, bright orange with a streak of dull blue across it, a thin cloud mixed with dust carried high in the air from the dried-out land below. Hanley's hands were dirty. The dirt and sweat of his palms made the yoke feel greasy. Red dust covered his clothes. If he moved his arms quickly, dust raised, creating a small cloud that fell to his lap and onto the seat between his legs.

Below was Sudan, a brown landscape, patches of green appeared, but were scattered. A long ribbon of green marked his passing over the White Nile, a sibling river, not great, but good to the land that touched it. Studying the charts of Sudan over the past year had given Hanley a good knowledge of the major features over which he flew, so different from what he knew. From the air, Africa was different from the other lands he crossed, as different as Greenland was from Ireland. In America, the land he flew over was much the same, looked much the same. He was glad he came. Fear aside, Africa thrilled him.

***

The old priest's knees ached, as did his arms. No one else will do this, he thought. Just me, the one that everyone waits for. There would be no water if I refuse to fix this fucking pump. Now I must also wait for the American. He's not coming, I think; saw the folly and stayed home to drink bad beer and watch American football. A joke, American football-helmets and padding.

Father Jean-Robert Robineau crouched beside the water pump, the various parts and pieces of which lay scattered about his scuffed boots, one with its heel glued on. The pump was essential to the mission. The water, whenever available, was produced by the vigorous and, for the priest, tiring pumping of its handle. Its surface was a mosaic of black paint, red primer paint and rust. At sixty-seven years of age, the priest was at least as old as the pump and worked about as well.

The box-wrench he pushed on slipped, his finger scraping against a flange in the middle of the pump shaft. A thick piece of knuckle skin curled back, allowing blood to well and then run around to the other side of the forefinger on his right hand. The priest felt the sting of the scrape, but did not stop, only put the wrench back on the nut and pushed again.

The pump was leaking water near the base. In Sudan, water was too precious to waste and so it was time to attempt an overhaul. The priest was aware when he started that he would be forced to improvise once he discovered the problem; a worn seal, a broken bolt perhaps. On his knees, his lips pursed, the priest stared at the pump. Over the past twenty years, he had experienced most of the failures the old pump managed to produce.

He scraped muck from the inside of the main shaft, a slight sewer stink coming from the filth. As he worked, he heard the two-way radio inside the compound's office building bleat static and then a voice began calling contact information for someone to hear. The priest's head snapped up and he got to his feet. The tingling of his thickened blood working back into his legs joined for a few moments with the arthritis in his knees to render him immobile. Again, his condition reminded him of Saint Francis of Assisi, who considered his body the weak, useless relative of his brilliant mind. "Brother Ass" was how the saint referred to his weak body. The priest could relate.

It must be Mr Martin, the American. He was due today, the priest believed. The priest could not remember the exact time. Too many things to remember, too many unimaginable things were happening now. It was not as bad here as in Darfur, but who knew where it would lead. The priest walked as fast as his tingling legs could manage, stumbling into the office and to the radio. He sat heavily onto an ancient wooden chair, picked up the microphone and answered, "This is the Mapuordit mission station. Is this Mr Martin, out?"

"Affirmative. This is Beech T806D on approach to the Akot airstrip. Who am I talking to?"

"This is Father Robineau Monsieur Martin. I will leave now but, it will take me about one half hour to get to Akot. It is about fifteen kilometers from here. We expected you today, but did not know your exact time of arrival. Please be patient."

The American acknowledged the response and said he would wait. What else could he do, the priest thought.

Hanley Martin would be bringing news of Father Robineau's family. The old priest was excited to hear about his niece Sophie and her English husband. The French priest did not think himself to be prejudiced, but, like many of the French his age, he was not especially fond of the British; or Americans, for that matter. He did not see anything wrong in feeling this way. Everyone did. He tried to remain contrite when it happened.

Sophie's father and mother had been concerned when she first mentioned Michael Campbell, thinking it was a temporary thing, a fling of sorts. After a while, their concern grew. When finally they realized this was a serious matter, Sophie's parents consulted Jean-Robert, first by mail and then when he had returned to France for a visit and some study. Eventually, the three conferred with their other brothers and sisters, discussing various ways to intervene. In the end, nothing came of it and, once married, all welcomed Michael to the family. When he thought of his niece's husband, he thought of him as *the* Englishman.

The plane must be getting close. It was almost dusk. The runway might be difficult to see. Finding the keys to the old

Land Rover, the priest picked up his hat and walked to the truck to make the drive to the airstrip. He was mildly aware that there was some danger being out after dark, but if all went well, he and the American would be back soon enough.

The finish on the old English vehicle was a dark green and dull, its faded swirls and cloud patterns covered the larger, flat areas of the hood and doors. The roof was white, a hedge against, but no real match for, the Sudanese sun and the heat they suffered through almost daily. The spare tire on the hood was soft and probably useless. He needed to patch it and spend the hour or two it takes to pump air into it by hand.

With an old rag kept under the front seat, he wiped the windshield of its thin dusting and then the driver's side door window. Getting in was hard for him. Crawling into the seat, he started the truck, found first gear and moved forward. Smelling of old grease and used oil, the truck traveled so many miles, the odometer stopped, showing only thirty-two miles, as if the old vehicle was new.

The drive was a difficult one. Two months ago, rain rendered the roads almost impassable. The rains stopped and now the rutted roads were hardened. The ruts assumed control the truck's direction, moving it from one side to the other. The priest gripped the wheel tightly, thinking that a run through the brush might be better than the road.

As the truck lurched forward, electric lines of pain shot across the old man's lower back, the sprung coils beneath the seat's heavy leather coverings offering little support. As he drove, he heard a heavy drone with thunderous undertones approaching from behind. The sound overpowered the sound of the truck's engine through a bad muffler and the rattles of its body. Faint for a moment, it quickly grew. A small wave of fear came over the old priest, making him feel ashamed. It was the American, faster than he anticipated. Yes, it was the of sound of an approaching airplane.

The noise continued to grow, a rhythmic beating of the thin Africa air, rising in intensity until the plane passed over the truck at a very low altitude, perhaps five to eight hundred feet. Involuntarily ducking his head, Father Robineau craned his neck, twisting to look out the windshield. A dark form flashed overhead, the noise startling in its massiveness. It beat down on the Land Rover and rushed ahead, seeming to push down the grass and bush, while the plane continued its descent. Until that moment, the priest had not thought of the condition of the landing strip, but now worried that it might be a hazard for the pilot. Would an American flier, accustomed to paved airfields, be prepared for what he would find in the middle of the Sudanese scrub desert?

Twenty more minutes passed before he neared the landing strip. Already, he could see the plane, sitting next to the small, crumbling building, a shack, that served as a terminal. Inside was a single table, a bare light bulb, an old Clansman crank-powered two-way radio and a telephone that connected the building to the mission and the office of the local government official. As the priest's truck cleared the last bit of brush to enter the clearing where the terminal stood, he could see the brightness of it, its shine a contrast to the dull brown surfaces of grass, brush and rock. Nearing the plane, Father Robineau stopped the truck, then got out, hoping nervousness wasn't showing on his old, dusty face. There was a hole in the front of the shack where tin had once hung, open like an eye, awakened by the noise of the plane. The plane itself was not what the priest had expected. It was dust-covered but otherwise looked new, not the kind of plane normally found in southern Sudan, old planes with faded paint over dents, oil blackened metal near motors that belched smoke. The plane was certainly old, but if cleaned of the dust, would be almost immaculate. To see a plane in this part of the world that looked like this was rare. A man was sitting in the pilot's seat, his head bent forward. He was obviously writing; or maybe praying, the priest thought. No, just writing.

After a moment, the pilot twisted around and then left the seat. The brush area of this part of Sudan had little noise outside the birds, crickets and frogs who sang to the evening wind. Now near the plane, Father Robineau could hear the pilot walking down its length. He heard the sound of the rear door opening. The door was lowered to rest a foot or so from the ground, held there by a strong cable. A middle-aged man peered from the doorway, saw the priest and smiled. He stepped from the plane and walked toward the priest. As he neared, he extended his hand and said, "Hi, I'm Hanley Martin. You must be Father Robineau."

"Yes, yes, I am." The priest was immediately aware that his accent probably sounded thick to the American. The priest hoped his English was good enough for the American to understand. They shook hands and briefly looked each other over.

"I must admit, when I passed over this airstrip, I thought about returning to the Port of Sudan. And believe me, that's not a place I want to see again anytime soon." Hanley's smile seemed odd to the priest, like he was hearing a private joke, but one he did not enjoy.

The priest said, "I was afraid the shape of the runway might prove to be a problem for you. I'm pleased you are in a good condition after landing."

"Oh, it was bumpy, but manageable. The gravel helped. I'm glad to see you made it out here. I didn't want to sleep in the plane tonight. Let me get the plane secured and we can go."

In front of the plane was a large stone buried in the ground with an iron ring secured to it with a hasp imbedded in the center of the visible surface. Twenty feet of chain was attached to the ring. The stone itself, or what was visible to Father Robineau, was an oval about six feet in length. The entire stone must be enormous, he thought as he watched the American drag the chain toward the front of the plane. The pilot must have seen the stone and taxied to it.

"How will you secure the plane?" the priest asked.

"I have a lock. It's an S&G 833, made for outdoor conditions. It can stand up to about anything, would be hard for someone, anyone, actually, to pick or cut," Hanley said. "Let me show you my plane."

Following Hanley up the steps, the priest watched as the American retrieved his duffle, his keys and an old brown leather satchel. He also took the large padlock from a metal chest behind the bulkhead.

"I've had this briefcase forever," Hanley explained. "It's been handy for carrying all my papers, including my flight log." The back part of the plane's interior was empty, save for two seats attached to the bulkhead, the partition separating the cargo area from the cockpit. The cargo area flooring was a highly polished wood, the interior walls painted a light grey. The cockpit seats, the instruments and the various levers and knobs all shined, with two small screens in the center of the instrument panel.

The priest followed Hanley out of the plane. After locking the plane's rear door, he threaded the chain from the large rock through a section of the right wheel strut and padlocked it. "This will do, but even if it doesn't, it's all that I have," he told the priest. He smiled and again the priest thought the smile odd, the American's face sad, but smiling nonetheless.

Picking up the duffle and the old satchel, Hanley Martin said to Father Robineau, "I'm ready if you are." As they walked to the truck, Hanley asked, "Do you think the plane will be safe, I mean, will it be vandalized?"

"I would doubt it. There are few if any rebel factions operating in this area. Most of them are in the Darfur region, west of where we are. The people here are still respectful of the mission. We have told those visiting the mission of your coming and they know the plane will help them. So, I believe they will honor its presence here and not disturb it. They will come to see it, starting tonight, perhaps, certainly tomorrow. Now they certainly know you are here. How could they not? My hearing is bad and I could not have missed your arrival." The priest smiled and put a hand on Hanley's shoulder. He said, "Let us return to the mission, we will find something for you to eat and drink and you can tell me about my niece, Sophie."

Stopping, the priest allowed a small, low cloud of dust to catch up to him, adding another fine layer of dirt to his dull boots. Squinting from some minor discomfort brought on by age and the thought in his head, he said to Hanley, "Tomorrow or the next day, you will meet Sister Marie Claire. She is a person of some force, or forcefulness. She is determined regarding some things, determined to makes changes. Sudan does not change easily. She knows this. It does not stop her; nothing stops her, not even the bishop. She will talk to you about these changes. Be careful with her. She means well, but be careful."

4

A thrill slid up Hanley's spine, chilling the back of his neck. Since leaving Crete, he had been too busy with the travel, customs, the fear and the anticipation, to think about her. The old priest snapped her back into Hanley's consciousness, holding his attention tight, freezing his stomach, forcing a rigid smile to his face. "I'm looking forward to meeting Sister Marie Claire," he said.

"She's not at the mission now. She is in Rumbek gathering supplies, drinking water and food, paper products, that sort of thing. She will be back later tonight or tomorrow," the old priest said.

Hanley's first glimpse of the Catholic mission station at Mapuordit was a yellow lightbulb glowing in the distance, a stationary point he watched as he bounced around on the passenger seat of the old vehicle. Even anchored as he was by a seatbelt, his upper and lower body parts were constantly flung about. He tried to hang on to anything that would hold them in place but his attempts were mostly useless.

The single yellow bulb was screwed into a standard white porcelain fixture, hung from the eaves of the station's main building. It was a deep yellow glow, the kind he remembered glowing at night, marking the back doors of countless farmhouses all over Indiana. It was the color that bathed the side of his uncle's farm house night after night, year after year. The memory brought a twinge of nostalgia, the kind he felt when it was something he had not thought of for years.

"I'm sorry for this horrible road. You may become accustomed to it, but I will tell you, I have been here for years and I have not," Father Robineau yelled to Hanley. The noise of the ride was more irritating than the jostling. After weeks spent flying an old twin-prop cargo plane, he was surprised he could think that possible.

Hanley leaned into the voice of the priest to hear what he was saying. Before he could answer, the old Land Rover rolled to a stop beside the main building and the priest turned the key. Hanley said, "I've always been capable of adjusting to most things. It's a gift of sorts, or else it's that I expect less from my surroundings than most people. Don't worry. I'll be fine. As long as there are no snakes, I'll have few problems."

"There are snakes," the priest said.

"Great."

"Oh, please don't worry. We do not see many. Only a few in this area are really dangerous. You just have to be careful where you step or reach. Unfortunately, they don't have rattles that warn you like American snakes. I think your snakes are much more considerate of others. In Sudan, our snakes are rude. Of course, in France, we have no poisonous snakes," the priest said.

"I thought France had a couple of types of poisonous snakes," Hanley said, "I believe I read that somewhere."

The old priest's face assumed an offended look and said, "There is nothing poisonous in France, Monsieur. Let me show you your room and then we can have dinner with the staff which will be in one half hour or so. We eat late as we have much to do while there is daylight to assist us," the priest explained.

With his duffle and satchel gathered from the truck, Hanley followed the priest across the compound to a rectangular building made of plywood and metal, the roof a corrugated tin, faded a flat gray with streaks of red and orange where the rare rains caused rust.

A cheap wooden screen door, grayed with age presented a browned metal handle to open it, a single spring to close it and two hinges to hold it to the frame, the only decorations Hanley saw on the building. The priest entered first, leading Hanley down a hallway made entirely of unpainted plywood. Their boots thudded on the thin floor, creating a shallow echo between it and the earth below. They walked the length of the building, a dormitory of sorts, to the last room on the left, the room where Hanley would be living for the year or more he might stay in Sudan. Another thin wooden door opened to a small room, no more than eight feet square, with a cot, a small table and a shiny black metal trunk, the kind freshman haul to college.

Hanley's room was, he would learn, the same as that of the doctors and nurses at the mission, a small cell with room enough for the few comforts he saw before him. The walls were thin and the door was old, perhaps taken from another older building. Hanley found a thin foam pad covered his cot with a very thin white sheet and thin woolen blanket on top. A large net suspended from the rafters hung over the bed. On the small table, Hanley found a large candle and holder.

"This is your room, one of our best rooms, you should know," the old priest said. "It is a corner room next to a door leading outside. It has a window and gets sun in the morning. Quite nice for our small mission. I think you'll be comfortable here."

Hanley laid his satchel by the table and his duffle on the bed. "It reminds me of my room my freshman year in college," he said.

"Where was that?" Father Robineau asked.

"Ball State in Indiana."

"Like baseball? Did they teach sports at your school?"

Hanley hoped the priest was being sarcastic. "If they did, they weren't successful," Hanley said, recalling the school's record in any athletic endeavor he could recall.

Sitting on the end of the bed, the priest asked, "What do you know of our mission and of this area?"

"I know a bit of what you do here, of the nature of your operation. I'm sure Sophie and Michael have told you about my meeting Father Bertrand at their home. It's been almost two years now," Hanley said. This, Hanley learned through his talks with Father Bertrand, the head of the Fathers of Notre Dame, the Catholic organization sponsoring the mission at Mapuordit, as well as several other missions around the world. A chance meeting with the priest at the home of Michael Campbell and his wife Sophie Robineau started the conversations that eventually led to Hanley's decision to work for the mission in Sudan. Michael, as Hanley called him, were friends, having met when Michael worked for Beech and then Raytheon in America. Airbus eventually hired Michael who moved to France where he met Sophie, the niece of Father Robineau. They lived in France.

Hanley knew from his research the mission had several doctors practicing at any time, rotating in and out after a month or two, most coming from eastern Europe. On the ride back from the airstrip, Father Robineau told Hanley there was a doctor from Ireland at the mission, but Hanley already knew this. The nurses and staff were mostly French, a few were Italian. Over the past eighteen months, Hanley read as much as he could about the Mapuordit mission station.

Hanley said, "I know this mission is part of the Catholic Diocese of Rumbek, which is northwest of here. The mission operates a primary and secondary school as well as a medical clinic. I know you treat leprosy in a separate clinic across the road."

Hanley knew the mission at Mapuordit was founded early in the 1990s, the location selected for the understandable reason of being isolated, sparing it from attack by the Khartoum forces or the local militia such as the Janajweed, a group supported and protected by Khartoum. Through his research, Hanley knew even the Sudanese People's Liberation Army and the SPLM, the rebel movement in western and southern Sudan, were a threat to the Christian missions operating in the region.

Another chance meeting, this one with Sister Mary Kathleen O'Brien, started Hanley thinking of working for the Catholic mission in Sudan. They met on a flight from Washington D.C. to Indianapolis. It was then Hanley believed he saw a pattern developing to the events that would change his life. Eventually, Sister Mary Kathleen said she saw them too. Hanley became wary of Sister Mary Kathleen and her assertions.

Sister O'Brien taught International Studies at Notre Dame. She was born in Baltimore. When they met, she was on sabbatical from Wheeling Jesuit College in Wheeling, West Virginia. He also learned they shared a love for the Pittsburgh Steelers, a team she adopted after the Colts moved to Indianapolis. She claimed to carry her Terrible Towel with her everywhere, even sometimes to mass. He knew the Terrible Towel was a cloth talisman waved by loyal Steeler fans at the games on Sunday, where Sister Mary Kathleen said all good Catholics go after mass. "I believe God is a Steeler fan, I really do," she said with a look of genuine belief tinged with a small amount of shame.

"The mission at Mapuordit is on the trail refugees use to reach Ethiopia and Kenya," the priest explained. Hanley already knew this. Many late-night telephone conversations with Sister O'Brien and packages she sent to him containing background information gave Hanley much of the history and conditions he would come across in southern Sudan. From his research, Hanley learned the number of refugees passing through the area near the clinic recently ballooned as the mission offered the only medical care in the region. The Fur and Zaghawa tribes made up the majority of the non-Arab tribes in Darfur, and the majority of the refugees escaping across the mid-southern counties of Lakes and Yirol. The mission also served the local tribes, Dinkas and Nuer with some Atuot mixed in. "There is a serviceable road between Mapuordit and Rumbek. Yirol, the main town in the Yirol County region, was just northeast," the priest said.

"Sudan is a nation of numerous tribes, both Arabic and African. The tribal differences are the root cause of much of the conflict found in Sudan. In many parts of the Mideast, the dynamics of tribal conflict have been misunderstood by westerners, I'm afraid," the priest told Hanley.

"A friend of mine, Sister O'Brien, told me the American government discounts the role tribal conflict plays in all of this and blames religion and economics as the leading causes of the strife that has lasted hundreds of years," Hanley said. He knew from his discussions with Sister O'Brien that tribal ethnicity and the related issue of control caused much of the conflict in this region of the world, from Sudan to Iraq. The Muslim-controlled government in Khartoum faced strong opposition from the rebels in southern Sudan. She told Hanley the South was a source for wealth for the arid and unproductive north. Minerals, food and now, possibly oil caused the Arab controlled government to want the native African population to disappear, in whatever manner necessary. Genocide was as good a method as any to the Sudanese government, she believed.

"Come, let me take you to the dining room. You must be hungry," Father Robineau said.

"Yes, in fact I am. I could use some food and a drink if you have one."

"Unfortunately, the doctors smuggle in alcohol and not always what we need to tend to patients," the priest said.

A sudden wave of exhaustion overcame him, his knees bent slightly as he rocked back a bit, small waves of nausea pushed a small amount of acid up into his throat. His head ached. What a day this had been. He experienced some of what this part of the world could offer. He knew it might be much worse. Americans are so naive, he thought; unless they're from the inner cities or maybe Native American reservations, most escape poverty and persecution.

"Let me show you where you will be taking most of your meals. I'm not sure what you are used to, but I doubt it is this," Father Jean-Robert said. "After which, I am certain you will want to sleep."

The priest led Hanley to a large circular hut, perhaps thirty feet across. It was at least fifty yards from the sleeping quarters.

The noises of the African night were not dissimilar from those of rural Indiana, only more intense. Bug sounds, tree frog songs and a steady wind through the trees covered the southern Sudanese savanna with a layer of life more striking than Hanley had expected. A slight breeze cooled Hanley's face as they crossed the compound. Suddenly, he was hit by an object just above his right ear, toward his temple. Whatever it was, it felt to be about the size and consistency of a wad of bubble gum. Hanley stopped and said, "Shit, what was that?" He looked about him, but could see nothing in the darkness. The priest turned and asked what was wrong. Hanley explained that he had been struck by something, something large and then asked the priest how large the bugs were in Mapuordit. "Very large," Father Jean-Robert said and they continued on. Hanley could hear voices coming from the hut.

A dark wooden screen door set in a frame surrounded by small rough timbers allowed light and voices to reach Hanley as he approached the building. The light was a dull white, making the faces and hands below it glow while obscuring everything else in the room from view. As they entered, Hanley was surprised to see the hut had a wooden floor. In the center of the hut was a large, rectangular table. Several men and women were sitting, talking. They were eating, or had just finished. Two bottles sat near the center of the table; one was a bottle of what appeared to be red wine, the other a large bottle of water. As Hanley and Father Robineau entered, the talking stopped and everyone's eyes turned toward the door. This feels like the first day at a new school, Hanley thought.

"My friends, let me introduce our newest staff member. This is Hanley Martin," the priest said. Turning back to Hanley, he said, "There is really no need to introduce you. Everyone knows your name and where you are from. Father Bertrand provided us with some information about you. Yours is an interesting story."

One of the men stood and walked around the table toward Hanley with his hand extended. He appeared to be in his late thirties, dark with black hair and the heaviest five o'clock shadow Hanley could remember having seen. You must shave three times a day, Hanley thought.

"I'm Stasio Dzyak. I am a doctor from Slovakia. Three of us are from there. We came together to do the surgeries for the people here in Sudan. The war has brought more of a need for our work, I am afraid. You have brought a plane, no? Very dangerous, no?"

The priest interrupted. "Why don't we allow our new friend to sit and have something to eat and drink? He is very tired and hungry, are you not?"

Hanley took the initiative and walked around the table to introduce himself. There were three other doctors, two nurses and a social worker. Two of the doctors were those from Slovakia, the nurses from France and the social worker from Kenya. Another doctor was from Ireland. Hanley had been told there would be three nurses; the missing nurse was Sister Marie Claire.

Dr Thomas O'Connell's resemblance to his brother Tim was remarkable. Looking at the young doctor from Ireland was like looking at the bartender in Galway. A planned overnight in Ireland led Hanley to dinner at the hotel in Galway. There, he met Timothy O'Connell. The restaurant was crowded, forcing Hanley to eat at the bar. When Hanley explained his trip to the young Irish bartender, the name of his final destination caused the bartender's jaw to drop. "This isn't possible," was all Tim O'Connell could manage to say. While Hanley ate, the bartender called his mother to tell her of the chance meeting.

"Dr O'Connell, your brother Tim said that you need to write a letter to your mother. It seems she is unhappy with your poor communication skills." The look on the young doctor's face was what Hanley expected it would be. Dr O'Connell was dumbstruck.

"What the hell. How do you know that?" the Irish doctor asked. Hanley explained his layover in Galway and the chance meeting with his brother. "By God, that's amazing," was all Dr O'Connell could say.

Hanley sat in the only vacant chair and looked at the food. He was even hungrier than he expected. The meal looked to be some sort of roasted meat, with vegetables, including ears of corn. There was a plate of flat bread and small cakes. One of the other doctors, about the same age as the first, but taller and not as dark, retrieved a glass from a smaller table off to one side and placed it in front of Hanley. The glass was mostly clean. Since no one apologized for its condition, Hanley assumed this was an accepted level of sanitation.

After pouring some wine and spooning some meat and vegetables onto a plate, the American answered the barrage of questions that came his way. Everyone seemed to speak English moderately well.

"Tell us, Mr Martin, what do you think of our airport?" one of the doctors asked.

"I've seen worse. Believe it or not, there are a few airports in America that make yours look good," Hanley said. He dipped a piece of flatbread in the broth and began to eat, thankful for the food and his safe arrival.

"Really? I thought all airports in America were paved. Where is there not paved airports in your country?"

"They're everywhere, really, many are out west, some in the Midwest. Anyway, yours is not bad, as long as approaches are made during daylight hours. What kind of meat is this?" Hanley asked.

"Local beef. We don't have it often, as it's very scarce. It's Sunday and we thought you might arrive so we had something a bit nicer than normal," Father Robineau explained.

"Well, I really appreciate this. I must admit I am hungry. I ate last night and have had nothing since. My stop in Port Sudan didn't allow me time to eat. I thought I might be spending the night there, but things worked out and customs let me leave."

"You're fortunate," one of the Slovakian doctors observed. "We've been told when the customs inspector there is in a bad mood, say when his wife has refused him her love, he makes people wait for days before he lets them leave. You're a lucky man, Mr Martin; his wife must have been agreeable, no?"

"I'll try to remember to drop her a note of thanks," Hanley said.

A nurse sitting across from Hanley smiled and sipped from a tall glass filled a third of the way with the same wine Hanley was drinking. Watching her drink, Hanley was reminded of how Rocky sipped ice tea from a tall glass sitting at her patio table. He chewed his food a little faster and tried to focus on what was around him now.

The rest of the evening was taken up with more questions about Hanley, his past, why he came and American politics. Hanley asked few questions. As his exhaustion became too much for him, he apologized for his frequent yawns. He was taken back to the sleeping quarters. On the way, they stopped to see the building housing the showers, another large, unpainted wooden building, the interior divided with thin plywood sheets into rooms. One room was larger and contained sinks and a long table, the rest stalls with showers or toilets, amenities Hanley would soon come to appreciate. Long sheets of heavy, white cotton cloth were tacked to the rafters, creating a ceiling for the rooms and some small amount of privacy. Two white lightbulbs hung from cords attached to the rafters.

"We are fortunate to have electricity. It often fails and so we provide a candle and holder," the priest explained. "I have not had a chance to ask about Sophie; is she well?" he asked the American.

"Yes, she is very well. When I left them, they were both well and happy. She sends her love. She is a lovely, decent woman, Father."

"Yes, she is. Thank you," the priest said. "Tomorrow is a busy day here. It will be especially busy for you. We wake very early at Mapuordit. So, take your sleep while you can. There is one more thing which I will begin to explain tonight and continue to explain tomorrow. Monsieur, nothing could possibly have prepared you for what you will see here in Sudan. It is unlike anything you have ever known. You will need to control yourself because what you will see will both anger and sadden you in ways you did not know were possible. This country is in a terrible way. Terrible things are happening now. Everything you do must be done with care. When these things begin to affect you, then you must allow God to care for you. Good night."

5

Sand colored but a bit redder, the wall radiated heat, not like the welcoming warmth of toasted bread but the alarm raising heat of a large bonfire or a blast furnace full of molten iron, a tub holding the drippings from a careless and sloppy sun hanging overhead. Fear took hold of Hanley, a deep and instantly recognizable fear, the kind he'd known for as long as he could remember, a significant part of his memory album, conjured-up, an early memory of stumbling on a king snake in his parent's backyard, its sudden odd twisting unnatural flight or the odd-lost fear his parents would never come back from a dinner out without him. The wall's intense heat burned his face and then his hands, raised to protect and protest its radiant violence. But now he was awake, disoriented and tired, the gauze of the insect screening over his bed as obscurant as his dreams. Hanley longed for more sleep before the next day started.

***

The next morning Father Robineau introduced the American to Jumma, who was to be his young Sudanese mentor as they shared a small breakfast of tea and dried biscuits with sliced fruit. He found the young African was polite, but inquisitive, fascinated about everything it seemed, particularly anything American. Hanley liked him immediately. Jumma told Hanley

44

he had been at the mission at Mapuordit for almost six years and that his father, mother and brothers lived in Rumbek. The priest said Jumma was assigned to Hanley for the next few days at least. After breakfast, Hanley, Father Jean-Robert and Jumma walked the compound while Hanley was introduced to the workers and shown the other buildings.

"Tell me more about Sophie and her husband. I have not been back for more than two years. I know you said they are well and happy, but tell me of the last time you saw them," the priest asked.

Hanley explained that his first trip to France was over two years earlier. He was attending the Paris Air Show for the first time. He stayed with Michael and Sophie at their home in Saint-Nazaire on the coast of southern Normandy. He was also their guest for two days when he stopped on his journey to Africa. He told the priest of the dinner with Father Bertrand during the first trip which brought a smile to the face of the priest. Jumma sat and listened, his eyes never leaving Hanley's face for a second.

The old priest said, "My niece is a beautiful woman; not just physically, but in all ways. I'm certain you saw this, Mr Martin; everyone does. Her father is so proud of her. She is a doctor of psychiatry, did you know that? Yes? Then you know she does not practice and does not talk about it. Her experiences were bad and she quit her practice. She does not discuss it, nor does her husband." Hanley knew about it, but no details. Michael Campbell mentioned it to Hanley years ago, saying only that it was her decision and that he honored it, as well as her request not to talk about it. Hanley had told no one.

"Where is Sister Marie Claire?" Hanley asked.

"Sister Marie Claire is in Yirol today gathering some supplies for us. She will return this evening. Perhaps you will meet her then," Jumma said. The young African smiled upon hearing the name of the nun. Hanley wondered why her name brought the young man such happiness.

After the priest left them, Jumma began Hanley's tutorial of the Land Rover.

"Pump the throttle three times quickly and then turn the ignition key, please," Jumma ordered. With skin the color of a ripe walnut husk, Jumma's immaculate white shirt shone like newly cleaned silver in the midmorning sun. Hanley's lesson in starting the old Land Rover had just begun. Jumma was twenty years old, intense, with a wisdom only a childhood filled with unspeakable horrors can leave to one so young.

Modifying slightly what he was told to do, Hanley turned the engine over immediately. The smile on Jumma's face told Hanley his young tutor was pleased.

"Jumma, years of starting airplanes such as the Beech has given me a feel for such things, but I could not have done that without your expert guidance," he shouted over the rumble of the old engine. The young man beamed his delight and gave Hanley a thumb's up. Two of the fingers on his right hand were missing. Seeing Hanley's gaze lingering on his hand, Jumma explained, "My missing fingers are the result of torture by the Sudanese rebels. They wanted to know where my family had gone when we fled our village in southern Darfur. I was separated from my family during the flight and was picked up by rebel forces in a nearby village. I was thirteen."

Hanley's grip on the steering wheel tightened as he listened to Jumma calmly explaining how his father taught his children to mix the truth with lies, enough to keep the family safe. Jumma told his captors the family sought shelter in a village nine kilometers north of his home. "My father prepared his children well," Jumma said. "Many nights I lay awake and practiced in my mind telling the rebels or the Sudanese soldiers what my family had done to make a living or where they had gone if they were forced to leave our village," Jumma said. "After I was released and received medical treatment, I joined my family at Rumbek, at the Catholic compound, where we planned to meet should we become separated."

To Hanley, Jumma sounded too detached when describing the experience. The inside of the truck seemed suddenly to close in around him, Jumma's stories falling on Hanley like stones.

The early morning heat combined with the faint smells of old oil, gasoline and the African dust, filling Hanley's nose, a bitter taste on his tongue, its tip stuck to the inside of his front teeth. Rapid breaths filled his lungs with the dusty African air and he choked, coughed into his fist, tears appearing in the corners of his eyes. Wiping his damp cheeks, Hanley wondered if Jumma thought of his future in days or weeks and not years as Hanley did when young. "Sorry, I need some air," he said, stepping from the vehicle.

Reaching across the seat, Jumma turned the ignition to off. "Don't worry, Mr Martin, the air around Mapuordit must be taken in with much care," he told Hanley as he came around the front of the vehicle. "I can get a surgical mask if you would like one," Jumma said.

"What happened to your sisters?"

Jumma said he learned two of his sisters had been taken by Janjaweed soldiers. He said, "They may have been raped or killed or taken north and sold to slave traders. My father told me this. I have not seen them since we fled our village."

Jumma sat on the bumper, the hot morning sun behind the truck, its front still cool enough to be comfortable. Hanley straightened up, air now moving into his lungs. Wiping his hands on the front of his cargo pants, feeling queasy, the uncertainty of his situation resting just beneath his stomach, he stumbled, catching himself on the hot metal of the front fender. The day just started, his stay in Sudan just started, he was still catching up from the long, long flight. He was disoriented. The bumper was warm. Sitting down, Hanley was comforted by the closeness to a large machine, a peculiarity started on his uncle's farm, when he would sit against the large rear wheel of the tractor, shaded from the central Indiana sun, as he ate the lunch his aunt made, carried in a small, re-used brown bag. He sighed loudly.

Jumma said, "While in Rumbek, I learned French and some English from the Catholics. At fifteen, I was sent to Mapuordit to work at the mission."

"Jumma, I want to drive to the airstrip. Will you come with me?"

"Yes, Mr Martin."

Preparing to depart, Hanley adjusted the outside mirror, noticing it was cracked, struck by a rock or a branch, perhaps. As they slowly drove to the airstrip, Hanley saw a number of small camps that surrounded the Catholic outpost. There were some ragged tents and many huts made from branches, wood scraps and grass. A few had corrugated metal here and there. All were depressing to Hanley. A severe jolt sent Hanley out of his seat and the old truck off the road where Hanley stopped. Jumma had not moved at all.

"Sorry, I was looking at the camps where the people have settled. I wasn't watching the road."

Hanley's young friend smiled. "I know," he said, "I was watching you. I should be driving so you can see what you can see."

The ground around the Land Rover was dry, so getting back on the road was not difficult. Hanley paid attention to keeping the truck away from the ruts and larger stones. Sometime later, they approached the clearing surrounding the airstrip. Hanley slammed the truck to a halt. Surrounding his airplane were a half dozen men whose ages ranged from that of Jumma's to one old man who looked to be ancient. Some wore simple brown robes gathered at the shoulder, some a colorful beaded corset and nothing else. Their heads and feet were bare. They did not speak or look at each other. As Hanley stepped from the truck, the men all moved to the tail of the plane, where, together, they walked into the bush, vanishing before his eyes.

"They watched the airplane during the night; to protect it from thieves," Jumma explained.

Staring into the brush where the men disappeared, Hanley asked, "Who are they? Who asked them to watch the plane?"

"They are Atuot. No one asked them. The people know you have come from America to help. They also know this plane can bring them medicine and may save the lives of their children.

It has value to them. They will protect it. No one needed to tell them to watch," the young man said.

Slowly, Hanley circled the Beech, looking for any signs of vandalism. He saw none. When he came to the rear of the plane, he noticed some seeds laid out on the tail section, laid out in a pattern. At the end of the pattern was a mark. Moving in to inspect it closer, he saw the mark to be a rough outline of a bird, painted next to the right stabilizer. The paint was yellow and looked to be no more than mud.

"What does this mean?" Hanley asked.

Jumma looked at the seeds and the symbol. "They have blessed your airplane. They are feeding the bird so that it can always fly. They want this bird to live a long life."

"Yeah, me too," Hanley said. Looking up at the dull blue sky, Hanley wiped sweat from the back of his neck and under his jaw. The day grew hotter, a heat greater than he had ever experienced. "Jumma, have you ever flown in a plane?"

"No, Mr Martin, I have not," Jumma said.

"I think you will fly in this one. When I travel, there may be times I need help loading medicine or supplies or even need a translator, assuming the different dialects are not a problem for you. Yes, I think that someday you may fly with me. Well, then, let me show you how this one works and get you ready for your first flight, whenever that might be. Then I'll need you to return to the mission and bring me a sturdy wood box to carry some of my belongings. That sound all right with you?"

"Yes, Sturdy means strong. When I fly, will I be afraid?" Jumma asked.

"No, Jumma, you'll love it," Hanley said.

Jumma looked skeptical. The young African said, "Sister Marie Claire said only the French truly know how to fly. You are not French."

"She said that, did she? The good sister must have forgotten her history," Hanley said. "Come on, let's look at the inside of this old plane. There are things I need to retrieve."

6

Tightened by weeks of vibration, the screws holding the cover of the compartment concealing the five bottles of RedBreast whiskey took Hanley over thirty minutes to remove. To be alone for this, he sent Jumma back to the compound to find a box. The bottles were intact, protected by the padding he wrapped them in and a cheap nylon gym bag stuffed in with the bottles for the trip. Leaving the whiskey in their wrappings, he put them in the bag and zipped it shut, setting it on the ground next to the plane near his other bags and a box with books and pictures from home. Hanley then carried a small aluminum ladder outside and covered the engines with shrouds that would protect them from dust. He tethered each propeller to a landing gear strut, using a sock attached to a cord designed for that purpose, finishing his routine by locking the plane's rear cargo door. He would not be flying for a couple of days and wanted the plane secured until then. The idea of sleeping in the plane crossed his mind, but changed it after seeing the Atuot standing guard.

He learned that morning the first flight he would make would be to Kenya for medical supplies and to bring a surgeon to Mapuordit to assist in a complicated procedure designed to correct the birth-defected foot of an eighteen-month old Cic boy, the Cics a clan of the Dinkas. The next day, he would then fly the surgeon back to Kenya and return with more supplies. A gift from a Swedish charity allowed all this to happen, including the fuel for the flights. Hanley would refuel in Kenya and have a significant amount left when he returned to Mapuordit.

Kenya would be interesting, he knew. As a boy, he had read stories in magazines about exotic animals, big game. Stories about Teddy Roosevelt and Stanley and Livingston. In college, he read Isak Dinesen and Hemingway. The mystery of Africa and Kenya in particular were not lost to him. It was important that he notice, that all the beauty and misery around him mean something, have it sink in, allow it to find a place in his consciousness and rest there, be nurtured and take root. Understanding Africa and Sudan was necessary if he was to stay safe, do his job and understand its people.

Soon, he would meet Sister Marie Claire. He must control the feeling that was growing in him, the anticipation and excitement. He was a bit afraid of his reaction, that trapdoors in his head would spring open, questions and fears spraying over the nun, popping forth like confetti from a can, his insecurities fluttering to the ground.

In the distance, he could hear the faint rough humming of a vehicle approaching. A small bit of fear, ice pressed against the bottom of his heart, shortened his breath. Were there government troops in this area or was it the boy? Squinting, Hanley looked toward the sound through the thick brush, squat bushes with small yellow flowers mixed with dead scrub and tan grass, a slight breeze shifting and mixing it all through which he soon saw a light-colored vehicle approaching from the southeast. Bumping up and down over the rough, Jumma's white shirt shone through the dusty glass of the windscreen. The engine strained, the volume of its noise marking the boy's command over its progress. It raised dust shifting in the wind, a sheet falling and sliding away from the truck, replaced by another. Hanley smelled the grass and the brush, a baked smell, compressed by the heat of the day, unable to float for long, pushed for a while by the breeze, driven quickly to the ground by the heat.

Jumma was now driving the old Toyota Land Cruiser. Its paint was a faded cream color, but it was in remarkably good shape for its age, Hanley thought. Rolling to a slow stop, the engine cut off and the young Sudanese slid from the driver's seat. Smiling brightly, Jumma said, "Sister Marie Claire will not be back until tonight. Father Robineau said I should tell you this." They loaded Hanley's belongings into the rear and started back.

"This old machine's in good shape. Just how many vehicles does the mission have?" Hanley asked.

"We have three trucks; this one, the English one and a bigger truck for hauling supplies. It is German, I think. Sister Marie Claire drives the big truck. She can drive as well as any of the men, better than some, I believe." Jumma smiled slightly after saying this.

Hanley said, "I suppose she has never driven off the road and always pays strict attention when she drives."

"So you know of Sister Marie Claire?" Jumma asked. "Is she known for her driving in America?"

"I know of Sister Marie Claire, but not for her driving," Hanley said.

"How is it you know of her then?" Jumma asked.

"She has a friend, another nun, in America that is also a friend of mine. They met in college before becoming nuns. They were exchange students, visiting each other's family while studying abroad. They've been friends since then. Our mutual friend's name is Sister Mary Kathleen." Hanley pursed his lips and looked at Jumma. He asked, "Jumma, do Father Robineau and Sister Marie Claire like each other? I have the impression Father Robineau finds the good sister a bit difficult at times. Is that so?"

Jumma's face went blank and his eyes grew large, startled. "I cannot say," he said softly, barely audible against the racket of the truck.

"Have I made you uncomfortable, Jumma?"

Jumma looked at Hanley, shook his head and said, "Sister Marie Claire wants Father Robineau to be stronger, stronger for the people we help. The good Father tells her she can only be as strong as the church allows her to be. I have heard this. The Sister says that is not strong enough. She says, if the church will not be strong for the people, then she will be strong for them. That if the church will not help her, she will find the help by herself."

"What help does she need?"

"You must ask her that yourself," Jumma said. Picking up the wooden box Hanley filled with his belongings, the young man turned to load the box in the old truck.

***

In his room, Hanley discovered he overestimated the amount of space available for storing his belongings. The old black foot locker was not capable of holding everything. The gym bag full of whiskey went in first and then as much else as he could squeeze in. The rest remained in boxes which he stacked in a corner. Hanley felt no guilt for having smuggled liquor into a Catholic mission, telling himself there were probably many other bottles stashed in foot lockers and in holes all over the compound.

He laid a photo of Elizabeth and Carrie on the cot. From the leather satchel, he took the one photo of Rocky he had and laid it on the cot next to the other. Staring at them, he allowed himself to think just how far from home he was. Even if he flew the Beech to Cairo to catch a jet to the states, it would still take him two or three days to get home. Flying the Beech meant more than a week with no long stops, assuming the plane did not break down. The picture of his daughter and granddaughter was framed and he sat that on the small table beside the cot. The picture of Rocky had no frame. Hanley sat it on a ledge above his cot, the ledge created by a two by four used to frame the building. If possible, he would buy a frame for Rocky's picture in one of the larger towns when he had a chance.

Hanley left the barracks and found Jumma waiting for him sitting cross-legged beneath a tree. In his lap was a large book. Looking up, the younger man smiled and asked, "Do you know Julia Child?"

"Yes, everyone knows Julia Child," Hanley responded.

"I like to read her recipes. She is so thorough. I think she gives her work much thought. This is important, don't you agree?"

"Yes."

"I like to cook. Someday, I want to attend a school to learn to make great food. Maybe in Paris or New York. A place where food is so plentiful you can use it to decorate other food. We don't decorate in Sudan, not with food. Not with anything really, not now."

"Maybe someday you can study with Julia Child," Hanley said.

A smile that Hanley thought could not possibly get bigger did. "Julia Child teaching me to cook coq au vin would be a dream come true," Jumma said. He closed the book and rose effortlessly from the ground. "Let me put my book away and we will help with the children."

The wasteful practice of using food for decoration had not occurred to Hanley, but it had to Jumma. Hanley felt stupid. When you must fight each day to find food, it would matter. Sister Mary Kathleen told Hanley that starvation was now a weapon being used against the people in western Sudan. The war being waged in Sudan was ugly, even for war. Starvation, rape, mutilation and slavery were now weapons and tactics. Killers changed tactics and alliances to the point that understanding the nature of the conflict and its participants had become difficult. Human rights groups and relief organizations, including the Christian organizations operating in the area, struggled with identifying who to cooperate with and who not to trust.

**

Dinner at the mission that evening consisted of a thin soup, bread and fruit. Water in bottles was all that was available to drink. That people drank bottled water was not a surprise to Hanley; its availability was. Cigarette smoke divided the air in the room into two layers the smoke floating among the exposed trusses, creating shifting halos around the bare lightbulbs. A disinfectant smell overpowered the odors of the food, the bare-wood floor damp in the corners, small puddles reflecting the light bulbs overhead as quivering eggs in the pooled water beneath.

"How difficult is it to find bottled water?" Hanley asked no one in particular as they ate. The same group of people sat at the table eating as the night before, less one doctor, the younger one who fetched a glass for Hanley and Father Robineau. The doctor and the priest were visiting a family at their tent not far from the compound. A child was too sick to come in for treatment, requiring a house call, one of the other physicians explained. He was the oldest of the Slovakian physicians, nearer to Hanley's age. His name was Dr Ivor Malsoiak.

"Bottled water is not easy to come by," one of the French nurses answered. "We have been to Yirol and Rumbek several times in the past month and were able to stock up. When it's not available, we use tablets or boil the water. Bottled water is better." Her name was Estelle. She was also a nun, from the Mary Knoll Order, as were all the French nuns.

"Father Jean-Robert said a report had come in over the radio, saying the SPLA was in the area north of Rumbek, searching villages for supporters of the government. He suggested everyone stay near the compound for the next few days until we know what's going on," Dr Malosiak said.

This was the first such report Hanley heard since arriving. For some reason, he thought it likely he would find the compound surrounded and the countryside full of war.

"The SPLA must be running low on food. They try to fool the outsiders by disguising their confiscation of food and supplies as searches for government sympathizers. They're just looters like the GOS forces or the Janjaweed. They don't rape as many women or kill as many children, so they think they're the good guys," Sister Estelle explained to Hanley. Her look bordered between sad and bored.

The soup tasted vaguely like vegetable soup, but stronger. It was made of mostly onions with some beet or potato-like ground fruit and something long and green, but definitely not a bean; more like grass. It tasted strongly of pepper, but sweeter. In a chipped white bowl were apples and pears, all small and misshapen, sculpted by birds and bugs before picked by humans. Jumma was not present. He ate with the other native workers. This form of segregation was expected here and Hanley was certain he was the only one that noticed. He was hungry and ate his soup, which seemed to surprise the others. Not noticing until he was almost finished, he asked, "You all seem to be watching my progress through dinner. Am I making a mistake or is watching an American eat more entertaining than I realized. If so, thn I will be happy to entertain all of you each evening as long, as I'm fed that is."

Everyone smiled. Dr Milosiak said, "No, we don't find Americans especially entertaining, other than your *Saturday Night Live*, it's just that not many find this soup to their liking. We are pleased you like it, that is all. Tell me, Mr Martin, we hear you are very wealthy. Why would you come here to do this work? You're not hiding from something back in Coco Indiana, are you?"

"I'm not that wealthy. And, no, I'm not hiding. Please call me Hanley. I'm from Kokomo, not Coco; although my granddaughter would find Coco funny. A friend of mine says she thinks of monkeys whenever she hears the name Kokomo."

"But the plane is yours, is it not? It looks new even though it is old. You have the money to keep an old plane new, do you not? We have been told you left behind several businesses to come here. So, it seems you may be wealthy. We don't see many wealthy people coming to Sudan to work, that's all."

Hanley did not like the direction this conversation was taking. Not certain whether the doctor was merely curious or something else, he wanted to move off his past and why he was here. "I worked hard all my life and was lucky to have some success. I did leave my businesses to work here for a year, maybe a bit more, we'll see. It was a difficult decision, one that I wrestled with for some time. I am here and I want to make a difference, if possible. I was raised to believe that everyone must contribute. Even though I did that, I gave back by giving people jobs, paying taxes and doing it as honestly as I could; it didn't seem to be enough. Maybe this will tell me if it was."

Hanley realized the doctors and nurses knew of his background. Between letters from Father Bertrand to Father Jean-Robert and letters from Sister Mary Kathleen to Marie Claire, his background was known to the staff. Pilots willing to fly relief work in areas such as Sudan were rare. It was dangerous and other flying jobs, even in this part of the world, paid better. It was also generally known that Hanley was flying for the cost of his fuel only. That was not seen as unusual; many of the doctors that rotated in an out of the country were volunteers working through churches or relief organizations. He knew there was nothing really rare about that.

"Don't get me wrong, Mr Martin. I am glad you are here. I hope you will be with us for some time. Pilots are hard to find and even harder to keep."

"So I've heard," Hanley said.

***

Sometime before midnight, Hanley awoke to the sound of a large truck entering the compound. Hushed conversations followed and then the sound of people working; cardboard scraping across wood and metal, supplemented by grunting and the occasional laugh or curse; mostly, the sound of movement and eventually silence. Then came the sound of a woman singing, soft and clear. A song he did not recognize; could not. It was sung in French. It was her.

7

Hanley woke to a dull morning light, shivered under his thin blanket, knew he was awake for the day, rubbed his eyes. Since childhood, rubbing his eyes had been comforting. With his hands balled into fists and using a circular motion, he massaged both his eyes together. The massaging stopped, turning into a quick rub of his face, Hanley stopped, sat up, stood and stretched. Pulling on his pants and a shirt, he picked up his watch, wallet and pocket knife and left the room, pulling its door shut behind him.

His room was the last room used as an apartment on the end of the hallway of the barracks that would be his home for the year or so he spent in Sudan. Across from his room was another used as a supply closet. He knew he would look in the room across the hall someday, but not this morning.

A door at the end of the hallway led outside, where a small, square platform made a porch. The porch was an open box frame made of lumber with a plywood top. The box rested on dirt leveled to provide a stable structure when stepped on. It wobbled badly as Hanley stepped out, the early morning light as dull as that in his room. Sitting on the edge of the box, he took in his surroundings, the smell of burning wood, smoking campfires in the distance marking the small spots where people had stopped to rest and gather themselves, their families, their lives. There was no dew, no dampness of any sort. Small noises, people talking, children, not happy, no cars, trains, television, airplanes, the things he would hear every day. There were the noises of country, birds, bugs, wind. Closing his eyes, he listened and heard the sounds of his youth, the wind and the birds similar, the bugs somewhat similar but not quite; these were more of a presence, persistent, insistent.

He opened his eyes. A man appeared in the distance, near a crude shelter, beside him a small child. Hanley could not tell if it was a boy or girl. The child followed the man about as he moved around the camp, never more than a foot or two behind him. As he neared a fire used for cooking, the man stopped, turn slightly around and slapped the child hard across it face, knocking the child down. A few seconds passed before a thin, faint wail reached Hanley's ears. The man moved on leaving the child lying in the dirt. "The child is not his," Jumma said from the corner of the building. "He is making certain it doesn't become too close to him. Did I say that correctly?"

"You meant attached. Close is right too," Hanley said.

"Have you eaten?" Hanley asked.

"Yes, but I will go with you if you want." Leaning against the building, the young man stared toward the crying child, his face blank. Hanley wondered how many children Jumma had seen slapped in his young life; countless probably.

"Is Sister Marie Claire in the compound this morning?" Hanley asked as he stood, rubbing his hands together, watching the child, now standing, crying while looking about, lost. The child's helplessness made him think of Carrie his granddaughter. He did not want to start that.

"Yes, she's here," Jumma said. "If she hears that child crying, she will be at that camp soon."

"Yeah? I guess that's not a surprise from what I've heard. Come to the canteen while I find something to eat."

"Canteen?"

"The dining room or whatever you call it. Come on, after that, we'll look at our first flight. It will take some planning. I'll need to file a flight plan by telephone and I'll need your help. Then we'll need to go over the plane, review its operation and what you can expect," Hanley told Jumma.

"You talk as if I will fly with you. Why? I do not know if I will fly with you. No one has said I will fly with you. Father Robineau has said nothing about that. Has he?" Jumma's expression appeared to be one of true alarm to Hanley.

He smiled, "No, he hasn't. I've been thinking about it; you should fly with me, often, I think. Maybe always." Jumma, sweat now dotting his forehead, looked, squinting into the washed-out sky, as if gauging its ability to support him. After a moment, he looked at Hanley and said, "If I fly, I'll see new things. I'll look down and see what a bird sees, see what is beyond the trees, see what I can't see standing here on earth. That should be better should it not?"

"It doesn't always help," Hanley said.

**

The cement block building where the children were examined and treated was on the eastern edge of the compound. Forty feet long and twenty wide, it had a wooden roof and beneath its eaves were long openings for windows, but the windows had no framing or glass. Off to one side, perhaps twenty feet away from the far end was the remains of another building, a pale brown mud brick, a dull, roasted color. The bricks were rough, some misshapen, the exposed beams even rougher. There was no roof and one end wall and a portion of a side wall were gone, the rubble lying about in the scrub grass around the old building.

Hanley came around the new block building and stopped. It was just after noon. He skipped lunch, believing he was not missing much as far as the food was concerned and he did not wish to face the Slovakian doctors again. He came to look over the new building and to find Jumma whom he had left in Father Robineau's office around ten o'clock. What stopped him was the singing.

The same voice he heard the night before while lying in the dark of his room was coming from somewhere near. It took a second but he soon realized the singing was coming from the ruined building. It sounded like a lullaby, soft and flowing, soothing. Hanley walked toward the sound, transfixed. Conscious of his intrusion, he softened his steps as he neared the old building.

The wall facing him was intact, with two openings for windows high up to allow for the movement of air but to keep the rains out, when it rained. He walked to the end where a wall had been and stepped around to look inside.

Sitting on a stool in the middle of a dirt floor was a woman of forty or so, slender, with a back as straight as a child's, wearing a plain blue dress and a white scarf around her head. She was holding an infant of about six months, bathing him with a sponge, a bucket of water at her feet. On her hands were latex gloves. The baby's dark head was practically bald; its wet scalp reflected the sun's light as if painted a bright gold. The child made no noise but waved its arms around as the nurse sponged water over its body and head. A towel lying across her lap, under the infant, was soaking wet. The woman sang as she worked, the song flowing over the child with the water. Hanley could only stare. It was like a scene from one of his dreams; for some reason beautiful but strange.

From the side, Hanley saw that the face of the woman, once fair, was now brown from the Sudanese sun. She had deep wrinkles at the corners of her mouth and eyes. Her hair was light brown, with some gray showing where it was visible just above her forehead. Years of hard work in places such as this had rendered her features weathered, but she was still lovely he thought. Her eyes never left the face of the child. The singing stopped and she said in French accented English, "You're the American, the friend of Mary Kathleen?"

"Yes, I'm Hanley Martin. You must be Sister Marie Claire."

"You do not look as I thought you would." She had not turned to look at him, had not seen him as far as he could tell.

"She said you were handsome. I suppose I expected someone else. My friend has a very odd sense of humor. She said you were sincere and sincerity goes a long way here in the bush. This child has leprosy and that is why I'm bathing him here and not in the clinic." She told him as if he had wondered.

It had not occurred to Hanley that the child might be sick.

"Shouldn't you be wearing a mask or something?"

"Or something? Right now, it's not a concern, at least not for me. He comes from a family where there is leprosy; his grandmother. She has been caring for him for the past three months, since his mother was killed by the Janjaweed. His aunt brought him to us because she could not care for him or did not want to. It should matter but it doesn't. He's been here for almost a month. I don't think it's a threat to me. His bathwater contains an antibacterial solution. His aunt said the grandmother covered her mouth and hands with cloths when she handled him. She boiled the cloths each night. It wasn't enough. I didn't say that right, did I?"

"Sounded right to me. I have to say that I admire your courage; or your commitment. The work being done here is truly amazing." Hanley's appreciation was genuine.

"My courage is nothing compared to the courage of the people here. I have no courage. Their lives have been turned into a hell on earth. They face constant persecution and starvation. Many Europeans and Americans could not comprehend what these people face almost every day of their lives. They are being chased from this land in the name of a god that must cry or scream at what's being done here, at the cruelty."

As she spoke, her voice grew louder with a deepening intensity. Suddenly, the baby in her arms began crying, a sudden, loud wail of fright. Sister Marie Claire stopped and began to whisper to the child, gently rocking him back and forth. The baby's scream turned to sobbing as the nun comforted the child. She put the boy to her shoulder and stood, walking back and forth beside the stool. As she stood, the wet towel fell to the ground and she kicked it away as she walked. Hanley moved to where she had been and picked the towel up at its edge with two fingers. He laid it across the stool and said, "When was the last time you wrote to Sister Mary Kathleen? She always complained that you didn't write often enough. That seems to be a common complaint of the people with friends and relatives working here."

"Wait and you will see. Time to write does not come often. I hear Jumma's been assigned to help you become acquainted with the mission and the area. He's a good one to have for that. He's one of the brightest we have taken in. I have much hope for him, but schooling is difficult. Money is always an issue and a position for non-Muslims at the university is difficult," she said.

With the boy now quiet, his head resting on her shoulder, the nun, turned to Hanley and asked, "Will you carry the stool and the bucket back to the clinic for me?" She leaned and retrieved the wet towel, then walked with quick strides to the open end of the ruined building. "Just pour the water out on the ground." She instructed and went toward the clinic.

Doing as he was asked, Hanley dumped the bucket and took both it and the stool as he followed the nun to the cement block building. She already disappeared through a door near the end. The sound of children crying had been a faint noise behind their conversation, registering a mild discord as they became acquainted. Entering the clinic, the dismay and fear of children being ministered to surrounded him, their sounds again reminding him of his granddaughter. A nurse was taking the child from Sister Marie Claire, who removed her gloves and washed her hands in a nearby sink, then turned to her next patient, a girl of either fifteen or sixteen years. The nun held the girl's face in both hands and asked her something in a language Hanley did not recognize. A frightened look was the response, with eyes wide and uncertain, her face dark and thin, with high, pronounced cheek bones and a thin, straight nose. Hanley thought her features had the echo of some other heritage. Small straight scars were visible on both cheeks. Her hair was cropped short. Keeping a hand to the girl's face Sister Marie Claire reached into a pocket of her dress and produced a small light, the kind used when examining patients or searching for car keys inside a jumbled purse. The nun asked another nurse, the African, for something in the same language that Hanley could not understand. She shined the light into the girls' eyes, then her ears and finally her mouth. The other nurse came with a long swab, the end of which was soaked in something orange and swabbed the girl's throat. Throughout the process, the girl appeared scared, despite the nun's attempts to comfort her. She only relaxed when she was told she could get down from the stool. She smiled somewhat uncertainly but her face did not relax. Hanley watched the nun write a note on a form clamped to a clipboard. She hung the board on a small brass hook screwed into the end of a long table. Hanley looked at the counter top, saw very few supplies, saw the despair in the wanting. He was surprised by his reaction. Whenever he had seen a doctor, he always took note of the amount of supplies kept in the examining room. Open cardboard boxes always dripped latex gloves onto the counter, antiseptic wipes wrapped in small packets strewn about and tongue depressors, striking in their uniform perfection, held by the dozens in large glass jars. Here, there was no such excess. Only a cloudy drinking glass with three tongue depressors propped up on the side, waiting in loneliness for replacements next to a box of tissues. Hanley hoped the cabinets beneath the counter top held more supplies, medicines and ointments, something that would at least give these people a chance, some hope.

"She's lovely is she not?" the nun asked Hanley.

"Yes, she most certainly is. Her features look as if she has something other than African in her. Is she local?"

"She is from west of Rumbek, more toward the Darfur region. Her name is Naja. What you see is the result of the rape of her mother by men from the north. This war is old but the consequences of war are still young. She is here now because her mother was raped again and then murdered; beaten to death with an axe handle, her sister also. She ran off and was not molested. A miracle. The women go into the brush outside the villages to gather firewood and sometimes wild food at a great risk every time but these are necessities for their families and so they do it. Heroes are not always in movies Mr Martin. When life is difficult, they are sometimes everywhere."

"Yes, I once saw a political cartoon that showed a professional basketball player standing next to a shabbily dressed woman holding a bucket. Under the basketball player was the description, "Paid millions to play a child's game;" under the woman was the caption, "Single mother who put three kids through college." Under both was the question, "Who is the real hero?" Maybe, when times are tough, just doing what needs to be done is a bit heroic," Hanley said.

"This has all turned to madness. I'm certain there are reasons that God will not show us, but the faith required is great, greater than I can maintain at times, if I have enough at all. We believed we are what we should be but most of the time we delude ourselves. Delude is the correct word is it not? *Oui? Bien.* So, what do I do to understand all of this? Tell me. Americans have all the answers, or so they say."

"Who says? I doubt that I or any American have answers for you. I have none for myself most of the time. I believe the rest of the world doubts that America knows what it's doing. At least they don't seem to think so, not to me, not anymore. Do you want to know what Americans don't understand? Why do people dislike us so until they need our help? I mean, when people do need help, then they call on us first. When things are good, we are the people everyone hates."

"Hate? I don't think Americans are hated. The actions of your leaders are questioned and often misunderstood. Your country does more than most. My own country does little for the people here and in other parts of Africa. America is not doing what it should. No one is. America shares its indifference towards Sudan and Africa with the rest of the world. I think Rwanda was a lesson no one learned."

"They had only people and not oil, which was their problem. Even in the Balkans, everyone hesitated to become involved until it was late in the day. I think the US's involvement had more to do with the politics of appeasing Muslims as with humanitarian matters," Hanley said.

"That may be true but it seems so cynical don't you think?" Sister Marie Claire asked.

"Every decent, reasonable man is ashamed of the government he lives under or should be," Hanley said.

"Do you really believe that?"

"Maybe. It's a quote from H.L. Menken, I…"

The wood of the doorframe above the head of another nurse exploded, raining splinters over everyone nearby. Just as the wood began filling the air around the door, Hanley heard the faint crack of a gunshot; the distance was significant as the report was faint. Someone screamed, a child, but only one. Everyone in the clinic reflexively squatted down to the floor, everyone but Hanley. Sister Marie Claire hissed, "Get down" to the American but he stayed up, and turned toward the sound of the gunshot, on tip-toe, trying to look through the small, high window for the shooter in the bush beyond the clearing. A second bullet hit the cement block wall with enough force that Hanley felt it through the dirt floor into his boots. It would have hit Hanley just below his rib cage but for the impenetrability of the block. Hanley ducked down, a feeling of nakedness a surprise to him as he wondered what he should do. He thought that perhaps only an American has a first reaction of regret at not being armed when faced with attack. He would trade anything for a rifle at that moment, the bigger the better he thought. There was another crack of rifle fire but this shot failed to hit the building.

"Stay down," The nun instructed as she and the other nurses made certain the children remained on the floor and did not run for the doors. No one made a sound. The children did not cry but remained composed, their sullen expressions nurtured by a short life filled with the threat of violence. Another round struck the building and then the sound of automatic gunfire could be heard in the distance. Three short bursts, ten seconds of silence and then a single shot. No one moved for another minute or so. Hanley stood slightly and walked, bent over, to the door and went outside. "No," the nun said but he was past her and out before she could move. Outside, Hanley moved down along the gray block, straining to hear any movement, the approach of men through the brush. He heard nothing. The entire compound had gone prone, waiting for the appropriate number of minutes to pass, a unit of time that experience randomly chose as enough. Hanley, bent over as he walked, made it to the corner of the building and surveyed the compound. He saw several people lying on the ground, others sitting behind trees, away from where they believed the gunfire was coming; some lying beneath a large truck, the one that had arrived late last night, he suspected. No one moved. Hanley slowly peeked around the corner of the building and looked in the direction from where he thought the shots had come. He stared into the bush and trees, squinting, trying to force his eyes into being more efficient. He could feel his eyes resisting. Maybe they didn't want to see what was out there he thought. "You've always been good, but I didn't realize you were also smart," he said aloud to his eyes.

When a hand touched his shoulder, Hanley twisted around quickly, producing a pain in his lower back, causing him to reach back to find the muscle that cramped.

"Are you trying to get yourself shot?" a harsh whisper asked. Sister Marie Claire held on to his shoulder, which did not help the pain.

"No. Do you really believe I would?" Hanley said rubbing his back muscle to make the pain go away. The shirt he was wearing was soaked through but he hadn't notice until he grabbed for his back. The nun hung on, pulling Hanley back from the corner of the building. The pain started to fade and he turned, wrenching his shoulder away from her grip.

"Let go, will you?" Hanley turned to the nurse. Her face was composed and stern. "I will not be ignored," she said. "You cannot have had any experience with this type of thing Mr Martin. You will get yourself killed and you haven't been here a week. We have spent some time developing a plan for you. If you're dead, you're of not much value to us."

"I wanted to see if anyone needed help and I was checking to see if anyone with a gun was heading this way," Hanley said. "Anyway, it's touching that you should be so concerned, especially considering you've invested that much time in putting together my job description." Hanley moved back to the corner and peeked out again. Sister Marie Claire moved up and punched him in the shoulder. Hanley pressed his lips together hard, his expression of annoyance was washed over lightly with exasperation. He shook his head slightly back and forth. The heat of the day was now intense, dust rising from the ground seemingly on its own, searching for something to cover or penetrate. The hard dryness of his mouth was suddenly there, his tongue stuck in place against its roof, as a cigarette sticks to a dry lip. Swallowing several times, trying to conjure up some spit, he said, "A friend of mine in college, who was educated in a Catholic High School in Ohio, said all nuns were sadists."

"Well, then get shot, I really shouldn't care," she said. He expected to hear her walk away but she stayed right behind him. Hanley saw that the man who had found shelter behind the tree was starting to move. Slowly he slid down to lay on his back and then carefully rolled over making certain most of his body remained protected by the tree. He then slowly peered around to look in the direction of the gunfire. The man and the tree were maybe sixty feet from the children's clinic. As Hanley watched, he noticed the tree had sustained damage but the harm was not new; the bark was marred, badly marred. "The trees have saved some lives it seems," Hanley said. "How often does this happen?" he asked.

She did not answer and Hanley turned slightly to see why. The nun was moving back toward the other end of the building, toward a dense bit of brush at the edge of the clearing near the far end of the clinic. Hanley watched her movements for a second and then looked beyond toward the edge of the clearing. An arm and hand protruded from the dense brush, the dark skin stark against the light brown grass and dust. The nun was running, shouting for help to the others in the clinic. Hanley ran for her, knowing she was about to put herself in danger.

As he cleared the edge of the building, he stopped and crouched, looking to where the shots had come from. Jolted by an immediate shame, he straightened and ran hard to where the nun had fallen to her knees. She had not stopped, had not hesitated for an instant; but he had. She was half into the high grass, bent over the head of the child, pushing down on the grass, creating some space to work. Hanley caught up to her and when he saw the girl's head he turned away, bile rising to his throat. His mouth wide open, he gasped for air and choked back the acid rising to his lips. Spitting out the sour waste, he was aware of two more nuns running past, silent and scared; they had seen this before; this kind of death, a child's death, wasteful, horrid, stupid. The kind of death men cause; the kind women don't understand but have learned to deal with. No one should learn to accept this, Hanley thought.

It was the girl the nuns had just treated before the gunfire started, the girl from west of Rumbek, the beautiful girl whose mother had been raped and beaten to death. The entire left side of her head was missing, the bullet, the one that had not struck the building, had pierced her skull just above and slightly behind her right ear; it made mush of her brain and exited taking most of her head as a souvenir.

Sister Marie Claire stood and said something to the other nuns that Hanley did not hear. She stepped from the grass, her face white and rigid. Another nun, sobbed and Sister Marie Claire snapped something at her and then said to Hanley, "Get used to this Mr Martin. This is Sudan. She is Sudan; she *was* Sudan."

Two of the doctors came to the edge of the clearing, examined the body of the girl for a minute and then left. Three Sudanese men placed the body on a stretcher and carried it away, draped with a green sheet. It was now an hour since the gunfire had killed the girl. Movement was returning to the compound. Hanley sat in the Land Rover waiting for Jumma to ride with him to the airplane. After the girl was taken away, Sister Marie Claire told Hanley he would be meeting with Father Robineau, one of the doctors and her that evening to discuss his stay at the compound and his schedule, including his first flight for the organization.

8

Hanley wanted to see the plane; he needed to see the plane; he needed to see and touch something that made him feel normal. This feeling was certainly not normal. While planning for his move to Sudan, Hanley had thought that, at his age, he would be better prepared to handle what he knew he would see here. Now, as he sat in the old truck in the heat of this awful day, he knew he would never be prepared. He was soaked in his own sweat, the sweat of being near murder. It was strange that he was shocked but not surprised by what happened. He was also disappointed that he did not handle it better. Now his reaction was homesickness. It was a need to be back in Kokomo, to see Elizabeth, to hold Rocky, to walk his old dog. He was scared. Fear, his fear, of anything, was always a disappointment. Hanley most feared his weaknesses. Could he handle this, day after day for months? In his mind, he had always assumed he would be there for a year, maybe longer. Now, he questioned if he could stomach that kind of commitment. The thought of climbing into his plane and flying home had entered his head and while, at first, he liked it, the thought soon frightened him as much as the girl's murder. Giving up this soon was unacceptable. It would make a mockery of those he left behind in Kokomo, those people he loved who supported his decision, those whose lives he had disrupted. It would cheapen the effort of those who were working here, those who would stay, who were dedicated to helping these people. He could not leave, he knew that; it wasn't homesickness; it was wanting to be somewhere else, anywhere else.

After Sister Marie Claire turned away from Hanley and sent one of the other nurses for a doctor, Hanley saw Jumma leaning against the wall of the clinic. With his rear pressed against the block, the young African leaned over with his hands just above his knees, his legs straight down to the ground; his eyes were fixed on his sandals. Hanley noticed Jumma was shaking slightly as he approached his young friend. "Where were you when the gunshots started?" Hanley asked.

"I was near the front of the large truck when I heard the first shot. It sounded closer than many of the shots we hear but then I heard a scream. I fell to the ground to wait for more shots. You see, Mr Martin, we never know if these are bullets just passing through on their way to somewhere else or if they are meant for us. We never know, it seems strange to say that but it's true."

Jumma straightened up and started to move away from the building toward the truck. Hanley said, "I want to check the plane; will you go with me?"

Turning slightly toward Hanley, the young man said, "Yes, I will meet you at the old Land Rover in a few minutes. I want to put some water on my face before we go. Please wait for me; I would like to go with you."

In the truck, Hanley stared dumbly at nothing, unfocused, unsettled. He came around to again notice the driver's side mirror was cracked. The edge of the mirror casing had a half-moon shaped gouge in it; a bullet had cut through the edge of the metal and cracked the mirror. Hanley began looking around the old truck; at buildings, trees, vehicles even rocks; everywhere was the small round stamp of war; the pockmark of that human disease, that scar peculiar to man and his ways. He had not noticed before but now worried he would see them everywhere. Someone approached.

Jumma got in and sat still for a moment, then said, "These are the times when I think I will never see what is beyond the horizon. I will never know what I might become because soon life will have no more time for me. That girl, she thought she had time, everyone thinks they have time. I don't think that way, not any more. I think I will never see Paris. You have been there, tell me about Paris."

Water hung from his ears and sat in tiny round disks on his cheekbones. He was still shaking slightly and stared at the dashboard of the truck, his eyes now unfocused.

"I know little of Paris." Hanley said. "I can tell you it is beautiful; different. I can tell you there are places on this earth, cities, mountains, canyons, that, when you see them, you know they are special places. There's just something, you feel it in your chest as well as your eyes and in your brain. That's Paris. You know that no matter where you look, wherever you go in that city, it will be special; and that, if you don't look, you'll regret it. I know because I didn't look and I wish I had. That's all I can tell you."

"That is enough. Thank you. It is what I hoped you would say." He wiped his brow with an old handkerchief, the water and his sweat now simmered to a blend by the day's heat. Hanley started the truck, turned around in the grass of the compound and set off down the track in the direction of his airplane. Dust followed them; dust blew over the road in front of them. That part of the year that brought the rain was just ending. The rain fall was much lower than normal this season, as happened last year and the year before. Drought, it seemed, was now another weapon to be used against the people of southern Sudan, but by what enemy, Hanley wondered.

Once past the compound, everything appeared as it had the day before. Today there was less cloud cover and more sunlight; more heat. Today there was a greater sense of everything baking. It was only the end of March. What would the summer be like, he wondered? Hanley knew the plane would be like an oven inside. Tomorrow he would fly and he welcomed that; the dangers in the air could not be any greater than on the ground, he reasoned. It would be something familiar, something he could control. Control; would it be a problem for him now? Was that it? All his adult life he believed he had been in control. He was wrong. Belinda, his ex-wife and Elizabeth were proof he had had little control over his life for the past twenty-five years. He had controlled his businesses but his businesses weren't his life, not his real life; business was just a means, an effort. Someone had once told Hanley that eating and sleeping were the biggest wastes of a man's time. Even though he had benefited greatly from it, there were times when he considered business the third. He had been, was, proud of what he accomplished but it did not have the meaning it once did.

Ruts like logs strewn across the dirt road caused the nose of the truck to begin swaying back and forth. When the brush alongside the track cleared, Hanley drove the truck off the path and the ride smoothed for a bit. Dust covering both sides of the windshield made seeing difficult. Squinting in an attempt to see better, he could feel the pain of the headache he had growing in strength between his eyes, just above the bridge of his nose. He was sweating a lot and the dust was beginning to cake in the wrinkles that spread from the corner of his eyes onto his temples. Sweat was running down his neck and his back. He could feel the heat escaping from beneath his shirt around his collar. He had not been this hot in many years; not since working on his uncle's farm during the summers as a teenager. Air conditioning in his home, office and his truck had shielded him from even the relatively mild heat of the Indiana summers. This heat was something else. He would need to adapt, to train himself to bear it. Suddenly, he was as thirsty as he could ever remember being. "Did we bring water?" he asked.

"Yes, there is a can and a cup in the back. We always have some water. We never go anywhere without some water," he said.

Flashes of light appeared and disappeared from a distance as the truck neared the landing strip. The sun light reflected by the plane's surface was broken by the brush and trees as Hanley and Jumma approached. Hanley's headache had matured into a distinct pain at the front of his head, a pain like a thumb pressed between his eyes. Trying to see the plane, the flashing light made his head hurt even more. Pushing the truck faster only made things worse but he wanted to get there, to make certain it had not been damaged, to know that he could fly home if he wanted. Earlier, as he watched the two doctors walk back to the main clinic after examining the murdered girl, the idea that, if his plane was ever damaged, if it could not fly, he would feel trapped. Repairing the plane would be difficult if not impossible. Parts and the skilled labor needed to affect the repairs would be tough to find. That thought was the start of his headache. Now dreading what he might see, Hanley ignored the road's deplorable condition and pressed the truck hard into the clearing.

No damage to the plane was immediately apparent as the truck entered the area near the old shack, the airstrip terminal. Two young Sudanese men sat near the plane, both different from those Hanley had seen the day before but whose dress was similar.

"Are they from the same tribe?" Hanley asked.

"Yes," Jumma said.

Without looking at the truck, the young men rose and walked away into the bush. Turning off the truck's engine, Hanley sat and enjoyed the silence for a moment and then said, "I need some water."

The water was warm but Hanley didn't care. He drank two cups and then stopped. You'd better learn to pace yourself, he thought. His thirst was still strong, so much so that he wondered how he would ever adjust to it. Thirst had never been something to be afraid of. Now he started to fear it. It's just a reaction to everything that's happened today, he told himself. The wind blew off the plain, bringing dust and spores, irritating his eyes. The headache moved around a bit and settled into a different, more painful position. Rubbing first his forehead and then his eyes, he walked to the plane.

Everything looked as it had yesterday. Hanley wondered just who knew he was here. Were the SPLA or the Janjaweed aware of his plane and the mission's plans to use it to move medicine to the compound and doctors back and forth from Kenya and Ethiopia? Hanley was aware that Khartoum was supplying the Janjaweed with shoulder-launched missiles which they now used to down planes flying in food and other humanitarian supplies. The Beech was small, too small to bring enough food to make a difference in a conflict like this. As he stood rubbing a spot just above his left eye, he thought that perhaps this shiny plane that he loved so much would look better painted a dull gray or something that would be difficult to see at low attitude; something that would not reflect the relentless Sudanese sun; something not easily shot down.

The heat from inside the plane rolled over Hanley as he opened the rear door. He walked to the cockpit and opened the side windows to get air moving inside the plane. Outside again, he sat under the wing and hoped for a breeze to cool him. None came. He would wait fifteen minutes before returning to the cockpit. Jumma sat under a nearby tree, writing on a tablet held to a clipboard. Jumma's intensity interested Hanley. Their conversations were always light, with the young Sudanese always smiling. When he would begin working, his concentration was startling. This was now particularly noticeable as he sat writing. With a furrowed forehead and lips pursed, he wrote slowly, seemingly with great care. Occasionally, his lips moved as he formed the words he deposited on paper. He was alone; the world around him had disappeared. Jumma stopped writing with the pen poised above the clipboard, the look of concentration gone. Slowly he rolled his eyes toward Hanley and stared at the American for a second and then lowered his pen.

"What are you writing?" Hanley asked.

"I'm sorry; I was just making some notes. Did I miss something you said?" he asked.

"No, I'm just trying to cool-off after being in the plane. No luck with that though. You look so serious. Must be important stuff you're writing about."

"No, just a list of the things I know I must accomplish today and tomorrow. Sister Marie Claire wants these things done

and I must do them. She is not one you want to disappoint."
Jumma said with a smile.

"I believe that." Pushing himself up, Hanley got to his
feet and turned his attention to the outside of the plane. As
he began his inspection, he noticed several spots of dried bird
droppings on the wings and tail section. The drops were small
and almost pure white. Retrieving a cloth from the back of the
plane, Hanley scrubbed at the spots until they came off or at
least until most of it came off. He realized keeping the plane
clean would be difficult. Water was too precious to waste on
an airplane. Thankfully, most of the dirt will be dust and it will
come off as he flies, he reassured himself.

"I saw you rubbing your back while you were hiding behind
the children's clinic with Sister Marie Claire. Had she hit you?"
the young man asked. He was now standing behind Hanley,
the clipboard held at his side. His head was cocked to one side,
his hand shielding the sun from his eyes as he watched Hanley
scrub the bird shit from his plane.

"No. Well not at first. She did later. Why, does she hit people
a lot?" Hanley asked laughing. He found the question humorous.
He assumed a nun was capable of hitting, but he normally
thought of nuns that hit as older women in severe black habits,
smacking boys with their rulers in hallways, while children in
classrooms smothered their laughter for fear they would be next.
He didn't see Marie Claire that way, at least not yet.

"If I tell you something, you must promise not to tell the
Sister. Do you promise? If you tell her, I will have to leave, I
think. Do you promise?" Jumma was starting to think that
perhaps he had started in a direction that he would regret and his
panic was beginning to show. He did not know this American at
all and was already offering to share secrets. Maybe this is why
America is so successful, Jumma thought; they get you to trust
them but for no reason and then they are always a step ahead.

"I won't tell. You can trust me."

Jumma was still uncertain even after the older man's
statement. Trusting someone was difficult to do in Sudan,

especially a stranger from another country. Now Jumma was really nervous. He had stopped trusting strangers when very young; perhaps now was not the time to start again.

"She hits people when they don't do what she says. She only hits men; the white men. Usually the doctors and never a Sudanese or a priest; especially not a priest. The doctors talk about it when she is not around. They say she is a frustrated woman. They say she uses her fists because she cannot use her lips. They call it a nun's kiss. One said it was the hand of God because God will not come to Sudan himself. They all laugh about it when she is not there to hear." Jumma looked nervous about what he had just said and Hanley knew it was because he was feeling exposed, having just entrusted a relative stranger with a secret that could cause the young Sudanese some embarrassment if it got out.

Hanley said, "My grandmother was a hitter. She hit only her grandsons. Never anyone else as far as we could tell. She would punch us in the arm or slap our stomachs with the back of her hand. Never hard. I don't think she started it until we were all bigger than her. She was small anyway. I haven't thought about that in years. I really believe these were gestures of affection. Some people aren't normally the type who touch and I think this was her goofy way of doing it." Hanley explained.

"Goofy?"

"Unusual."

"Then Sister Marie Claire is making certain she is goofy while touching the doctors because you can sometimes hear her touching them from another room."

Smiling at Jumma's description of Sister Marie Claire abuse of the doctors, Hanley turned back to the plane and entered through the rear door. A little more than five minutes had passed, yet the heat still cooked him as he walked to the cockpit.

"Jumma, come here will you?" Hanley shouted down the length of the old plane. He guessed his young friend was curious enough about the inside of the plane that he would not mind the heat. Jumma stuck his head through the front door, grimaced at the wave of heat that greeted him and answered, "Yes Hanley, did you call to me?"

Swinging his head back toward the voice, Hanley asked, "Come on up here, will you?"

9

The late afternoon air was still, hot to the touch, or so it seemed to the American, whose clothes always seemed wet, dank, smelling of sweat and tension, for tension had a smell here in the bush, like hot metal on an electric alarm clock, hot from ringing its shrill tone for years and years, with no one waking, no one to turn it off. Hanley heard it all the time, a high piercing sound, uncomfortable, deep inside his head. It was tinnitus, something he inherited, he supposed - his mother suffered from it. When he concentrated on the sound, he felt uneasy, felt he might begin to slip into a place where he might stay, a place where he could not control it.

Having carried an old aluminum folding chair out to the shade of the barracks, Hanley unfolded it with some trouble, the frame sticking, pressure on the cheap plastic liners, rods and grommets forced against each other, pinching and impeding, making it difficult. The chair was a bit bent, the nylon strapping frayed and faded, from white and blue to a dirty cream and denim, it was uncomfortable in its precariousness, but better than the hardness of the old box back porch or the ground. The webbed seat creaked like a horse saddle when he sat down, allowing him to sink, giving Hanley a sudden tightness in his gut, anticipating he might fall through. His small descent stopped and he relaxed. A search of the storage room in the barracks yielded only one chair. He would give it to the nun if she came.

Hanley watched the activity of the mission compound, breathing the heated air, still surprised to feel the air he inhaled to be measurably hotter than his tongue. He was tired, sleep difficult to find. A small child cried somewhere near, the crying of children a constant piece of the workings of the mission. He would never tune it out, he knew, never ignore it. His days were filled with the same noises; children, shouting adults, bugs, a slow persistent wind, the noise of the heat, the madness over the horizon; his imagination.

Coping with the change in his daily routine was proving to be challenging, more than he had thought, the years of the same routine so deeply stamped into him. He never noticed how repetitive his daily life had been; waking at six o'clock every morning after a bad night's sleep, toast and coffee for breakfast, quick necessary murmurs between he and his then wife, Belinda, each ignoring the other for years. Shaving, a shower, sometimes walking the dog, many times just chaining him to the corner of the garage, then the trip to his office, the meetings, the deals, the accomplishments. Would he ever settle into a routine in Mapuordit?

He waited for the nun. He needed to talk to her, needed to ask her questions, had to get his courage up. Yesterday, at lunch, he asked her about her history, tried to find out who she is, what she believed about her work at the mission, why she stayed so long, why the church kept her there? He was curious about what she knew about him, his reason for coming to Sudan, what it might mean, about his success, could he give enough back. "How long have you been here? I may have heard that along the way but I can't recall," he asked.

"I've been here for more than eight years, the longest of anyone but Father Robineau. My first months here were hard, but then all of Africa is hard, at least for Europeans, whites. Soon, I gained some comfort, at least with my work; never with the situation," she said. "I have been in other countries, in

Senegal and then Zimbabwe, but those stays were short, at least compared to my stay at Mapuordit. I hate this country, but love the people. So, I deal with the people and try to avoid dealing with the country."

The sun was low, hanging over the clinic building, a globe of bright orange cupped in a tree, the bare branches applying a filigree pattern to its lower half. A goblet. Gnats swarmed him, lighted on his lips, one lodged in the corner of his left eye, slamming it shut, the first knuckle of his right hand digging in to push it out. Feeling it moved out, Hanley wiped it away, dragging a tear with it, the relief momentary as the gnat swarmed again. Pushing himself out of the low-slung comfort of the chair, Hanley moved ten feet away, waiting for the gnats to follow. Hovering low over the ground, the gnat seemed to forget about him. The sun was sliding down the tree trunk, split, bulging from each side. The gnats stayed away; so did the nun.

Her humming reached him first, soft and melodious. She had a good singing voice from what he heard, singing to the children, to the workers unloading a truck. Hanley wondered if she was trained to sing, like an athlete trains to run. The humming stopped, followed by the sound of a knock on thin wood.

"I'm over here, beside the building," he called out. There was a creaking of wood and then silence. She stepped from behind the building, smiling brightly as she saw him.

"A man of your age risks much sitting in a chair like that, don't you think?" she asked.

"Yes, I suppose so. But men of my age take a risk just by getting out of bed in the morning, assuming we wake up at all." Her smile widened a bit more. "Sit here," he said, as he pushed himself up and out of the chair. Hanley sat on the ground beside the chair before the nun could protest. He noticed her shoes, well-worn running shoes, split where the thick rubber soles joined the nylon tops, once white, now a dull grey. Beneath, the nun wore dark blue socks, her dress was a light blue, on her head the same white kerchief he had seen her wear before. The kerchief was always bright and clean.

"I thought we might talk before dinner. I have questions. You are the person I believe has the answers," he said as she sat in the chair.

"I have the answers? Oh, my, you could have picked a better chair than this. I will need help when it comes time to stand up."

"There wasn't much to choose from. Your friend, the overwhelming Sister Mary Kathleen O'Brien, said you, more than anyone else here, knew what was what, as they say."

"She did?" The nun turned to look at Hanley. She shook her hand to dislodge a fly that landed there, gripping the arm of the chair tightly as the chair swayed with her movements. A shout from the camp beyond the clinic caused her grip to tighten even more.

"My conversations with her were full of references to your command of the political and social situation here. And, as I'm now your aerial courier, I thought it might be beneficial if I learned some of what you know. I'm about to meet and interact with people in cities in this country and others as I move about, carrying medicine and people. I simply thought it might be to my advantage to understand a bit more about this country, above what I learned on my own or with the help of the good Sister back in Indiana. A little bit of nuance may go a long way," he said. The sun was now half-hidden behind a low hill, the tree a black shape in the low evening light. Hanley stared ahead, listening to the sounds of the camp and the chair as Sister Marie Claire shifted her weight seeking comfort.

"By the country, you meant the government?" she asked.

"Yes, the government."

"The local leaders, even the leaders in Rumbek, are not bad but they do little to help. Perhaps they cannot. Perhaps I expect too much," the nun said, looking off toward the clinic and the campfire beyond. "Yes, I may expect too much."

"What about the church? Do they do as much as they should?" he asked.

"What did Kathleen say?" she asked, the use of her first name only surprising him. Hanley thought he heard caution in her voice. He wanted to look at her face, to gauge her reaction, but didn't.

"She said they did what they could, more than most," he told her. "I had the feeling she was somewhat more defensive than she needed to be when answering the question. You know, the old 'I think thou dost protest too much' or however it goes. Like, she was defending the church but not sure she should."

Movement to his right made him look, squinting into the setting sun. Two of the doctors and a nurse were walking to dinner, laughing together at a remark, the nurse a full head shorter than both physicians. She wore a blue baseball cap, her blonde hair done in a ponytail and held in place with some sort of tie, pulled through an opening in the back. He estimated she was in her early thirties, some years older than his daughter. Her face was brown and freckled. He thought she was pretty, her body trim, not quite petite, but close. She looked over at Hanley, saw he was with the nun and frowned. Odd, he thought.

"We all defend the church as we defend ourselves. Our lives are the church," the nun said. She stood with her hands pressing the small of her back, bowed backward as she stretched. "That chair is dangerous," she said. "Are you hungry?'

"Since I've been in Sudan, I'm always hungry but I'll adjust. May I ask you something?" He waited a second and said, "This may sound odd to you, but, as you are a person of faith, I thought you might find this interesting. I…"

The nun held up her hand to interrupt and said, "My faith is not as strong as you may think. Sudan is draining my faith from me, takes a drop each day or so, it seems. I try to stop it, pray that I don't lose more, but it leaks from me as I walk about, as I sleep, as I pray. I may not be the best person to ask."

He blinked and said, as if she had not spoken, "I have for years wondered about my good fortune, about why I succeeded when many others didn't. My success was, it now seems, effortless, at least. So much so that luck must have played a major role in it. So, I began wondering if I should do something to make up for my good fortune."

"Why would you?" she asked. "If your good fortune was God's will, should you not accept that? Giving back is something we all should do. You are no exception. I would not recommend that you think there is something special about your circumstance." Turning away, she said, "I'm going to dinner. Please join me."

Getting to his feet, Hanley said, "I don't think I'm special. I just feel this deep need to repay fate or God or whomever for my good fortune. I've been lucky, that's all. Too lucky, it seems." Hanley noticed how dark it had become. Hurrying to catch up with her, he said, "I just need to know if I'm doing enough, that's all. I thought, with your background, you might guide me." Night sounds swelled around them, dampening the sound of their walking, overcoming the sounds created by the few humans scattered about the mission.

"A woman walks into the bush to bring water back to her family. In Africa, the path leading to water is known as the Death Path. A lion, having found the remains of a dead cow near the water, does not bother the woman as he is no longer hungry. That is luck, good fortune. Her life is spared, her children still have a mother to love them. Yours is not luck or fate. You're simply a wealthy American, confused, but wealthy still. You can afford to fly your plane to Africa and indulge yourself in a search for an answer to a question that is no more than self-interest. You can search for the answer while you're here, but do not allow it to get in the way of helping people not as fortunate as you." The nun walked away.

The words stung, the rejection a mild shock, then anger followed. His face flushed, Hanley felt the pressure in his head growing, the blood surging in his temples. Staring down at the sparse grass and dirt, he sucked in air through teeth, filled his lungs to clear his head, to damp down the urge to fight, an urge he seldom felt. Looking up, he said, "Fuck this" and followed the nun to dinner.

***

Hanley watched her striding toward the dining hall, looked back at the silhouette of the tree that moments before held the sun in its grasp, saw it appeared thinner in the dimming light and thought he should change his approach. After coming this far, he could not fail to find the answer. His commitment to the work was important and he would do it. The work was the payment. She should understand that. The answer was something else; it would not affect the work.

As he walked, a slow wind pushed at him from the south, warm and dry, carrying a smell of dried vegetation and even drier earth. There was an undertone of wood smoke and something else, something less recognizable. Hanley thought it might be the smell of wildness, pungent, rendering the air of Sudan elementally different from the air back home, as wild game differs from the chicken sheathed in plastic in a supermarket. Was there wild game nearby? How wild? Would he be eaten alive before being shot by the local militia or rebels? A rattle from the brush made his heart thump, but he saw nothing there in the failing light. Walking faster, he caught the nun just before she mounted the steps to the dining hall.

"Has anyone ever been attacked by a wild animal since you've been here?" Hanley asked, a bit of an edge to his voice.

"We lose a doctor a week on average," she replied, looking back over her shoulder. As the nun entered the dining hall, she said loudly, "The doctors are weak and the lions carry them away, but bring them back as they taste bad, especially the Slovakians."

"Why don't you taste one for yourself and see," said one of the Slovakian doctors. "The lions do not appreciate a good-tasting doctor, although, in the lion's defense, Slovakian doctors are an acquired taste."

"Like the Mopane," a nurse said, causing those at her table to smile.

"Yes, very much like that, now that you mention it," the same doctor said, smiling down into his bowl of soup.

"You're a pig," the nurse replied, realizing why the doctor smiled.

Sister Marie Claire laughed and said, "Let's not offend Mr Martin. Pilots are more difficult to come by than doctors." She wandered over to the small table where the prepared food sat. Little steam rose from the food that had been set out some time before she and the American arrived. There was a small kettle of soup, a thin broth with what appeared to be cubes of potatoes or turnips, some steamed beans and small pears, brown on the large end and green near the stem. Picking up an old white bowl, the nun ladled in some soup and picked a piece of flat bread from a plate, selected a dulled gray spoon and sat at a table where no one else was seated. Hanley took some soup, two pears and bread and sat with the nun.

"Have you told Mr Martin of your reputation with men?" another doctor asked the nun. There was smoke in the air of the dining hall, cigarettes in the hands of some of the doctors and nurses, the ceiling fan idle, leaving the slow wind through the screened door little help in clearing the air.

"I'm aware of it," Hanley replied, then to the nun. "I have heard about it, you know." He tasted the soup, grimacing, crunching what turned out to be a variety of turnip, undercooked and bitter.

"What have you heard?"

"Well, about your reputation with men. You're known to be demanding and not afraid of confrontation and you're a 'hitter'. You like to punch an arm to express your surprise or dismay. Relax, my grandmother did the same thing. Otherwise, you're known to be dedicated and a bit unhappy with the church's role, or lack of it, in helping the people of Sudan. And, while you defend the church, publicly, at least, privately, you believe the church could be more of a force for change in Sudan," Hanley said, holding a pear by the stem, twirling between his fingers while he talked.

"Sister Mary Kathleen talks too, much I think, at least she talked too much to you."

Biting the pear, Hanley grimaced again. "Is everything bitter in this country?" he asked.   "Everything," she said.

Scratching the worn surface of the table with a fingernail, Hanley looked at the pear, considered another bite, then placed it next to his bowl. The smoke in the room caused his eyes to burn and water. He looked around, noting the faces and occasional smiles, the rigid mechanism of the smokers, the rotation of the forearms, the cigarette clamped between two fingers, the jet of smoke from the pursed lips. The clink and scrape of the nun's spoon against the bowl brought him back to the conversation. He felt his anger rising again. "So, you think I'm just a spoiled, rich American, indulging himself, assuaging his guilt, trying to forget the thousands of people he screwed climbing to the top? Is that it?" Hanley asked as she placed a piece of bread in her mouth.

Chewing for a moment, she said, "Not exactly. I know you have issues with your good fortune, that you wonder why you were so lucky while many around you were not, why you can't understand the sequence, is that the right word?"

"Yes."

"Remembering the sequence or chain of events, or at least remembering exactly the decision you made that made you successful. Looking back, trying to remember only makes it all seem even more out of control, does it not, Monsieur?" she asked, staring intently at Hanley, who was again twirling the wounded and bitter pear by the stem. "We don't understand, because, I believe, we are not meant to understand, at least not fully understand. In each of our lives, there are too many factors that affect what happens to us each day, things we are not even aware of. A man in a car bumps another man in a car and one of them is delayed in placing an order for airplane parts and so another man places the order for him, but calls your company instead. You are not aware of the two cars hitting each other, but you benefit from it. How can you know? These mysteries happen a million times each day, endless mysteries. They are God's hand in our lives and we are not meant to know. We are expected to accept this fact. Mysteries flow from God's hand as sand from the hand of a child playing on a beach." Tearing off another piece of bread, Sister Marie Claire looked down at her bowl, dipped the bread in the broth and ate it. A nurse, listening to the nun, watched the American's face, saw his clenched jaw and the rapid scratching of his finger across the table top. Hanley picked up the pear by the stem and twirled it furiously in his fingers.

"I had an uncle, he's dead now, who told me I needed to give to others as a form of payment for any good fortune I have. He said that working hard, being a good person was not enough, but was a start. He called it 'the debt' and that I needed to remember that as I got older. I loved him, but I wish he had not said that to me. I listened, hell, I was just a kid, I'm surprised I listened. What he said stuck in my head like a splinter, festered, never working itself out. The combination of wondering why I was so lucky and what I needed to do to pay back that debt has eaten away at me for years," he said, the pear spinning between his fingers.

A sound came from outside the dining hall, causing everyone to stop talking, the small hums and creaks of the building vying for the attention of the diners, then the sound came again, the low roar of a lion, distant, causing the skin on Hanley's neck to crawl.

"I wish I had my 8 mm with me," one of the doctors said. The listening continued for a moment, then the nun said to Hanley. "What your uncle said is true, we all must give. We all must give, no matter that our luck is good. Even when our luck is bad, we should give. Giving is all that matters. It is the taking that matters little."

Gathering her bowl and spoon, the nun stood, moving to a sink in a corner of the room where she rinsed her bowl in a tub of water and placed on a small table nearby. Squeezing the shoulder of a doctor as she passed, Sister Marie Claire left the dining hall, the screen door's sharp bang signaling her departure. Hanley watched, thinking about what she said, concerned that he was making little progress in finding his answer. Maybe there was no answer.

***

Insomnia was nothing new to the American. The rickety porch moved as he moved, sitting with his legs out stretched, propped against the door into the barracks near his room. Small red lights pierced the darkness beyond the compound, campfires of irregular shapes provided irregular warmth, he supposed, to the poor people sleeping nearby. It was the middle of the night, a small amount of chill to the air, comfortable enough to sleep if he could sleep.

After the nun left the dining hall, Hanley sat by himself for a time, listening to the talk of the doctors, nurses and nuns, who smoked and told stories of their lives back home in Košice or Charleroi. When he got up to leave, the talk had turned to the church's role in Sudan and in the plight of its children. As he was rinsing his bowl in the tub, he heard a doctor say, "The Diocese is still dealing with its troublemaker," which caused a momentary silence around the table. A nurse asked if she had been a rebel in the convent or had Africa brought this trait out in her. The conversation stopped for a moment, a break Hanley saw as an opportunity to leave. He said goodnight over his shoulder as he left, the silence changing to murmurs and then laughter.

"God, what am I doing here?" he asked softly, keeping the question on the porch and to himself. No one cares and why should they. "Perhaps you're making too much of this," he said aloud. His approach to the nun had not worked. She saw his need for an answer as purely self-interest. I must try something different, he thought. But what?

Still, the question remained. Was he here for the wrong reason, here to help himself more than to help others? He would talk to the nun again. He would work on his approach.

10

The next afternoon, Hanley sat listening to Father Robineau and Sister Marie Claire discuss a letter from a doctor in Italy who planned to visit the mission in July. As he listened his thoughts drifted back to Kokomo and his old life and back, again, to *the* question. Letters from his daughter and staff told him his businesses were doing well, as well as could be expected without him, he supposed. He was proud of his success, as proud as his upbringing would allow him to be. For as long as he could remember, there had been strings attached to all he had done, strings that came from his parents and grandparents, strings that controlled, to an extent, the decisions he made, how he dealt with people, his business, certainly his family. These attachments ruled his life, he thought, which was natural. Then there was his uncle. What he was doing now was because of his uncle.

Summers, his young summers, belonged to his uncle and aunt. They were farmers, more full- than part-time, part-time because his uncle worked at the county's only farm supply business to help them make a living while maintaining the farm. Hanley moved in with his aunt and uncle each summer, beginning when he was twelve years old and each year thereafter until he left for college in Ohio.

Small, perhaps eighty-five acres of rolling land in southern Indiana, the farm was divided into twenty acres of grazing pasture, sixty acres for crops, mostly corn and wheat with a new crop, soy beans worked in and a small bit for the farmhouse and buildings.

He remembered that his farm life began at five o'clock each morning, starting the morning after he arrived. Mending fences, bailing hay and tending to his aunt's large garden along with the many other things involved in keeping a farm going, kept him busy and tired each day. The work was hard, but he enjoyed it, for the most part, knowing it helped two people he loved and knowing it made his parents proud, The mornings were actually the hardest part, getting up while it was still dark, the chill of his room, the window open as there was no air-conditioning, rolling up in the thin blankets and the nubby quilt, shivering, thinking of how nice another hour in bed would be, hearing his aunt in the kitchen, the muffled bangs and crackle of paper, the smell of coffee and the small resentment of relenting to this ritual of forced responsibility. Lying in bed back then, he thought he knew what responsibility meant, now he knew it was meaningless. Growing up, he believed, was taught, that being an adult was a state, an age that bore a title earned through the ritual of progression and effective development. It was, he came to realize, only the experience of being an older human being. Nothing accomplished so much as having survived day after day, accumulating enough experience to successfully dodge misery and pain, to find a bit of happiness among the harsh times and disappointments. Lying there, he never realized the importance of that moment, or of any of the moments that had passed since his youth. His life seemed like water to him, running through his hands, sliding away, the clear and sweet, the painful and embarrassing flowing freely, out of any control. As much as he tried to remember the important moments, they were often as vague as his dreams, only not as frightening. His life passed without his permission. He thought his life had been rude to him, in spite of all his good fortune, like someone handing him a hundred-dollar bill and then shoving him to the ground. He wasn't sure why he felt that way.

He had a large bedroom all to himself for the first two years and then shared that bedroom with one of his cousins, Rick, fellow summer laborer. He remembered Rick, blond, slim and smart but without direction. Rick was his aunt's favorite; she protected him from his uncle at those times when Rick's day-dreaminess got in the way of the work. When Hanley was in college, Rick was killed in Vietnam, shot in Saigon by another American soldier, a kid from Stockton, California, drunk or stoned, carrying a cheap, throw-away 32-caliber he thought he needed for protection. Rick had looked at the prostitute the kid from Stockton was feeling up at the bar and was shot for that look, one month to the day from setting foot in the country.

He still remembered much about that time, remembered that first morning, standing on gravel, shivering in the early morning light, mist obscuring the fence lines and the cattle, lowing out their presence, calling to each other and to the house, getting some reassurance from the other cattle lowing back and from the echoes coming back to them from the buildings. He stood, head down, staring at his new boots, a gift from his parents that year and each year thereafter, boots that would last through the fall and be discarded sometime around Christmas. The boots were always a reddish brown, with a low gloss to them, the toes of these boots that first morning showing a beading of moisture from the dew. Almost daily, his uncle would remind Hanley that hard work was the glue that held the world together. His uncle, lean and farmer-strong, had a thin face, with deep wrinkles around his eyes and mouth, their effect heightened by his deep tan which never faded, even in the winter when Hanley would see him again at Christmas. They liked each other, but showed little affection at first, but grew closer as Hanley became a teenager. His uncle began his discussions about responsibility that first summer. Over the years, especially the last two summers before Hanley left for college, his uncle talked a great deal about what he called the debt.

***

"Did you finish fixing the wire down by Indian Rock?" his uncle asked.

"Yes sir, it's fixed."

"Will it hold?"

"Yes sir."

"Did Rickie help you?"

"Yes, he helped me."

"Did he? Hmmm. I'm not sure who is worse, you or your aunt. You're not doing him any favors, covering for him the way you do. I can't do anything about your aunt, but I might change you if I work hard enough."

"Oh, he's all right. His mind is on other things, that's all."

"I'm aware of that. Can't say where his mind goes, but I know it isn't around when I need it. He'll never be a giver, just a taker." His uncle frowned, as he wound a new pull-cord around the wheel that sat on top of his lawnmower, the cord Hanley would be pulling tomorrow when cutting the grass around the farm house.

"What do you mean by that?" Hanley stopped putting away the wire cutter and a small come-along he had used to repair the barbed-wire fence. Hanley was fourteen. The come-along and the cutters were both much older than he.

Looking up, his uncle stared out the garage window above his old work bench. Clouded and smudged, the glass yielded some light and a limited view of the pasture beyond. Hanley saw the jaw muscles tighten on his uncle's face and then they relaxed. His head dropped again and his uncle said, "This farm is not much, but it's all we have, all we'll ever have. Your aunt and I have worked hard all our adult lives to have this. We're proud of that. It isn't the owning we're proud of, you know. Not that. Hell, the owning is gone the moment we are. It's the work, the effort that matters. No one gave it to us. We have never been a burden to anyone. We pay our way in this life and that's important. We try to do more, to give back when we can. That's important too; maybe the most important. If you can keep yourself and those you love, then you've done your job. If you can give back too, then you'll have done your best. That's all you can do in this life. Work hard and try to make a difference." Looking up at Hanley, his uncle raised his eyebrows, smiled and shrugged, then went back to his work.

Watching his uncle, leaning against the marred, stained wood of the bench, his old tools, greasy rags and baby jars filled with nuts and washers around him, Hanley felt his own jaw tighten as he realized just how much he admired the man. The lives of his aunt and uncle were simple and hard. It was that way, he thought, because the plan and purpose of their lives was simple also; be good and work hard. All else that follows or is the result of that effort will be of a similar nature. Over the next few years, they would have many conversations about work, responsibility and making a difference. He remembered all of them.

***

"I feel bad about leaving so soon. Things aren't finished. There's still the wheat to harvest and we haven't completed enlarging the pond. There's more brush to clear and…"

"Don't worry, college is important and we knew you had to leave sooner this year. We're proud that you're going. Bob's coming over to help and Rick will be here for another ten days or so. Your aunt has been helping with Bob's kids since his wife took ill and he won't cost me much. If the brush sits until spring, it won't hurt anything. I would like to get the pond done before winter. Take advantage of any snow melt next spring to fill it up. We'll manage," his uncle said.

"How bad is Bob's wife?"

"Pretty bad, from what your aunt says. Maybe won't recover. All those boxes of canned goods and clothes you saw stacked on the back porch were for them. When you and Rickie leave, we don't eat as much, as your aunt cans and we've stocked piled plenty of fruit and vegetables. We won't miss it and they can use it. The clothes are those collected by the church. It's small, compared to what they need, what they will need." Hanley looked at the worn top of the kitchen table where they sat talking, an old oak table, scarred in small places, the varnish thin and yellowed. A brown lump of what looked like a bread crumb nestled in the crevasse formed by the split that allowed the table to be pulled apart and a leaf put in.

"It's good of her to do that for them."

"She doesn't do it to be nice but because she should. Her being nice may be part of what Bob sees, how he feels about it. Your aunt doesn't mind that. She does it because she should. It's part of the debt we owe and she pays it. That's all."

"What debt?"

"The debt most of us owe, for being fortunate, for our lives and our loved ones. Just knowing that things could be worse, we need to remember any considerations we receive in this life. It's a hard thing, living, harder than any of us expect. If we do well, if our families don't suffer much, if we're happy most of the time, then we *are* lucky. What we can do for others in need is just paying back what we owe for our good luck. A child born with a horrible illness may never know what good fortune is. How do you account for that? You don't. All you can do is help where and when you can. Your great-grandfather once said to me that there are only three things of value in this life; your family, your reputation and your education. Most people believe that, but don't live their lives like they do. They think money and what it buys is as important. They're fools. You know that, don't you? Don't be a fool Hanley. Remember who you are, realize what you have that's important and what you may owe. When it's all said and done, just pray you can look back on your life, you family and your deeds and be satisfied with what you've done."

***

The schedule for the flights for the coming month sat before Hanley on the table in the mission office, the low light of the early evening from the small windows enough as he scanned his destinations, already familiar with the names, visualizing them on a map in his head, then switching quickly to the sight of the runways lining up before him, the nose of the Beech down in descent, the leveling out and tilting of the plane's nose back to the sky as the tire skittered on the pavement or spewed the gravel behind them upon touchdown. Touchdown had been synonymous with safety until he arrived in Africa. Now, safety had little to do with it, he thought.

11

"Have you seen the airstrip since we've repaired it?" Hanley asked the nun. "I wanted to have it ready before the first flight."

"No, I have no reason to go to the airstrip, except now, with you," she said. "Jumma said it looks like new, although I doubt he has ever seen a new runway before."

"I appreciate your coming out. Jumma was a great help with getting it done. My language skills being what they are, he was indispensable, you know," Hanley shouted to make sure she heard him. "Jumma is proud of the work."

The Land Cruiser bumped along the road to Akot and the mission airstrip, Sister Marie Claire fighting the steering wheel, trying to miss ruts, hitting others. The jolt of the tires smashing through clods of roan-colored dirt should have tossed Hanley into the air, but for the old seatbelt holding him down. The black vinyl seat was hot, making him sweat through his shirt. His back was wet enough that he slid back and forth across the seat as they drove. "It's only 11:30 in the morning and already so hot, I can barely breathe," he said, wiping the moisture from his forehead with his wrist.

Departing from the airstrip would be difficult, the track needing maintenance, always requiring inspection, which took time. Walking the airstrip for the first time, two days after his arrival, Hanley mapped the larger ruts and holes, the soft spots and brush having grown too near the track. Ever watchful for snakes, he noticed the large number of hoof prints, clumped together as the cattle grazed, or strung out as they walked in line along the runway. Stones had emerged here and there, the result of the rains, and Hanley noted them as ovals on the drawing he made of the landing strip, the blueprint for the reclamation project he would oversee. It would be hard, hot work. Even starting early in the morning was no protection against the heat. Now the spring rains passed, Hanley, Jumma and a small crew of workers from the mission could repair the ruts and holes in the track and have the work last. They filled them first with dirt, then with gravel from the back of the large truck, gravel Hanley bought in Rumbek, The repairs took several days to complete, the time extended by the number of trips made to buy the gravel. The improvements were enough to make the departures and landings manageable.

"Is every building in Kokomo air-conditioned?" she asked.

"Just those that need to be."

"It's the same here in Mapuordit," she said, smiling. "Sister Mary Kathleen tells me her office at Notre Dame is so hot in the summer, she keeps a bucket of ice under her chair. She claims it's the administration's way of preparing her for Hell, which is where she believes they are trying to send her."

"I doubt she needs their help," he said as he held on to the armrest, hoping to anchor himself for the remainder of the ride. Every bump produced a loud clang from the rear of the vehicle, the tools banging inside an old metal box bolted to the floor. Hanley's uncle taught him that loose toolboxes in trucks running over fields were dangerous. For a long time, he had not given the issue of dangerous toolboxes much thought, not until his first ride in the Land Cruiser, when a horrific bang and then the sound of metal sliding reluctantly along metal registered with him instantly. Instructing Jumma to stop, Hanley used an old piece of rope found beneath the front passenger seat to secure the wayward box to the back of the seat until he could manage to bolt it down, which he did.

The smell from the bush reminded Hanley of bailed Indiana hay, lying hot in the summer sun. Dust too was carried into the truck, sticking to his sweaty face and arms, a thin irregular line of brown forming along the underside of both his forearms.

He watched what appeared to be sparrows, but bigger, flying in and out of the brush along the road, never seeming to light, as if resting were too dangerous. The day before, he saw what he thought was a vulture, circling above the compound. Jumma said it was an eagle, a steppe eagle, which Hanley never heard of before. At that moment, Hanley realized how many things in this world were still mysteries to him and that fact would never change.

"Will you be taking Jumma with you tomorrow?" she asked.

"Well, I had to think about that. I wasn't sure taking him on the first trip was wise, not knowing what I might encounter. I don't look for any problems, but then, you never know. Since he has not flown before, I didn't want his first time spoiled by an unpleasant memory. But since the first flight is into Ethiopia with no stops in between, I thought it would be alright, so, yes, he's going with me," Hanley said.

Her hands were red from the tight grip on the steering wheel, her gaze intent, watching the track before her for problems; replacing blown tires and broken suspensions was expensive and parts hard to come by. "He's excited, but nervous. He wants everyone to believe he's not afraid to fly, but I think he is. Since he first came to us, Jumma has worked hard to prove his worth to the mission, that he is intelligent and capable," she told Hanley. Never taking her eyes off the rough path before her, Sister Marie Claire's voice rose above the noise of the trip, the clanging and the roar of the engine, the air crashing against the box shape of the truck. "Jumma really likes you," she said. "Because he has no real experience with Americans, you are like a man from Mars to him. Your success and the fact that you flew your own plane from America to Africa astounds him. He does not want to disappoint you. That is part of the fear. He does not want to fail at anything, but especially on his first flight with you."

"I know how he feels," Hanley said.

Rolling to a stop by the old terminal shack, the nun relaxed her grip and smiled. "You know, I don't have a driver's license. I had no need to drive before I came to Africa. But I do well, don't you think?" she asked.

"Yes, you do well. I doubt this experience will help you in France. Not a lot of kudu crossing the roads there I expect," he said. "Come on, let's look at the airstrip."

The grasses around the terminal and the airstrip were beginning to green from the spring rains. Small cups of water lined the side of the strip, uneven in their placement and would be gone by mid-afternoon if no more rains came that day. The day was heating up. Beads of sweat lay across the bridge of the nun's nose. Walking along the strip, she stopped, hands on her hips, the tunic she wore over slacks bunched beneath her hands. Examining the strip, she said, "Only once have I been to the airstrip in the past two years. There was no need, really. But, what I remember of its condition, this is much improved. The workers did well, I believe. Now I see why Jumma was so proud."

"Thank you, sister. They did work hard. The young men of the mission take a good deal of pride in what they do, that's obvious. I was glad to have their help," he said.

Turning to face Hanley, Sister Marie Claire said, "Now that you have a good runway, make good use of it." Looking into his eyes, she smiled, bent down and plucked a small white flower from a stem growing next to the gravel, turned and walked back to the terminal.

***

"Okay, Jumma, we've inspected the plane, looking for any signs of wear or fatigue, for any potential problems. As I explained, it's better to discover them while the plane is on the ground then when it's in the air. Trust me on that. Now, we're going to review what is called the pre-flight check list. It is in this book, a binder, really. Here, take it. I'll show you how to go through it and check the plane's systems before take-off," Hanley said, handing a small three-ring binder to Jumma. The binder was the size of a small-town telephone directory, covered in black vinyl, the pages inside held in clear plastic envelopes with holes for holding them to the rings. Jumma opened the binder, placed it on his lap with his head down low to examine the print. Running a finger down the first column, Hanley watched as his lips moved, reading the words. The check-list index looked like this:

Checklist – Beechcraft C-45 Expeditor

Pre-Start Checklist
1. Cabin Door – CLOSED
2. Controls – FREE
3. Landing Gear SW – DOWN
4. Parking Brake – ON
5. Bat. & Gen. SWS – ON
6. Gear Safe Light – CHECK
7. Fuel Quantity – CHECK
8. Fuel Selectors – MAIN
9. Crossed – OFF
10. Anti-Ice Fluid – CHECKED
11. Trim – SET > T/O
12. Flap Switch – NEUTRAL
13. Throttles – 1/8 OPEN
14. Mixtures – RICH
15. Props – HIGH
16. Manifold Heat – COLD
17. Oil Shutters – HOT
18. Oil Shutoff Valves – OPEN
19. Circuit Breakers – CHECKED
20. Electrical Switches – OFF
21. Alt. Static Source – NORMAL
22. Oil Bypass Valves – AS REQUIRED
23. Warning Lights – CHECKED

Start Checklist
1. Fuel Boost Pumps – ON
2. Magnetos – OFF
3. Engine Sel. SW – RT or LT
4. Starter (2 Revs) – ENGAGE
5. Magnetos – ON
6. Ignition Boost SW – ON
7. Primer – AS REQUIRED
   (SAME PROC. FOR OTHER ENGINE)
8. Fuel Boost Pumps – OFF
9. Warm Up Engines – 1000–RPM

After-Starting Engines
1. Oil Pressure – UP
2. Fuel Boost Pumps – OFF
3. Lights – AS REQUIRED
4. Radios – ON
5. Tailwheel – UNLOCKED
6. Parking Brake – UNLOCKED

Run-Up
1. Temps. & Press. – GREEN ARC
2. Props (rpm) -EXERCISE
3. Manifold Heat – CHECK
4. Vacuum – CHECK
5. Volt/Ammeters – CHECK
6. Mags. (rpm)- CHECK

Before Take-Off
1. Controls – FREE
2. Mixture – RICH
3. Props. – HIGH RPM
4. Friction Locks – SET
5. Oil Shutters – AS REQUIRED
6. Manifold Heat – COLD
7. Flaps – UP

8. Fuel Selector – MAIN TANKS
9. Oil By-Pass – CLOSED
10. Trim – SET
11. D.G.'s – SET
12. Instrument – CHECK
13. Navs. – CHECK / SET

Take-Off
1. Time – RECORD
2. Fuel Boost Pumps – ON
3. Landing Lights – ON
4. Inverter – ON
5. Transponder – ALT
6. Tail Wheel – LOCKED
7. D.G.'s – R.W. – HEADING
8. Pitot Heat – AS REQUIRED
9. Throttles – 36.& RPM
10. Oil Pressure – GREEN ARC
11. Oil Temperature – GREEN ARC

Climb
1. Gear – UP
2. Flaps – UP
3. Manifold Pressure – 32"
4. Prop. RPM – RPM
5. Fuel Boost Pumps – OFF – PX CK
6. Landing Lights – OFF
7. Airspeed – 120/MPH
8. Flight Plan – OPEN

Cruise
1. Manifold Pressure – 28"
2. Prop. RPM – RPM
3. Mixture – Lean
4. Oil Shutters – F.
5. Manifold Heat – AS REQUIRED

6. Fuel Quantity – Manage

Approach / Descent Checklist
1. Customs Code – OBTAIN
2. Fuel Selectors – MAIN TANKS
3. Mixtures – ENRICHEN
4. Manifold Pressure – 26"
5. Manifold Heat – AS REQUIRED
6. Altimeters – SET
7. Navs. – SET
8. Flight Plan – CLOSED

Before Landing Checklist
1. Fuel Boost Pumps – ON
2. Landing Lights – ON
3. Props. – RPM
4. Landing Gear – DOWN/GREEN
5. Manifold Heat – OFF
6. Heater – CYCLE
7. Brakes – CHECK
8. Flaps – AS NEEDED

After Landing Checklist
1. Fuel Boost Pumps – OFF
2. Landing Lights – OFF
3. Inverter – OFF
4. Transponder – STBY
5. Props. – HIGH RPM
6.   Oil Shutters – F.
7. Flaps – UP
8. Pitot Heat -OFF
9. Taxi Lights – AS REQUIRED
10. Time – RECORD

Shutdown Checklist
1. Parking Brake – SET

2. Radios – OFF
3. Mixtures – IDLE CUT-OFF
4. Magnetoes – OFF
5. Battery/Gen SW's – OFF
6. Tailwheel – LOCK
7. Controls – LOCK
8. Tie-downs – (3 POINTS)
9. Chocks – ALL WHEELS

Airspeeds – Miles-per-Hour
Vne 257
Vyse 122
Vmc 86
Vno 205
Vyxe 110
Vle 160
Vy 135
Vlo 160
Vx 119
Va 153
Vfe 120
Vso 75
Vs 80
Max T\O Wt: 10,100
Max Lnd Wt: 9,800

"Hanley, what does Vne 257 mean?" Jumma asked.

"The number, 257, is miles-per-hour. The Vne means never exceed airspeed. After 257 miles per hour, the wings may fall off," Hanley explained.

"Then we should not go 257 miles per hour," Jumma observed.

"Don't worry, we won't. Let's start with the simpler stuff, okay? Even though the first thing is closing the cabin doors, we'll wait until we're set to roll and then we'll close them," Hanley said.

"Set to roll?" Jumma asked.

"Just an expression. When the plane begins to move, I say it's rolling. Now, we'll wait to secure the door due to the heat. So, let's start down the list and I'll show you how we check everything. Experienced pilots check each and every item. That's how they become experienced. It's a pilot's joke, Jumma." Seeing the blank expression on the young man's face, Hanley said, "Overlooking a problem may kill you. New experiences tend to elude the dead. Never mind. Let's get started." Hanley took them through the checklist, letting Jumma ask questions as they went. Hanley thought he noticed Jumma seemed less tense as they worked their way through the list.

Reaching over to flip switches as he checked through the systems, Hanley said, "When we were inspecting the plane, you watched as I swung the propellers. I was checking for any problems with the hydraulics. Some people believe in swinging the props more often than I do, but my experience has shown a problem of that nature will show itself quickly. I brought oil with me, several cases that I stored at the mission. These engines use oil, but most of that occurs turning the engines over, starting them. Unless there is a leak. Radial aircraft engines are great, they run for hundreds of hours without a problem. The starting procedure is not that complicated. Some pilots think it is, but a little experience, again, shows it isn't hard at all. I usually prime the engines eight times, throttles opened until you hear a click in the gear system, turn on the fire suppression to the engine you're starting, hit the starter, wait for a half dozen rotations and hit the magneto switch and it will kick over. I always start the right engine first, it's farthest away and I can listen for problems without the roar of the engine in my ear." Jumma's eyes never left Hanley's face as he described the ritual for starting the Beech's engines.

When Hanley started the right engine, the entire plane shuddered, the vibration familiar to Hanley as it ran though his body. The noise was overpowering. A friend of Hanley's once described it as like riding down a road bracketed by ten Harley

Davidson motorcycles. Jumma grabbed the steering yoke as if afraid he would be ejected from the plane. Patting the young African on the shoulder, Hanley gave him a thumb's up signal, getting a faint smile in return.

The entire procedure, from initial inspection to starting both engines took almost an hour. As Jumma gained knowledge and experience, Hanley thought it might shorten the time needed to prepare the plane and depart. One item worried Hanley. The Beech was a tail dragger with a tailwheel that was locked for takeoff. The airstrip, with its graveled surface would be challenging.

Hanley took a headset from behind Jumma's seat, plugged it into a receptacle in the control panel and put it on. He retrieved a second set from behind the seat and gave it to Jumma, watched as he put it on and helped him adjust it to fit, then showed him how to turn the unit on and adjust the volume. Pointing to a small red button on the steering yoke, Hanley demonstrated how Jumma could talk by pressing the button and listen when it was released.

"Okay, Jumma, we're about to begin our departure. I will taxi out and line the plane up with the landing strip, lock the tailwheel and power up. The plane will roll forward slowly, but only for a moment and then surge forward, pushing you back, against the seat. It will take most all of the airstrip to get off the ground. Don't be alarmed if it appears we're running out of room, we'll make it." Jumma's smile faded even more.

Setting the Friction Locks, Hanley pulled the throttle back, the reverse of most planes whose throttles are pushed forward. The big plane began to move, the pulse of the large engines rhythmic and impressive, a force that pushed everything around it back, the wind generated by the triple blades causing the grass and the brush to bow before their power. Noticing Jumma's arms straightening as the big plane gained speed, Hanley glanced over to see Jumma pressed into the seat by the thrust of the plane's momentum. Hanley thought he saw both fear and wonder on the young African's face.

The shuddering smoothed out slightly as the tail of the plane rose, the pilot and his young co-pilot now seeing the airstrip passing beneath them in a blur. Hanley pulled back on the yoke and the plane's nose came up, the first loss of contact just detectable. The end of the runway was approaching fast, then the Beech was airborne, the sway of the plane loose of the ground, a minor shift as the Beech cleared the bush below, sliding sideways, slipping into the wind.

Pressing the red button as he was shown, Jumma said, "We have fled our mother earth into God our father's hands. I hope he does not drop us."

As the plane gained altitude, Hanley watched the gauges, searching for any indication of problems. "You don't have any Canadian geese around here, do you?" he asked.

"I don't believe I've ever seen one," Jumma answered.

Turning southeast, Hanley pointed the plane in the direction of the mission. "Jumma, if you watch out the window, you will soon see the mission beneath us. I will circle overhead so you will get a good look. Then we'll be on our way to Ethiopia," he said. Jumma did not appear to have heard Hanley, staring out the window at the earth falling away beneath them. Then he nodded twice and gave Hanley a thumb's up, never taking his eyes off the scenery below. After another minute, Jumma pressed the small red button and said thank you, his eyes still fixed on what was passing below them.

The mission soon came up in the distance, looking small and isolated, grouped together along a light gray squiggle of road appearing out of nowhere, returning to the same. Hanley kept the plane at one thousand feet, knowing there were no altitude restrictions in southern Sudan. As they passed over the mission, Hanley dipped the wings of the Beech, circled the mission once, then, setting course almost due east, began the journey to Ethiopia. He heard the click of the headset being keyed and Jumma's voice saying, "The mission buildings looked like papers scattered along the road. I could see the people, like tiny bugs crawling among the papers. If people look like bugs to me, what do they look like to God?"

"Dust, I imagine," Hanley said.

The start of the flight to the Jimma University's hospital in Jimma, Ethiopia, was uneventful, the day clear, the air smooth, little turbulence to bother Jumma on his first flight. Hanley's first trip was to gather supplies and meet the people he would be dealing with in Jimma. "I'm afraid I'll say Jumma and not Jimma when I'm there," Hanley said, smiling.

"Just say JU and they will understand you mean Jimma University," Jumma said.

"Would you like to attend JU?" Hanley asked.

"Maybe, I don't know," Jumma answered.

Southern Sudan turned somewhat greener as they moved eastward, part of the East Sudanian Savanna, a large dry wooded area. The As Sudd, a swamp during the rainy season, was dry. This was not what Hanley had expected. In preparing for his journey, he spent most of his time researching the political environment, not the ecological. He thought of all of Sudan as being more of a desert, which the northern half certainly was. The terrain turned even greener as they moved eastward.

The Beech felt good, the heaviness of the vibrations and noise balanced by the lightness of the plane lifted and carried through the air. There were few clouds, but much haze below, the earth beneath them masked by it, the greens and browns fading as they rose to altitude. The flight would be approximately two hours.

Once trimmed, the Beech was a remarkably stable plane, requiring, in good weather, little adjustment during a short flight. Hanley would be contacting the Jimma airport within the hour, maybe a bit longer. The flight was going well so far, Hanley thought.

***

They were scheduled to depart for Mapuordit just after 3:00 p.m. Hanley waited in the small private aviation terminal to escape the African heat. Jumma sat nearby, leafing through the C-45's flight manual, turning each page slowly.

The heat was on everything, an invisible coating of high temperature. The tarmac in the African sun felt like he imagined a hot stove top might feel through his boots. Sitting inside the terminal gave little relief. A copy of the *International Herald Tribune*, discarded by someone, a passenger or pilot, maybe an American, allowed him to catch up on world events. Reading the headlines, Hanley felt a small amount of panic, a tightening in his chest, as he again realized how removed from his family he was. As he read, he occasionally looked out across the airfield, the image of distance hills and trees altered by the shimmer of the boiling air.

The events in the newspaper were of the normal kind; a multimillionaire became the world's first space tourist, a war criminal surrendered to the police, a spacecraft was still heading to Mars. It was the same self-absorbed bullshit that covered the front of every newspaper everywhere. He looked back to the distant hills, the low slopes all a uniform dingy plum color, the deeply burnt grass and shrubs darkened a grey by the dirty air, dust swept up to form a constant veil through which Africa was seen. From Egypt to Botswana and South Africa, he knew the view would be the same; sitting in any airport, he would see this continent through a dusty lens, the distance as obscured as its future. Africa was appealing and grim at the same time.

***

The airfield at Akot was forty minutes out. Hanley would start the routine, try raising the mission at Mapuordit, never easy, but necessary. The need for vehicles at the Mission meant he could not leave one at the airstrip, resulting in a wait for a ride back to the compound, sitting in the heat somewhere; in the plane was out of the question, even though it provided the most security. There wasn't that much danger, the shifting presence of the militia and rebels always an uncertainty. Knowing where they were was never an easy task, information was slow and came through the flow of refugees from the northwest. The mission experienced little in the way of direct contact, the one instance, the killing of the young girl near the clinic, the major exception, and it was major. Seeing the girl, her head destroyed by what was probably a stray bullet, sickened him, frightened him more than he could have anticipated. He wasn't prepared for it, but how could he be? Had he been to Viet Nam, then maybe he would have been ready. Kokomo had not prepared him for much, but this instance was understandable. Still, the disappointment lingered, the question he now had was would he be prepared for the next time.

***

"Well, how is my new aviator?" Sister Marie Claire asked Jumma as he walked past the mission chapel, carrying his notebook and an old backpack, one of his few personal possessions. Just having completed her evening prayer, the nun was waiting by the chapel entrance for one of the mission nurses, her evening's dinner companion. She knew Jumma had just returned from Ethiopia with the American. "Did you enjoy your first flight?"

Stopping, Jumma looked at the nun, looked around as if afraid he would be heard and said, "Yes, in a way. Sister, when we were flying, when we were leaving the ground, Mr Martin did not look where we were going. And sometimes he would not steer the plane, would not even hold the steering wheel. If I am to fly with him, I would like him to be a more serious flyer. Maybe he thinks God is protecting him. But how does he know if God is protecting me?" the young man asked.

The worry in Jumma's face was genuine. The nun saw this and, for a second, controlled her reaction, then tilted her head back and laughed. The laughter surprised the young man for a second, then a smile spread across his dark face. Taking his face in both her hands, she said, "I will talk with the reckless American tomorrow. This is not America, Jumma, is it? He had better watch where he goes in Sudan."

"Yes, I think that would be better," Jumma said.

12

The rash, now two days old, stretched from his ankle almost to his knee. With his pant leg pulled up, Hanley examined, then scratched the area lightly, making it itch worse than it had before. "You should have a doctor look at that," Dr Dzyak said.

Sitting on the small porch near his room, Hanley watched as people moved about the compound, the Saturday evening air cooling quickly, white smoke curling above the fires around the mission, the smell of dinner lingering, children crying or murmuring as they played. The laughter of children in Sudan was different, Hanley thought; it had a subdued tone to it, still laughter, but not as free, not as freely given as the children in Indiana. He thought he heard Jumma's voice nearby. He had not seen Jumma since early in the afternoon, when he and another young man took the Range Rover to Juba for bottled water. After dinner, Hanley and the older Slovakian doctor, Dr Dzyak, sat on the little box porch and drank Hanley's whiskey from dirty glasses, smudged with prints after being twirled in their dust-covered fingers for almost an hour. Hanley was beginning to feel the effects of the alcohol, the ringing in his ears now more pronounced, his neck muscles more relaxed, an odd combination, Hanley thought.

"When I was in America several years ago, I tried to find an America beer that tasted like real beer. There was one with a man on the label, a revolutionary. It was good, the rest not very, I'm afraid. America is a strange country. You have much, a lot, is that right?" Hanley nodded.

"And it is beautiful, what I saw of it. I have seen pictures of the western states, Utah, you know. And your government works well, well compared to most. But your people lack passion, it seems to me," Dr Dzyak said. "I don't mean to offend you, my friend. I mean, I am drinking your good whiskey. But Americans seem to always be sleepwalking or sleep-driving." With his legs pulled up and his arms resting on his knees, the doctor sat, leaning against the wall of the barracks, looking up into the evening sky. Wiping his nose with the back of his hand, he said, "It's dusty here, always much dust."

Hanley said, "America has grown lazy, I'm afraid. We have enough to live our lives very comfortably, at least until we get older. Some Americans have way too much, more than they'll ever need. We have lost our balance and certainly our sense of urgency. When our lifetimes were shorter, we valued our time more. When our children wanted, we wanted to give them more, we fought to give them more. Now, we spoil them and teach them that owning a car is more important than learning the rhythms of poetry. We've lost touch with ourselves, with what is truly meaningful in our lives. I'm sorry, I'm getting drunk." Hanley's head rested against the side of the building.

"Don't apologize, I like Americans drunk, they're more like the rest of us that way," the doctor said.

Hanley's first month at the mission in Mapuordit passed quickly with the flying and the other work he was taking on. Watching the daily operation gave Hanley a sense there was order to the work being done, but not efficiency. Knowing he could and should not involve himself in the medical or spiritual side, Hanley thought he might help with the planning and scheduling. A little order in a life never hurts, his aunt would say to him at some point each summer. It was one of those sayings heard in childhood that people carried to their graves. Perhaps he could be the mission's efficiency expert. Many hospitals use them, he reasoned, why not a medical mission in Sudan. He though the whiskey might be getting to him.

"Doctor, I have the impression Sister Marie Claire runs this mission. I know that Father Robineau is the actual manager of the school and the clinic, but it sure seems to me she is in charge of most of the activities here," Hanley said. He watched the doctor who was tilting the glass to his lips. The glass came away, leaving a drop of the brown liquid hanging on the edge of his lower lip, which he quickly and quite deftly, Hanley thought, pushed back into his mouth with the forefinger of his left hand.

"In some ways, she does run things, but not all," the doctor said. "It has to do with Father Robineau's age, some with the time they have spent together. He relies on her because he trusts her to help manage. I have only been here a few weeks, but I know of this. I belong to a network of physicians in Europe, a group that donates our services to the Fathers of Notre Dame. We talk, you know, we share our experiences. The situation here is known to us. It's not gossip, Mr Martin, it's preparation." Another sip and the doctor sighed, saying, "The diocese in Rumbek is not as trusting of the nun as the good Father is. But even he worries about the other issue."

"Other issue?"

"The children. The good sister has an obsession of sorts. Over the years, it seems, she has watched the devastation this war has taken on the people of Sudan and she is angered. The pain and suffering of the children, which affects us all, has affected Sister Marie Claire more. That pain has caused her pain and has become intolerable. Rumor has it she has become part of a movement, no that's not right. She has joined a group, an underground, that helps children. Gathering them up and moving them to safety, giving them shelter, food and medical treatment when needed. I have noticed that sometimes we will see children at the clinic in groups, brought by one or two adults. Sometimes the same adults. No one says anything, no one asks questions. The children are cared for and Sister Marie

Claire always talks to them and the adults that bring them. There is something there, we know this. Exactly what that is, we don't ask," the doctor explained.

From somewhere came the sound of a vehicle, Jumma and his companion returning with the water. Hanley pulled down his pant leg and pushed himself from the box. Stretching, he walked to the corner of the building, leaning against the weathered plywood sheeting, the chipped edge biting into his shoulder. Still holding the glass, he judged by its weight there was a sip or two remaining. Swirling the whiskey around with a barely perceptible rotation of his hand, Hanley thought about his granddaughter, wondered if there would be anyone who would care for her under such circumstances as now existed here in Sudan. Looking into the glass, he thought of her, ached for her a bit. Turning back to the doctor, Hanley asked, "Does the diocese try to stop her from helping the children?"

"I have heard they have ordered her not to be involved. I do know she ignores those orders. Father Robineau does not intervene, allowing the nun to deal directly with the bishop in Rumbek. Father Robineau's relationship with the head of the order shields him from the diocese, who are left to fight the nun on their own. It is not a fair fight, as they say," the doctor said. Swinging his legs over the side of the box and onto the grass, Dr Dzyak stood, twisting his upper body in a swiveling motion to stretch and then he turned to face the American. Taking his pursed lips between his fingers, he looked at the ground, seeming to Hanley he was contemplating what he was about to say. Looking up, he smiled and said, "As I am sure you are starting to see, things are done differently in Sudan. A place like this has no rules, the rules are made up as needed. Otherwise, people would not survive. Sister Marie Claire knows this. She knows there are no limits. And she appears to be willing to go to any limit to help these children. Their needs are unlimited and so is her desire to help them."

"One more thing, doctor, please. If the diocese is not helping her, who is? Is she doing this alone?" Hanley asked.

Shaking his head, Dr Dyzak said, "I don't know, really. I hear things, we all do. Supposedly there are others involved. Who, again, I don't know. Perhaps you should ask her. I do know she does not talk about it, at least not here."

"Maybe I will. Thank you," Hanley said. Dr Dyzak walked away toward the clinic. Darkness was on the mission now, the night clear and warm. Looking up, Hanley searched the sky for the constellations he knew, which would be difficult. Here in Mapuordit, he was close to the equator. Here, his point of view was different.

***

Jumma walked along the road to the mission, a spiral-bound notebook in his hand, watching the group of children and two adults ahead of him as they neared the compound. The adults, a man and a woman, were perhaps thirty, maybe a bit older, the children were all very young. No one in the group spoke, their pace was brisk. All the children were dressed in bright colored tee shirts and beige shorts, with rubber sandals on their feet. Jumma followed behind, monitoring their progress but also watching the road behind them for dust or listening for the sounds of a vehicle. Seeing dust might give him more time to get the group off the road and hidden in the brush, if need be.

They were a half-mile from the mission, another twenty minutes, Jumma estimated. This was the first group in over a month. In the three months before that, there had been seven groups, almost forty children, all led by two adults, almost always couples, but twice just men. Over the years, the pattern was much the same, sporadic in the sense that there was no set schedule, but the effort apparently constant. The network was in place, the people involved dedicated to their purpose. They stayed at the mission for a few days, then moved on. Each time, a truck came to the mission and took the group, including the adults, away, heading south to Kenya and the refugee camps. Jumma knew this because it was his job to know. Jumma was helping Sister Marie Claire with the children. It was how he came to Mapuordit. He had been rescued while still separated from his family. Now he helped. It was what he could do for the nun, for having saved him. She would always have his help for as long as she needed. Forever if necessary.

***

He saw her coming from across the road, from where the lepers received treatment, a white cloth in her hand, her face rigid, showing stress, he thought. He was beginning to understand. There was now a mission for her beyond the administration of medicine, beyond the simple act of healing those fortunate enough to reach Mapuordit. Hanley wondered if her commitment to the children was now stronger than her commitment to the order she served. He wondered if Sudan was now the alter she stood before, the violence its sin, its children the souls to be saved.

Hanley saw his first group of small souls the day before. Children, some barely older than his granddaughter, led by two adults, a part of Sister Marie Claire's network, he supposed. There was a quiet tension that surrounded them as they were guided to tents, the care for the children beginning immediately. The young Irish doctor and a nurse examined the children while the nun spoke with the adults. He also saw Jumma, standing at some distance, watching the group and those tending to them. He did not appear to be involved, but watched intently as the examinations continued and the children were fed. Jumma sat watching and then writing in his notebook. What is he writing, Hanley wondered.

As the nun approached, Hanley waited by a small bush near the edge of the roadway. Nearing the bush, Sister Marie Claire looked up, saw the American and smiled. Wiping her forehead with the back of her hand, she asked, "Have you been waiting long?"

"No, not really. You've been working early enough. The sun's just rising," he said.

"If we see the sun in the morning, then we are the fortunate ones, no?" she asked

Each day at the mission started at dawn. By the time the sun had crawled above the hills enough to be seen, the compound was up and moving, fires in the outlying camps glowing brighter as the chilled people added wood, the children huddled near the heat, hoping for something to eat. The mission's kitchen fed as many people as it had food with which to feed.

"Have you had breakfast?" he asked.

"No, I'm not hungry," she said.

"Where are you going now?"

"It's a bit early to be so inquisitive, is it not?" she asked. Her head was down, the look on her face unchanged. He noticed her grip on the white cloth caused the knuckles on her hand to whiten, the tendons visible through her thin skin, the hand shook. She was trembling.

"Are you all right? Let's stop for a second. We can sit here and talk," he said.

They stopped, Hanley looking for a spot, dry with enough grass to be comfortable. He offered his hand to help her sit.

She said, "Are you worried I might collapse or do you want to draw me into another conversation about you and your cosmic obligations?"

Hanley, now more prepared for his conversations with the nun, smiled and said, "I was a boy scout, you know. Helping old ladies cross the street was beat into us as a thing we must always do. So, it may surprise you, I still have the urge to help whenever the occasion presents itself."

She smiled, took his hand and sat, her movements fluid, like a dancer. Hanley sat beside her, legs bent at the knee, wrapping his arms around them. He wore an old faded khaki-colored jacket, a field coat, adorned with pockets of various sizes and purpose. His boots bore a mosaic of scratches from walking through the bush, covered by a thin layer of dust. He looked at the boots, trying to remember the day he bought them, where it had been. He couldn't.

"I saw Jumma yesterday, watching a group of children who had just arrived at the mission. He was taking notes as he watched them. Why would he do that?" Hanley asked.

"I don't know. Did you ask him?"

Hanley looked at her, at her face, now more relaxed, the cloth hanging loosely in her hand. So, it will be like this, he thought. Always like this. "No, I just thought it was curious, you know. Maybe he is conducting a study of sorts, noting their condition, how they behaved. I just wondered why he did it from a distance and not closer where he could observe more, talk to them. It just seemed odd," he said.

They sat for a moment more, then the nun stood, brushing grass and dirt from the back of her skirt. She raised a hand to her brow to block the rising sun, turned to the American and said, "Jumma believes the mission helps the people of this country and it's his desire to help. Perhaps he is writing their stories so that the world will remember a country it has already forgotten." She walked away, leaving the American sitting alone.

"I don't think so," Hanley said to her as she walked toward the mission.

13

The ride to Juba took a long two hours. The road was graveled and relatively smooth, mostly straight, occasionally rough. As they were about to leave that morning, Hanley asked to drive, telling Sister Marie Claire he needed to learn the routes and the terrain. Looking at the Land Rover, she said, "You should do well, this is the easiest of all the vehicles to drive. If you show promise, we will teach you to drive the big truck." Getting in, she smiled and said, "Jumma said you do not watch where you're going when you fly. It worried him. He thinks you believe God will watch over you as you fly. I think you will need to watch where you're going today if we are to get to Juba."

As he slid in behind the wheel, Hanley said, "You know, I've never been a 'God is my co-pilot' kind of person. If God will let a jetliner full of people auger itself into the ground, why worry about me? I hate these seatbelts, you know?" From the corner of his eye, he saw the nun smoothly extend her seatbelt, heard the sharp click of it fastening. He struggled for a moment more, then fastened his own.

The nun said, "Let's not waste any more time, I have much to do today."

It was still early in the morning, the dim gray dulling the image of the distant hills. The light would soon be bright; Africa seemed to awaken quickly each day, Hanley thought.

Driving away from the mission, he watched as a woman and two children, a boy and a girl, gathered wood from an area just beyond the old clinic, with its collapsed walls and exposed beams. The children were throwing small stones into the air, trying to hit them with sticks, cutting arcs in the air the way baseball players do, their faces stern with the effort. Connecting with her swing, the crack of the stick meeting the stone brought a grin to the girl's face, a thin white line in the faint light of the early morning. Good, Hanley thought, you probably need something to smile about. The boy was not happy and swung harder at the stones.

With a small dark green zippered notebook open in her lap, the nun read from handwritten notes, tracking the words with her finger. The sentences appeared written in French. The writing was small and neat, precise, garnished with numbers and drawings, maps, he thought.

"Don't you find it hard to read while driving?" he asked.

"I'm not driving, you are," she said.

Hanley's lips compressed to a straight line across his jaw. He could feel the pressure rising inside him, her remark setting off a chain of reactions inside his head, none good, he knew. He always found it curious that, when angered, he could see, feel his anger coming on, knew he should control it, but could not. It was like a tide rising within him. Nothing could stop it, he would deal with it after it had stopped. Pushing the clutch to the floor, he let the Land Rover roll to a stop in the road. Looking at the nun, seeing her eyes closed, her hands spread over her notebook, he was about to speak when she said, "What is it? We cannot afford to waste time. I have a schedule to keep. Please, let's continue."

A count to three and he said, "Look, I understand you've been here forever and that you're in charge. Or at least in charge of a number of things at the mission. And I know it's not easy. We all recognize that, trust me. I can guess that you have had a multitude of obstacles to overcome, that progress has been slow and hard won and that most people you deal with need to have their asses kicked, but for God's sake, try to be at least civil to someone you hardly even know." He felt better and worse at the same time. Knowing he may have damaged what little relationship they had, he was immediately worried. Standing his ground and establishing boundaries were necessary. While having taken a measured approach to dealing with matters, he seldom allowed himself to be pushed around by anyone. Finding first gear, he started off again, the whine of the transmission filling the void between them. Sister Marie Claire closed the notebook, rolled down the door window, resting her forearm on the sill. She looked over the Savannah, greening now, the new sprouts highlighted by the taller brown grasses, the canopies of the acacia trees budding. There were clouds in the distance; more rain coming, late for the season. The rain was a bother, a necessary bother. It always came hard, making a mess of the roads, traveling even more difficult than normal, the creases and ruts not worn away enough to make driving tolerable until it was time for the rains to come again.

"Do you see those clouds in the distance, Mr Martin, yes? The troubles of Sudan are like the clouds. You know they are coming, but you cannot stop them. The rain they bring is necessary, even though it is sometimes destructive. This war has been here eleven years and only brings destruction. We must prepare before it arrives. Some people do not believe it will ever arrive here in this part of Sudan, but it already started. Perhaps not like Darfur and I pray it never does, but it is here. So, if I am, what is it, short with you, I'm sorry, I have much on my mind. And, besides, I was in fact not driving, as you said," she said.

Hanley, keeping his eyes on the road, said, "I suppose that's an answer. If I'm going to be of any help to you and the mission, if I'm to be any help at all, then I think we, you and I need to come to an agreement, an understanding of how we can work together. Okay?" Something crossed the road, an animal, he could tell, dark and large, a quarter of a mile or more away. He slowed the Land Rover, squinting to see better, his neck stretched over the steering wheel. "Did you see that?" he asked.

"See what?"

"Something crossed the road ahead. Looked large, like a cow. Are buffalo here?"

"Yes, but they're rare. It was a cow, I am sure. I want us to get along, is that right? To work together is, I agree, essential. Now that you're here. But I will tell you, I did not want you coming. I told the diocese this, wrote a letter to Father Bertrand in which I stated my objections," she said.

"What were your objections?"

She tried reopening the notebook, fumbled with it for a second and spread it on her lap. Thumbing through the pages, Sister Marie Claire moved forward and then back, searching, the white pages covered in blue and black ink, the words blurred as she flipped through them, finally stopping, she began tracking again with her finger. She began reading. She stopped and said, "I listed the reason here before I wrote the bishop. Really, I knew Sister Mary Kathleen liked you, quite a bit. She admired your determination to follow through with your plan, to pay back a debt she knew you believed you owed. She admired your belief that you should help others. And I will tell you that her opinion means much to me. But I didn't understand; I still do not. If you needed the money, or wanted to establish yourself as a pilot to start a business, I would have understood that. I was afraid that your motive was not strong enough, you would not be committed to the mission, that you would either leave soon after arriving or stay and not do the work." Looking up from the page, her expression concerned and weary, she said, "I know you want to discuss this with me, help you make sense of your need and decisions. I'm afraid I'm not the person to help you. I do not want to lead you on falsely and I do not want to disappoint you. I will tell you this. I believe the work is what can carry you through each day in a place like Sudan. The work and your commitment to it. Do the work; the answer will come to you."

Both his thumbs were pressed hard into the steering wheel. He wasn't bothered by the revelation she opposed his coming to work at the mission. Hell, he'd been married and divorced;

rejection was nothing new. What bothered him was the idea she might question his tenacity, which pissed him off. Letting the anger boil off, he said nothing.

He turned away from her to watch the road. Don't worry, he thought, I'll do the work.

***

Hanley sat in the old Land Rover, the morning sun now high overhead. Warm breezes blew in through the open windows. There was still a small crescent of mist in the upper corner of the windshield. Sister Marie Claire sat in an ancient Fiat, faded from red to rust, parked twenty feet away, talking to a man, his face obscured by the reflection of the sky on the windshield. She arranged for the meeting, she said, to pick up medicine. They were just outside the city of Juba.

Watching the cloud patterns moving across the Fiat's windshield, seeing the gray smoke pattern, reminded him of spring days in Indiana when the damp air was just warm, a breeze, heated, carried the smells of the newness. That moment, when he realized it was happening, the smells, the warmth, it would catch him, stop him for an instant and he would smile at the realization. He could smell the newness here, at this moment, felt it, knew it but without the smile. He thought he gained some ground with her, made his feelings known. It would be hard, dealing with the nun. He knew that.

Hanley saw the nun's hands moving, waving in animation, white birds fluttering about inside, between she and the man. She talked with her hands, he knew from their first conversation. Poor guy, Hanley said to himself. He wondered if the man had been through it before, dealing with her, perhaps talking about the children. That's what this was all about he guessed; helping the children. He knew without being told, there had been many such meetings in the past, trips for medicine or supplies, meetings where more was exchanged than just water or aspirin. He wondered how many people were helping? There must be a fairly large network of those engaged, committed to the cause of these children. Who were they and how big is this group? Hanley realized he could spend all morning, guessing about Sister Marie Claire and her cause.

The dull click of a door handle being raised brought Hanley's head up. He could see her face, still talking to the man, her foot outside the car and on the ground, the toe of her dirty shoe dug into the dirt. As she exited, bent, her head still inside, a hand on the door bracing her, a small brown paper bag in the hand, she said, "*merci*", got out and closed the door behind her, all done in one fluid motion. Lithe is the word, he thought watching her walk to the Land Rover.

"Thank you for waiting," she said, as she sat down, placing the small bag on the floor beneath her legs. Opening her notebook, Sister Marie Claire leafed back to the next available blank page and began writing in her small, neat script.

"Are those illegal drugs? Because, if they are, I'd like to know. If I'm embarking on a new career path, I'd like to remember the moment," Hanley said.

"Yes, they are illegal in a way, but, sometimes it is necessary to apprehend drugs this way," she explained.

"I'd stay away from the word apprehend. *Obtain* drugs in what way? What, exactly, is in the bag? Who do I need to worry about? Is there a Juba drug unit? I'm telling you, if we're caught, I'll cut a deal and give you up in a slim minute," Hanley said, more exasperation in his voice than worry. He stared at the nun until she stopped scribbling.

"There are fifty, codeine-based pain pills in the bag. The man works at a medical clinic in Juba. He took them for me. No money is exchanged. It is done to help. Others at the clinic take medicine and sell it or take it themselves. He does not. If he did not, many people we treat will suffer. And anyway, if he did not take them, others would." Closing the notebook, then twisting her body, she placed it on the back seat, turned back to look at Hanley for a moment. Her face darkened, making him think she was struggling with what she was about to say.

"I am not certain of what you may be thinking. How could I be? What I do, what I am, what I have become are what I must live with. I made a decision some time ago, a difficult one. I may have put my soul at risk. It is so hard to tell, the lines are always blurry it seems. Finding a way to help these good people has become my calling. It may seem that is how it has always been but that is not so. The church is committed to saving souls and helping the poor along the way. Politics, especially the politics of Africa, make the church's approach different. There is a different level of commitment in Africa. Frankly, it infuriates me. Doctrines of prejudice are not the doctrines of Christianity," she said. Her face, now darker than before, her blue eyes wide, she sat completely erect, the rigidity an extension of her anger. Another moment, an exhalation and she relaxed, the back of her hand brushing the hair from her forehead.

The man in the Fiat had driven off toward Juba. There were still wisps of acrid smoke from its exhaust hanging over the stones of the road.

"Are you ready?" Hanley asked

"Yes, we should go back now. Thank you," she said. A gift, a small smile, was given to the American. It lasted a second and then she turned away to look at the cloud on the horizon.

Starting the old truck, Hanley turned a broad turn across the road, off into the greening ground bordering the track and back on again. It will be a long ride back he thought.

14

Tearing the sheet of paper from his notebook, Jumma read the single paragraph it contained, smiled and folded the sheet over once, running his thumb along the edge to sharpen the crease, the paper pressed to his bare leg, the contrast of the paper and his skin a reminder of the differences in his life.

The right engine of the Beech was spinning as Hanley prepared to depart for Kenya; Hanley and Jumma were returning a French doctor to Nairobi. The physician was strapped into the jump-seat behind Jumma. Working through the checklist, they paused as the engine warmed up, giving Jumma a chance to read the paragraph he wrote the night before. The note was a snippet of his short life, the words, written in the French language, as best he could, were remembrances, small pictures, he liked to think, allowing him to glimpse a past now glazed with time. Tucking the folded sheet into the notebook, Jumma placed it into the pocket on the wall of the cockpit beside his seat, finding his place on the checklist.

"Why did you tear the sheet from your book?" Hanley asked.

"I will send it to my father in Rumbek," Jumma explained. "It is of something I remembered. We took a walk together, he and I, when I was small, very little. We held hands and I remember seeing a dog, an old dog, carrying a stuffed animal in its mouth. This was in our village, Uwayl, which is not a village, it was larger. Our home is near the edge, near a large field where vegetables and wheat grew. From there, it was the bush. The dog walked along the street, carrying the toy. When he came to the street he must cross, he stopped, put the toy down, looked for traffic, both ways he looked, then picked up the toy and crossed the street. My father's laughter could be heard everywhere, everywhere. I remember that laugh always. My note will remind him of the dog that made him laugh." Telling Hanley this while looking at the checklist, he smiled broadly, the sound of his father's laughter in his head, a moment of contentment, a small pleasure he could hold, like a cool stone in his hand. Then they continued through the list, checking the various functions that came into the play of putting the plane into the air.

Once airborne, and after many minutes of monitoring the plane's condition, rechecking the charts and the weather, Hanley keyed the small red button on the yoke, asking Jumma, "Was the dog that made your father laugh your earliest memory?"

"No, my earliest memory was being chased by a snake, a brown and red snake. That may have been a dream. It seems to be odd to think that a dream and a memory may be the same. What do we believe?" he asked.

"Listen, I've known a lot of people who dream their way through life."

A small crack from his headphone announced an air traffic controller in Nairobi was contacting the Beech. Hanley responded, leaving Jumma to think. Turning to the window beside him, he watched the faded brown and green of southern Sudan pass slowly below them, the patterns irregular, natural, showing little influence on the land other than nature's. The land where Jumma was borne was different, so brown and dry, his memories of the green plots of produce were among the clearest.

These memories were a mix of comfort and torment. They led to daydreams of what might have been, which were worse than the memories themselves. He thought of his memories as a landscape; his yesterdays were his yard, his village, his youth the mountains in the distance. No matter how long he gazed at those mountains, he could not see them clearly, could not remember what he had hoped, only remembrances of little security and true peace. There were impressions of times of happiness with his family, their love, which he longed for again. There was something else he longed for; the feeling that the ground he stood on, the earth beneath his feet, that his country was a good and safe land, a land he could be proud of belonging to. He wanted a country that gave its people hope for a good life, a safe home. A country he would never think of leaving. When he looked at Hanley, he could not understand why he left America to come to Sudan.

The snake was as surprised as the child. Asleep beneath the wood piled against the large hut, the snake, jagged scales, brown, red and round-headed was hidden, unnoticed by the boy. Neither were a danger to each other, but did not know it.

The end of the stick is what caught Jumma's eye. It was the color of butter, a favorite of his, when his parents had it. Pulling the stick from the pile brought the snake out, its nose against the end of the stick, the squatting child in its path. Before young Jumma could move, the fleeing serpent sawed his way through the dirt between the boy's legs, fast enough to be past him before the child could move. So frightened was Jumma, he wet his shorts, spraying the ground beneath him, missing the quick snake. Frozen in place, bawling hard enough that he shook, Jumma remained there until his mother came running to find him squatting and crying. Seeing he was near the wood pile, she took him to a grassy area, stripped him of his tee shirt and shorts and checked him for bite marks. Seeing none, she carried him, still wailing, to a communal water pipe, rinsing her son and his clothes. Dressing him again in the wet shorts and tee shirt, Jumma's mother then continued her work, the sobbing and wet boy trailing behind her, his hand out, wanting to be held. Jumma remembered all this like it was yesterday.

His other childhood memories were not as clear. Those were jumbled, from between the day the snake taught him what fear was and the day when strangers continued the lessons. The one notable exception was the day the dog made his father laugh.

When the troubles came to western Sudan, they spread rapidly throughout the region. Those nights were spent listening to his father explaining what he knew of the war, the various reasons and who was involved. The government in Khartoum and their support of the Baggara and Abbala tribesman who formed a group called the Janjaweed, murderers riding horses and camels. One night, while the family ate its evening meal, a mush of wheat and goat meat, some fruit and bread, all bathed in the yellow light of four candles, Jumma's father began talking of the war, and what might happen. Jumma was ten years old. They would not leave their home, he told them. This war is the work of men who want what farmland and water there is in western Darfur, a fight among tribes, he said, as he chewed his food. "This will not come to visit this area," he said. Jumma's mother and two sisters listened, his mother's head bowed low, her dark eyes closed, as she worked a string of beads through her fingers, red and black with tiny holes drilled through each, black thread, knotted on the side of each bead, holding them together, minutely spaced, someone's prideful work. The beads were decorative and she was nervous.

***

His father drank water from an old blue metal cup with white speckles, a cup Jumma had seen his grandmother drink from, then said, "I know I have said the troubles will not visit us here. But, this has changed. We must talk of how we can protect each other should the war make its way to this village. We will talk about it, we will practice it, like we practice your school lessons, for someday, you may need these lessons to help each other. We must not be afraid, but we must be smart. Do you understand?" his father asked. Jumma remembered nodding at the question. Drinking again, his father reached for him, rubbed his head and smiled. Jumma also remembered the warmth of his father's hand, could still feel it, the recollection of the touch brought him joy, as he flew with the American to Kenya.

The discussion and the lessons of his father continued in the days before the men on horseback arrived. The instructions, the lessons, were simple suggestions repeated each evening. If separated, they were to make their way to Rumbek, farther south, away from the fighting. Each family member was to say their father worked as a laborer for a company that constructed roads and dug wells. If caught, they were to say the family went to Abyei, the ancestral home.

His father worked in a shop in Uwayl, making sandals, belts and pouches. The shop, like a cave, dark and deep, its walls were a faded stucco, his work table near the rear, kept the family fed. He did not talk of moving. Their home was sound, a good place for Jumma and his family. A small productive garden, some chickens and goats also helped keep them fed. It was a good life. Their good life may have continued, had the war not come to them. His mother called the war the loss of sunshine, or sometimes the darkness.

Blinking rapidly, Jumma woke to a rattling sound in the distance. There were gaps in the sound, no rhythm to it. The duration of each packet of sound lasted but a few seconds, a thrumming, like rocks thrown against cement blocks. Listening, he heard the sounds of the house in between the rattles, the creaks and murmurs, the sound of breathing, his sisters and parents. Years later, he would remember the sounds of his family breathing, the last comforting sound before the darkness descended on his family.

It was autumn in Sudan, not a season much noticed. Light gray smoke rose from the fires between the huts, the sun faded by the thin clouds hovering from dawn to dusk, a pale pink cast around the blunted sun. The gunfire, arrhythmic and ominous, came and went for two days, growing louder and then fading, marching around their village, hidden in the distant bush. The families of the village huddled together at various times,

mothers and children mostly, worried looks cast toward the
bush, consoling and planning, spreading intra-village rumors,
the children frightened, reading the feeling of their parents,
sensing their emotions as small children and dogs sometimes do.

On the morning of the third day after the gunfire began,
a man from Uwayl was found on the road to the village, shot
repeatedly, his hands severed, set beside his head, sitting on
end, steepled as they would be in prayer. For several hours,
people passed the body and praying hands until a truck arrived,
an old International pick-up carrying two men. Covering the
body in a yellow blanket, they placed the dead man in the
back. The oldest of the two men laid a towel next to the hands,
kicked them onto the cloth, wrapped them quickly and placed
them next to the body. The truck then turned back toward the
town and drove off. A group of children witnessed the recovery,
Jumma among them.

An hour after the corpse was removed from the road,
several men on horseback appeared in the distance, all clustered
together. Beyond them were two men sitting on what appeared
to be camels. Jumma stood on a chair he pulled from his
hut, the additional height giving him a better vantage point.
"Jumma, get down from there," his mother shouted from
inside their home. Two of his friends were there, all three boys
the same age, old enough to be frightened, yet trying to show
some bravery, as they expected young men should . Turning,
Jumma looked into the hut to see his mother gesturing
violently, pointing to the ground, her hand tracing ovals in the
air, a blue cloth in her other hand, eyes wide and then growing
wider as she looked past Jumma. Whirling back, he saw the
horsemen separating into two groups, the larger moving to his
right, the smaller coming straight toward the village. Dust, the
color of the dried grasses, rose behind them, drifting away to
the right, following the riders moving away from the village, a
spectral dust dog following its master. Behind him, he heard air
escaping from his mother, as if someone punched her hard in
the gut, the exhalation blunt, as the two boys standing beside

the chair twirled where they stood, spun by the hand of fear, running away to their own huts. Jumma jumped backwards from the chair without looking, his quick motion tipping the chair over in the direction of the riders. Landing on his feet, his momentum carried him back into the doorframe of the hut, hitting his head hard enough to stun him momentarily. Jumma started to fall, his right arm extended to catch himself when he felt a hand wrap itself high on his arm, jerking him up and into the hut. His mother pulled him back into the large room that served for the family's communal time together and into another smaller room, the kitchen. Shoving her children under the table, Jumma's mother returned to the door of the smaller room and lowered a rough burlap cloth that was its door. Arming herself with a large, dark metal knife, she waited near the opening, wiping the perspiration from her face with the blue cloth. Jumma watched her mother, listening to the heavy breathing all around him, a harmonic chugging, fear's chorus, singing the praises of the fate about to fall on them.

The young boy wondered about why he could feel the sounds of the horses hooves but not hear them. It is a strange thing, Jumma thought, hunched beneath the table with his two sisters. There is no storm coming, no thunder. Feeling the pounding of the horse's hooves as much as hearing them, Jumma listened as his sisters' breathing turned to sobbing, they clutched each other, their heads pressed hard together. Had he known it would be the last time he would see one of them, he would have studied her face, touched her hand, held her close in his arms. He wished he had done all of that and more. Her face was now lost to him. Trying as hard as he could, he could not remember his sister's features. He tried drawing them, but couldn't. Jumma carried his failure every day, a blister, raised and filled with remorse.

The first screams he heard were from a child. He tried to tell who it was, the shrillness masking the identity, it lasted but a few seconds, then stopped abruptly. For another second, there seemed to be a perfect silence, then gunfire, savage and large, hammering everything around them. Now there were screams everywhere. Jumma clamped his hands over his ears, squeezed his eyes shut, trying to block out the terror growing around him. He thought someone threw stones through the walls of the kitchen, then knew it was bullets hitting the floor and spraying dirt over his bare legs. The screams of his sisters loud in his ears, he opened his eyes to see his mother pulling the girls from beneath the table. Jumma scrambled after them, his hands clawing at the dirt, legs pumping, he seemed to go nowhere, the air thick, a crystal gel he could not move through. As his mother pushed her daughters through the burlap door, two men entered the hut, rifles held against their sides, pointed straight ahead of them, the bore of the barrel looking surprisingly small to Jumma. They were dressed in tan military fatigues and traditional headdress, the scarf wrapped over their faces, showing only heavy brows over large black eyes. Instantly, the men began shouting, ordering them to fall to the floor, spittle arching, cascading to the floor before them. Crossing the large room, one man grabbed Jumma's mother, throwing her to the floor, while the second man went for his sisters. Jumma, standing in front of his sisters, was knocked to the ground by the second man, short and stocky, who smelled of cattle. As he was hit, Jumma closed his eyes, hitting the floor on his side and did not see the man's boot coming for his head, felt the pain of the impact and then knew nothing else.

Jumma lay on a hilltop above a village he had never seen, the hill higher than any he knew of in Sudan, the village below bathed in a dull light, maybe early evening, he did not know. Lying on his side, his head resting on his arm, he studied the village; it was not his. The ground beneath him began to shake, immediately violent, rolling him over. His head hurt and he felt as if he might vomit, his stomach aching, his chest beginning to burn. "Wake up, you little shit," a voice above him said. "Wake up, we're going to talk."

The smell of cattle was strong in his nostrils. Jumma opened his eyes to a dark ceiling, covering a small room with dirty white walls, a short squat table and an old brass oil lamp, dented with no glass to brighten the flame. Three men stared at him. Jumma tried to sit up, was pushed back down by pain shooting across his forehead. Rolling to his right side, he managed to push himself into a sitting position, leaning back against the wall for support. He was too frightened to speak. Looking again at the men, he realized one was a boy, perhaps fifteen years old, not much more, he thought.

"Where is your father?" one of the men asked. Dressed in a khaki green uniform, he wore a holster on his belt, a black handle visible beneath a flap, also black. Two pens protruded from a shirt pocket, the pens apparently leaking, as there was a large stain beneath the pocket. Several other stains covered the front of his shirt. Jumma looked harder, seeing the stains were not black or blue, but brown. Blood. The boy's clothes were clean, a tan camouflage, looking new. The second man's uniform was covered in brown spots, in sizes from tiny to one large one at his armpit.

"Get him up," the man with the pens said, ordering the other two into action. The boy moved first, crossing the space quickly, bending to take Jumma by an arm, his grip strong like Jumma's father, pulling him to his feet. Jumma stumbled and was caught by the second man. Lifted from the floor, they carried him to the third man, now seen as the leader by Jumma. Holding him off the floor, they stopped before the leader, who asked, "Where is your father?" Jumma looked dumbly at the man who made a fist and hit him hard, the blow landing squarely in the middle of Jumma's forehead, knocking him unconscious.

When he woke, the pain in his head was unbearable, causing him to cry, the fright and pain so disorienting, he stopped thinking. Shock was setting into Jumma, a shield thrown around his mind to protect itself. With his arm over his eyes, he wept loudly, his chest heaving, gasping for air. "Momma," he cried out.

"Shut him up and bring him here," the man with the pens said, his exasperation clearly showing in his voice. Jumma was pulled from the floor and carried across the room, then slammed down on a chair. He screamed "Please" as a hand grasped his wrist, pulling his arm up, then pinning it to the table. Two other hands held him by the shoulders, the thick fingers digging in, the pain as bad as the pain in his head.

"Boy, where is your father?" he was asked. Jumma cried, tears and snot flowing down his young face. "One more time, where is your father?"

The room was silent except for Jumma's sobs. A hammer wielded by the younger bandit smashed the third finger of Jumma's left hand as flat as a cracker, blood spewing from the tip as it burst from the pressure, the nail splintered, the small bits and pieces pushed into the pulped flesh. Mercifully, Jumma passed out again.

***

The French priest and the nurse saw the body by the road, just southeast of Uwayl. It was mid-afternoon, a hot day, the sky clear and bright. They were returning to their mission post in Mapuordit from the small town, part of a delegation from the Diocese of Rumbek to minister aid to the people of the area, victims of the attack by the Janjaweed a week before. Stopping thirty meters from the body, the priest scanned the bush for others, people waiting near the road, the body simply a diversion. After a few minutes, the priest inched the vehicle forward, his head swiveling from side to side, checking as he drove. The nurse gasped, opening the door and jumped out, the old truck still rolling. "Wait," the priest said, grabbing for the nurse and missing.

Jumma lay on his back, wearing only a pair of faded orange shorts, his dark skin carrying a red sub-tone, the sun burning his skin. Lips puffed by dehydration and the sun were framed by a battered face, large contusions on the side and front of his head. His left hand, wrapped in a blood-soaked white shirt, lay out straight from the boy's body. It was covered in ants.

"Bring water, Father, quickly please," Sister Marie Claire said. Father Robineau, carrying a jug of water, walked to where

Jumma lay, still searching the bush for trouble. Pulling the nun up by the arm, the priest knelt, scooped the boy from the dust to carry him to the truck.

***

Jumma shivered, the chill of the cockpit always a surprise to him. The Beech had reached an altitude of eight thousand feet, where Hanley would cruise on their trip to Nairobi. The chill may have been a product of his memories, he could not be sure. Looking at his left hand, he could not recall having all four fingers. He didn't miss it.

15

"Honey, leave that poor dog alone. He's not feeling well and he doesn't really know you. Come over here and sit by me," Elizabeth said.

Hanley's granddaughter launched an old tennis ball which struck Weed on the nose and rolled under the couch in Rocky's den. Weed blinked hard and squeezed his eyes shut, hoping the little girl would go away. The sound of Elizabeth's voice was reassuring, but Weed would not relax until the child was somewhere else.

"Carrie, come over here and let me see your new outfit. Your momma says today's the first day you've worn it. I'd love to see it," Rocky said, patting the couch beside where she sat, smiling at Hanley's granddaughter. Carrie ignored her.

Rocky was trying to rescue Weed. Hanley's absence had been difficult for both of them but harder, it seemed, on the dog. Weed stuck to his rug most of the time and did not have an interest in much else. The usual enthusiasm for walks was dwindling. Weed's internal clock had told him that the normal cycle of Hanley's absence had passed some time ago. He missed his best friend and waited each minute for the sound of his truck to announce the cycle was complete for a while. He was lonely and even Rocky could not help.

Hanley had been in Africa for just over four months. From his letters, Elizabeth knew he was safe and into a routine of flying doctors and supplies to and from the mission.

Carrie huffed in exasperation at the old dog's unwillingness to take an interest in her. Playing was not what she sought. That was too inclusive. When Weed could not be motivated as she hoped, Carrie turned to her mother and Rocky for attention. Not before she nailed the dog's nose with the ball.

"Have you heard from your father this week?" Rocky asked.

"Yes, he called from Khartoum just before returning to the mission. He was about to meet a doctor from Germany and take him to Mapuordit. He seems glad the trips and his routine have fallen into a cycle of sorts. Dad asked if I'd talked to you. I told him we talked once or twice a week. He didn't have much time to talk. He did say he would try to call from Mapuordit when he could find a way to do that. God, I already hate that name. Did he call you?"

"He called from Kenya two weeks ago. He did sound tired. I can imagine why. The stress of these trips and just knowing where you're going would be enough. He will handle it. You can imagine how he misses everyone. Sitting in that plane for hours alone has given him enough time to think about this decision and what he's facing. He's there now and we can only count the days. I think Weed has already started." A visit to her mother had given Elizabeth the opportunity to drive north to Kokomo on her way back to Ohio and see Rocky. It also afforded her the chance to look at her father's house.

The thought of leaving her husband grew in her mind each day. She knew there would be no return to any sort of normal relationship. After her father had left for Africa, her husband Gary had gone to the West Coast. He returned after a few days and then left immediately for New York. Since his return, they had hardly spoken; only brief, harsh exchanges in passing. For the most part, her husband stayed away. She knew it was only a matter of time before they would start the discussion she was dreading. None of it would be easy, not now. Something was substantially different. It had the feel of permanence.

"I'm sorry you're the one left taking care of Dad's stuff after he decided to fly off to that godforsaken hole. You know, if he had decided to stay, it would have been because of you and not me or Carrie. I wish he had. The only time I've seen him happy for years has been just in the last year or two. You were the reason." Elizabeth said.

"No, sweetheart, that's not really right. If your father had stayed it would have been for you. Not me. Maybe Carrie or his parents. I think Weed may have been third or fourth. You were first. You've always been first. That's been the case since I've known you and always will be." Rocky said.

"Did you know that Mr Weekley sold Dad's truck and sent me the money? Why would he do that? I mean, is he not coming back? When the check came in the mail last week with a note attached, it scared me to death. I called Mr Weekley. He said that it was his idea. That it wasn't right for the truck just to sit there, that Dad could certainly afford a new one when he returned. Dad agreed and he sold the truck two weeks ago."

The dog began to snore and both women stopped talking. Carrie had also fallen asleep between them, her face, now angelic, was all rosy cheeks and long eyelashes. Rocky knew that if Hanley were here, he would melt. Despite behaving much like her grandmother at times, he still adored Carrie.

"I'll make some lunch, after that we'll look at your father's house. Stay with me tonight and I'll send you off early in the morning. We can talk things over if you like. Oh, don't shake your head just yet. I'd love it. Weed would too. Just stay and tomorrow you'll be fresh and ready for the drive. Besides, my seed catalogues came this week. It will be fun." Rocky said.

"All right, but I'll need to call mother and tell her. I'll leave a message on Gary's service. I'd like to stay. I've been thinking about Dad's offer. I probably should look at the house. Tomorrow being Monday, I can talk to Dad's attorney if I have questions. We'll stay."

"Good," Rocky said.

***

The mail was late, as always. The afternoon sun through the window of the dining room warmed her arms, crossed in impatience. Why is he always late, she wondered. He drinks, at least he looks as if he drinks, she thought. A typical, low-level French bureaucrat.

Movement brought her eyes to the wall surrounding her house, a hat, the top of which appeared and then disappeared, as the head it covered bobbed and wobbled, the mailman, owner of the head, finally on the street bordering her home. Stopping before the iron gate, he fumbled with the latch, his lips moving in back and forth motions, pink waves rolling across his fat red face. She could see from a distance he was sweating profusely. He paused to wipe his neck with a bare hand, scratched a spot behind his ear, squinting, even though the sun was behind him. Appearing to talk to himself, he marched up the brick walk to the front door. He is hungover, she thought. Yes, a French mail carrier would be drunk in the afternoon.

April in Saint-Nazaire was never hot. This week was an exception. Sophie Campbell noticed her mailman's sack was nearly full as he approached her front door. Hoping he would not fall and hurt himself, she turned from the window, walking to the main hallway of her house.

Struggling to push the letters and thick brochures through the weathered brass mail slot, the mailman belched, then pushed the last letter through. The pile of mail, slid a short distance and stopped, alone in the middle of the hall.

When she picked it up, Sophie recognized the battered condition of the letter, a sign it was from her uncle in Sudan. He would tell her again, as he did in almost every letter, that the trip through the Sudanese postal system was haphazard and a dangerous one for a poor letter and she should give these letters much care, for they have met with great disrespect along the way.

Sophie would need a cup of coffee while reading her uncle's letter. Hanley Martin would have been there for over four months when this letter was written. There was information in this letter she wanted to know, but feared; what an odd combination was fear and want, she thought as she spooned coffee into the glass press. It was only a few months, she thought; what could happen in so short a time? Then there was the why. Why was she worried about a man she hardly knew; a friend of her husband, a man who left his family behind to live in a place that was not kind to its own, much less a stranger? Why did she care? She would not think about it now. Perhaps she was not meant to know why. Sadly, she now had two people in Africa to worry about. She would pray for a million others, but worry about only two.

A smudge covered part of the envelope's flap. The flap itself had a wavy look to it, as though it had been wet. Steamed, she thought. She hoped that opening this letter had been difficult for them and that they were disappointed with what they read. It opened easily. The letter was handwritten on white notebook paper, torn from a spiral binder, her uncle's usual stationary. It was not smooth, but had the look of having been handled frequently during the writing, probably over several days' time. As she unfolded the letter, she noticed a stain that appeared to be in the shape of a winged bug of sorts near the top edge of the first page. Mostly brown with a slight edge of yellow on the right side, the mark was as if her uncle had chosen an odd and ugly stamp with which to personalize this letter. She was sure the bug had not volunteered its services. This priest uncle of hers was a hunter and would not have hesitated to swat the bug when it landed on the page. Did he kill the bug before he started or after? She began to read.

(Translation from French)

April 27th

My Dearest Sophie:

First, I hope you and Michael are well and happy. Second, I must apologize for the stain at the top of this page. It has been hot (always) for the past two weeks, more so than is usual. The bugs are horrible, worse than I have seen since I have been here. A beetle crawled onto the paper and I hit it even before I could think of what I was doing. I apologize for the stain, but I did not want to waste paper. This country teaches one not to waste anything (as if your grandmother had not taught me that many, many years ago).

Tell Michael that Mr Martin, the American pilot, arrived over eleven weeks ago and has been very busy since he arrived. After his first flight to Ethiopia, he has been flying several times a week, moving patients and doctors back and forth between our mission and elsewhere, mostly Kenya, then bringing supplies from Nairobi. Sometimes, he flies to Khartoum and Port Sudan. He said that the customs people in Port Sudan are especially fond of him. When he mentions this, he smiles an odd smile. He is a quiet man and at first, he seemed overwhelmed, but once he started flying, he changed. Then there is Sister Marie Claire; she and Mr Martin have become the talk of the mission. They are an odd pair. Antagonistic is the word I'm looking for, but that is not right either. There is a tension, yes, but it is not a bad tension; perhaps more a teasing. I do not know how to describe it. I think they are good for each other, even though they seem not to be when I watch them. She hits him, which is a good sign. The odd thing is that she has stopped hitting anyone else.

Sophie was surprised by this news. She knew of Sister Marie Claire.

The conflict here has increased of late. There is now gunfire in the distance, is now coming more often and often nearby. We have had two people killed here in the past four months. One, a young girl from the Darfur region, was a favorite of Sister Marie Claire. The good sister was devastated, both heartbroken and furious at the same time. It was Mr Martin who calmed her anger and since then, since he began flying, he has become more of a leader here every day. Now, the good sister turns to him for advice before the doctors or even me. He has a way of calming her, as I have said. She has been good for him. She teaches him of Sudan and its people and of the conflict, the nature of the conflict. It is hard to understand, hard especially for an American, I believe. When you have not experienced war, not seen this kind of cruelty and disrespect for life, it is hard to know how to respond to it. Even for us who have been here for some time, even we have not learned to understand why it is so cruel. The treatment of the children and the conditions they experience every day of their short lives, this is what pierces our hearts the most. The loss of hope and expectations is the worse. Seeing eyes that are empty of everything but fear is so tragic.

A problem is developing and it is causing me some amount of anxiety. The American pilot and one of the Slovakian doctors have begun asking why the church does not take a more active role in discussions with the governments of America and the European countries to intercede on behalf of the people of Sudan. These questions come now almost daily, on the evenings we can gather together, during and after the meals, when we have time to talk. Now the questions of why the church and the other nations refuse to help more than they do always dominate the talk. I tried to explain the role the church and others have played in seeking peace, but my explanations were met with more questions and apparent disappointment. I continue to explain, but I'm afraid Mr Martin and the doctors are looking for answers I cannot give. While she does not participate in these discussions, I'm also afraid that perhaps Sister Marie Claire sows the seeds of impatience in the pilot when they talk alone, but I do not know this for certain.

I should let you know that I may be returning to France in six months, perhaps less. The church has decided that I have been in Sudan long enough. I am afraid I am not disappointed. Our work here is important, but so difficult and frustrating. I miss you and our family. I miss France. Please write when you can. All my love to you both.

Jean-Robert

16

Looking like an old stove on wheels, each corner dipping up and down in counter motions, the dull white Land Cruiser moved down the track between Rumbek and the mission, following the sea swell ruts, small waves of African dirt, a land boat with two survivors aboard, Hanley and the young Irishman, Dr O'Connell. Bouncing along inside, they discussed a wide variety of topics, everything from the difference between Irish and Scotch whiskey to Hanley's preferred current topic of destiny and the role it played in his life. The young doctor was resisting Hanley's attempts to draw him into a conversation, too tired to talk after a long night tending to new patients, more children infected by measles.

Hanley was questioning the church's position on fate and Sudan, which led to the young doctor trying to explain the role of destiny or determinism in Christian beliefs.

"The church believes that God's divine providence carries man along as a swollen stream might. That man is free to swim against the stream, dog paddle with the current, try clinging to rocks along the way or float on his back and whistle or even drown. All of those actions represent man's free will. No matter what he chooses to do, he still is carried along by the stream. Some Protestants believe a man is placed in the stream by God and can only float or drown. He has no choice. That is predestination."

Hanley checked the fuel gauge, noticing again the Land Cruiser's large black steering wheel was cracked from years of heat and sweat. Hanley said, "Yes, that makes sense. I thought it was a heaven or hell thing, no grey area, God doesn't allow for wiggle room, tow the mark or burn. And, isn't that really destiny? I still think an omniscient did, somewhere along the line, add destiny to the mix, beyond the obvious overly deterministic predestination bullshit. Or is that man-made? I mean, I think some people just have a certain fate in store for them. Let me give you an example. When I was young, just out of college, I worked for a company, Thompson Machine, that manufactured machined parts, some of which were used in the aviation industry. It's where I got my start. I was on my way to Wichita, Kansas and stopped in St. Louis to see a company I hoped to land as a client. It was a disaster. It shook me up for weeks. It was probably as much bad luck as anything, but it was one experience, not the only one, but one that started me thinking about fate. I haven't stopped thinking about it since."

A young Hanley Martin had made a sales call to a company in St. Louis, one of his first stops as he headed west toward Wichita and its many aviation companies. As he waited in the lobby, the man he was to meet, the Purchasing Director, was killed by his wife in his own office, after she accused him of having an affair with his secretary. She punched him and, as he fell backward, hitting his head on the corner of his desk, killing him instantly. Hanley did not make the sale that day. Hanley said, "After that day, I have always wondered about the decisions we make in this life and if they are really random or are they influenced by forces we do not recognize or would not understand if we did know about them. I'm not talking about the guy that died. He knew why his wife was there, cursing, showering him with spit and anger. He was guilty of getting some mud for his turtle with his secretary, as we used to say in high school. Sorry. What leads us to be on a bridge that collapses, to be standing in front of a desk with hard corners and not a haystack when slugged by your wife or fly a plane to Africa? Is it truly chaos or is it a plan? I don't know. You tell me."

"What is that?" Dr O'Connell said, looking up the road ahead. Lying by the roadside, Hanley saw a form, indistinguishable at that distance, looking like a mound of dirt, dark, but with something bright in its midst, maybe a scrap of paper or cloth, weeds surrounding whatever it was, making identification more difficult. As they approached, Hanley slowed the truck, stopping beside what now appeared to be a body. The two men looked at it for a moment, the sadness connecting them tangible like webbing strung between, spun by the spiders of conflict that haunted Sudan. O'Connell said, "Let's take a look."

Covered in a coarse, mud-red blanket, a single foot protruding from beneath it, was the body of a boy, maybe twelve years old, Hanley thought. He was mostly skin and bones, his face gaunt, eyes protruding, staring at whatever lay before him in whatever world he now found himself. "He's still warm," the doctor observed after touching his wrist, feeling for any sign of life. "I didn't see him on the way into Rumbek this morning, did you?" Dr O'Connell asked Hanley.

"No, no, I didn't. Maybe he and whomever he was with hid in the brush when he heard the truck coming. Perhaps he thought we were soldiers or Baggara."

"Maybe. Will you open the back of the truck? We'll at least see that he's buried. We didn't do anything else for him, now did we? We can at least do that."

Hanley opened the rear door of the Land Cruiser, holding it while the doctor placed the boy's body inside. Arranging the blanket so it completely covered the boy, Dr O'Connell stopped, laid a hand on the cloth covering the dead boy's head and held it there for a moment. Then he turned to Hanley and said, "What he's facing today must be better than what he faced yesterday."

Hanley looked up and slammed the door closed.

***

"Jumma."

"Yes, Sister."

"Could you come with me to the clinic? I want to store the medicine and the supplies Mr Martin brought from Nairobi. We are fortunate the people at the Nairobi Hospital are generous in response to our needs and requests. They understand how severe our situation is."

Sister Marie Claire had found Jumma sitting alone in the dining hall at the main table, writing in his notebook with the black and white, speckled, hardboard cover. Now, with his head down, he continued to write as they spoke. Jumma said, "I think the people at the hospital in Nairobi may not be as good to us as you believe."

"What do you mean, Jumma?"

"Last night, two of the doctors were talking about the supplies and just how much was brought back in Hanley's airplane. One of them said he thought it was unusual, that is the word he used, 'unusual'. The other doctor said he thought Hanley was buying extra supplies. I don't know about this." Jumma did not look up from his writing, which she knew he loved, and so she was not insulted.

"Jumma, are you certain that is what they said? I do not mean to doubt you, it is just that this is a serious allegation, one that I must look into. Our relationship with these hospitals is important to the mission. It has taken the church some time to develop these ties. Why would you tell me this if you knew I would talk to others about it?" she asked.

"Sister, I do not know why I told you. I should have known it would upset you and I do not want to do that. I could not prevent myself from telling you and I do not know why," he said.

"Which doctors said this? Which doctors, Jumma?"

Two quick steps brought the nun to the table's edge. Placing her hands flat on the table top, she leaned forward, pushing her words toward him. "Jumma, tell me which doctors."

The young African stopped writing, twirled the pen in his fingers, his trouble drawn on his face, stopped twirling the pen, looked out the window in front of him and said, "Dr Milosiak, he said it." Jumma closed the notebook and stood. Looking at the nun, he said, "Sister, I really don't know about this. I heard the doctors talking, that's all."

Her jaw working back and forth, Sister Marie Claire stood up straight, turned and walked to the door. Without looking back, she asked, "Will you help me, Jumma?"

"Yes Sister."

The clinic was crowded, a line forming at the door, ran across the open space to a tree, around the tree and toward the road. Three doctors and two nurses were providing care that day. To alleviate the crowding in the clinic itself, one doctor and a nurse were working the line, screening the people to prioritize the cases.

Sister Marie Claire walked fast, so fast, Jumma could barely keep up. She stopped by the tree, hoping to calm herself before reaching the clinic. She stood with her eyes shut, her hands balled into fists. When she opened her eyes, she saw a man, standing in a line of people waiting to see the clinic doctor, staring at her. In his arms, he carried a child, a boy, thinned by prolonged hunger, his eyes now slightly bulging, his lips swollen and parched. The man looked so forlorn, she thought, so lost. As they exchanged looks, the man smiled a wan smile, a brief betrayal of his circumstance, offered to the nun as a gift, a gift without reason. It lasted only a second as the line began to move and the man was forced to move with it.

Jumma asked, "Sister, why is it that Hanley's kindness makes you angry?"

"I'm not angry, Jumma. I just wish Monsieur Martin had talked to me about this first. We have a good arrangement with the hospital in Nairobi. I don't want that to change," she said. "I am going to the office to call the hospital, then I'll come back so we can work. We have much to do this morning."

***

Playing with his two-way hand-held radio to pass the time, Hanley's face was covered with a fine layer of sweat. He sighed, smacked the radio against his leg, looked at it again, moved the dial again, heard nothing but static and then put it in a pocket of his cargo pants. "Forget it," he said to no one as he was alone. Looking up from the front seat of the Land Cruiser, he saw Sister Marie Claire striding across the grounds toward him. She looks constipated, he thought. As she drew near, he slid from the seat to stand by the truck. "Good morning," he said.

"Monsieur Martin, I have a question."

'Okay, shoot."

"Pardon?"

"Please, ask the question." Hanley smiled, but it was apparent the nun was in no mood for smiles. She stood before him, arms at her side, fists clenched, feet apart. Hanley thought she looked ready for a fight.

"The doctors believe you may be buying supplies from the hospital in Nairobi. The hospital has been generous and understanding of our needs. I'm afraid you may have caused us a problem."

"Why do you think that?"

"If they believe you are willing to pay for the supplies we require, if they think we now have a rich American, willing to spend his own money, then they may not be willing to donate these supplies. You may have harmed all the work we have done to gain a commitment from them, a commitment to our mission. You should have talked to me first. It was irresponsible of you. I'm sorry, but it's true. You don't know how it is here. This is not America—"

"Really; I hadn't noticed."

"—and things are done differently. Please don't hurt our efforts. I know, at least I think you want to help, but we have been nurturing these relationships for many years." While the nun complained to Hanley, he smiled at her, which made her even angrier than she had been when she started her explanation. Her eyes narrowed, her voice rising, her irritation clearly apparent to the American.

"Monsieur, you must believe I am very concerned. What we do here has many limitations imposed upon it. Relationships are fragile. Don't bring us problems; we have enough."

Hanley said, "I understand, I really do. I'm just trying to help. I have resources that have value here and I just thought that maybe I could, you know, make a difference."

"You are making a difference. Bringing us medicine and doctors, taking patients to hospitals for care, that makes a difference, a great deal of difference. I thought you would understand that."

"Sister, I understand, maybe better than you think. When I first picked up supplies in Kenya and saw how little they were sending, I thought of suggesting I could perhaps buy some extra, you know, a hundred extra tongue depressors here and there."

The nun shot back, "You didn't just buy some additional tongue depressors. There is much more than normal at the clinic. I contacted the hospital in Nairobi and was told I should speak to you about the arrangement. What arrangement?"

"I had the opportunity to meet the hospital's administrator at the airport in Nairobi. I was picking up the doctor from Sweden who had been at the Nairobi Hospital before coming here. The administrator had driven him to the airport. The administrator asked me if I was interested in flying their doctors to southern Kenya on occasion. They offered money, but I bargained for something else. They agreed to increase the monthly supplies for an occasional flight. Simple. They'll also buy the fuel. It was an easy decision, I thought?"

She stared at Hanley for a moment, her eyes wide and blinking rapidly. The tip of her tongue appeared between her lips, moving from one side of her mouth to the other. She looked down at her feet and said, "Thank you," then turned and walked away.

"You're welcome," he said.

17

African maize covered half of the garden plot, which was maybe half an acre, the corn now a foot high, the leaves small, covered in a fine dust, making them gray in the afternoon sun. The fruit, the ears were also small and would not be large he thought, not like the roasting ears found in Indiana and all over the mid-west of America. Maize was what his grandfather called rough corn. He knew enough history to know what he saw growing here came here from somewhere else, from somewhere in the Americas, an invention of the Mayans or Native Americans.

Hanley tried to think of the size of the garden in hectares, but couldn't get it right in his head. Sister Marie Claire was hoeing, digging out weeds between the rows at the other end. The American walked around, looking at the vegetables planted by the mission staff, tended by everyone but him. He recognized some beans, several types if squash, including pumpkins, if they were a squash. He thought he had known that once, but could not remember.

It was late afternoon, with no real wind to stir the hot African air. He saw she wore an old baseball cap over a solid red bandana, the tails made by the knot lying on the collar of her dark blue shirt. The ball cap was also dark blue with a very large red C on the front. Where did that come from, he wondered. Her jeans were dirty at the knees, where she had knelt to pull at the more stubborn of her opponents. She hummed something, he did not recognize it. Without looking up, she said, "Did you bring a hoe?"

"No, I never thought about it, actually. Too many years behind a desk, I suppose. Mentally conditioned to avoid manual labor. A subliminal thing, I guess. What do you think?" he asked.

"I think you can go to hell for lying, not just for stealing or cheating." Looking up, she merely shrugged, held out the hoe and said, "Here, try it."

Hanley stepped into the garden, the soil soft and shifting, his boots sliding beneath him as he searched for balance, like walking on a beach.

"You should be wearing gloves," she noted.

There were but a few weeds entrenched between the rows, making him wonder if she was busying herself to keep her mind from the matters that pressed her that day or maybe to think those same matters through. Holding the hoe up to inspect it, he saw the wood handle was completely unprotected by varnish, the wood dulled and grey with chinks in its surface, making gloves necessary if the hoer was to get through the day without taking on splinters. The old metal blade looked off somehow, more than bent, it was altered, was encrusted with dirt and rust, the edge showing a gleam from someone's attempt at sharpening, the edge visibly grooved, the file used to hone it rough, the wrong tool, probably the only file available. The hoe was heavy, another sign of age, made in a time when durability was part of the equation. It looked like every hoe he had seen in Indiana when he was young. "This hoe and I are the same age, I think," Hanley said. "We appear to be in the same shape." Looking for a safe spot for griping, he began digging out the few weeds he saw, careful not to damage the stalks, picking up the freed weeds and placing them where they could be retrieved when he finished.

Hanley felt the nun watching him as he worked, and she cautioned him to be careful around the maize. Following behind to pick up the weeds as he worked his way between the rows, picking up speed as he grew accustom to his new job. His right hand slid up the handle, the pressure pushing a splinter through the webbed skin between his thumb and the first finger. A low cursing and a shake of his right hand brought the nun's head up.

"Are you all right?" she asked.

"Yes, it's nothing."

She said, "The hoeing is not difficult. I have seen it done worse than you are doing it. You have gardened before, monsieur?" she asked

Stopping, Hanley straightened up slowly, pressing his lower back with a hand as he did. Using his wrist, he mopped sweat from his brow. "Yes, when I was a boy, I worked on the farm of a relative. I helped my aunt with her garden," he said. He felt dampness forming on his shirt, from between his shoulders to just above his belt. There were also ovals of wetness behind the knees of his tan khaki cargo pants.

"Is this too much work for you? A man of your age must be careful. Perhaps you should hoe more slowly," she suggested.

He ignored her.

"Mr Martin, I believe I owe you an apology. You must know, I do not apologize often. During our earlier conversations, I had been rude. I believe you Americans call it abrupt."

"We have other names for it," he said.

Pausing for a second to examine an ear of corn, she then said, "I know you are here to help us, I do realize that. I did not mean to be mean or, uh, uncaring, if that's the right word, to you as you look for answers to the questions you have, that you seek. It may be that I do not understand the question itself. Is that possible?"

"Anything's possible, I suppose. I appreciate you saying this. I didn't intend for this to be a problem. I can assure you this will not interfere with my work. It's just that I needed to know something. It's because I was so successful in my life. Am I somehow *required* to do something to justify my luck, to show fate that it had not made a mistake when it picked me to succeed? I was taught I must do something to, you know, pay back my good fortune. I just need to know what I must do. I couldn't find the answer before, at least not until fate appeared to step in. Two chance meetings, one was your friend, Sister Mary Kathleen. She was actually the second. The first was in France. Both seemed to point to this mission and then to you. I swear to God."

"Please, don't say that," she responded.

"I'm not making this up. I mean, I leave France, and on my way back to Indiana, I meet a nun that knows of the priest I met by chance at a dinner party in a place, by the way, I had never been before. The priest heads the organization that runs this mission, that put the uncle of my friend's wife here, put you here, a friend of the nun I met on the way home. Your friend, Sister Mary Kathleen, even lives in the same state I live in. Forgive me, but it all seemed oddly meant to be," he said. He leaned on the hoe, a hand covering the end of the handle, his chin on the hand. "Sounds nuts, doesn't it?" he said.

"Did you like Father Bertrand?" she asked.

"Yes, I did. The whole thing seems like a dream to me now. It was a bit surreal, especially the old lady. Her name was Paulinier, a local historian. Sophie, Michael Campbell's wife, really likes her. There were five of us at the dinner party; Michael and Sophie, Father Bertrand, Madame Paulinier and me. I was staying at Michael's home. For whatever reason, I decided to attend the Paris Air Show after years of avoiding it, letting my staff attend. I needed a change, I suppose, and went. I really enjoyed it, probably should have done it earlier. Anyway, the dinner party was a turning point for me, helped me make some big decisions. The dinner party and meeting our friend, Sister Mary Kathleen," Hanley said. "I'll tell you about the dinner party. It was interesting."

***

When he stepped into the dining room, the parquet floor squealed beneath his shoes, as if he stepped on a baby's toy.

Brightly polished, the floor reflected in small, irregular shaped ovals the chandelier over the table. The aromas from the table made his stomach churn, loud enough, Hanley coughed trying to mask the gurgle. It was a lovely simple dinner of leeks with light balsamic vinaigrette, small filet mignons with broccoli, brie with chestnuts and for dessert, chocolate mousse with strawberry sauce.

After some time, Hanley watched, fascinated as a bit of leek rode the corner of Veronique Paulinier's mouth, clinging stubbornly, refusing to fall. Apparently for Madame Paulinier, chewing was part of her oracular routine. He was seated to Madame Paulinier's right, at one corner of the table. He watched as she savaged the food Sophie had prepared. Madame Paulinier was a woman in her late seventies, thin as a communion wafer and just as dry. However, she appeared to know the entire history of the Loire Valley and Normandy and was prepared to share it with her fellow dinner guests. Her English was broken, but she persevered as she had a new audience. Some of it was interesting and Hanley was polite. She was very different from the other guest at his host's table

Short and wiry, Father Paul Bertrand was in his mid-sixties, with a slightly hawkish face. Hanley thought the priest to be quiet, but as they talked, he sensed an intensity below the surface.

Eventually, Mrs. Paulinier stopped her lesson long enough to attack a challenging piece of filet and Father Bertrand asked Hanley why he had come to Europe after all these years. Hanley looked at the cleric and arched his eyebrows, surprised by the question. Before he could respond, the priest apologized to explain he was aware of Michael Campbell's repeated attempts to have Hanley visit them in England and then France. He simply wanted to know what had changed.

"Many things changed in my life within the past year. My wife and I divorced and my daughter now lives in another state. I'm alone, except for my dog. His name is Weed. He and Michael have an interesting history. You should ask Michael to explain it sometime."

Some brie failed to make it into Michael Campbell's mouth as he looked up at Hanley. "Hanley is trying, as most Americans do, to be humorous. Years ago, he found a mutation, a mistake of nature, dropped on his doorstep one bleak winter night. Hanley thought it was a puppy, a cute one no less and took it in. Being somewhat of a freak himself, it was love at first sight. The dog, if that is what it really is, finds legs, apparently male legs, British male legs, irresistible. I had to carry a newspaper to beat the damned thing wherever I went when I stayed with the Martins in Indiana. It was memorable," he said.

Hanley paused to sip his coffee and said, "After my divorce, it seemed like I needed a change, something to do beyond my normal routine. When I can, I fly my planes for enjoyment, but I needed something more. My staff began discussing this year's air show in Paris and I made the decision to attend. The trip has been as much as I could hope for so far." Looking at the priest, Hanley said, "Sophie tells me you were the priest in her parish when she was a young girl. She and Michael have also mentioned the organization you run and your travels for the church. To a number of countries, I understand. It sounds as if you have had a challenging task for many years, especially in Africa. How do you stay with it? I mean, you must see and deal with things that are bound to shake your belief in all things human. It must effect even a man of faith. I assume you find strength in your faith in other things," Hanley said.

Father Bertrand appeared to consider the question. "My faith is also in other people and the goodness within them. I happen to believe that most men and women are good and actually do care for the plight of others. Women especially are caring and willing to help those less fortunate than themselves. So faith includes my belief in the good to be found in my fellow man, as well as God. If not for that hope, I might be building airplanes also," he said.

Hanley smiled.

Sipping some wine, the priest said, "The Fathers of Notre Dame have been a mission program since the late 1800s.

We press our faith into many remote areas, especially Africa. Currently, we have a number of missions operating in Chad, Benin, Mozambique, Ethiopia and the Sudan. Things are more difficult now than ever before."

A cough, then another stopped the conversation, as Madame Paulinier worked the roll she was eating down her dry throat. After a moment of struggle, she thought to lubricate her throat with wine, which smoothed the process.

Father Bertrand continued, saying, "Before, we struggled with poverty, disease and corrupt governments. Now, we also struggle with something bigger. Before, we were supported by our Muslim brethren, even though their beliefs are different. They knew we were there to help, to minister aid as well as faith. Now, some Muslim clerics see us as the enemy and our missions are now in an even more dangerous place." He looked at Sophie. She stared at her friend. Hanley saw her expression had changed.

"A dear friend of mine, Sophie's uncle, Jean-Robert, is in the south of Sudan, in a mission in Mapuordit. It is a small station with only one priest and a few sisters working with the children, mostly orphans. They also care for lepers. Fighting has left so many homeless and the children suffer the most. Currently, there are one hundred little ones receiving aid at the Mapuordit mission. This is but a fraction of the orphans to be found in that region. Many children are now afraid of seeking the aid of our priests and nuns. They have seen the punishments inflicted and will not risk being hurt or killed. Thousands have died due to their fear," the priest explained.

"Does the Sudanese government help in any way?" Hanley asked.

"No, we must contend with many different issues, from the government as well as the growing movement of radical Muslims and the SPLA. The SPLA is a particularly vicious group, formerly Marxist, now just thugs using violence to stay in power in south Sudan. They recruit children, boys of ten or twelve years, and teach them to be soldiers. They are not soldiers, Mr Martin. They are children raised to believe they can take whatever they want from others through intimidation and murder, if need be." Father Bertrand stopped to sip his wine.

Hanley thought that perhaps Madame Paulinier might seize the moment and begin again her discourse on the lore of Loire. But the old lady sat and waited for the priest to continue. She must have realized the conversation had moved in a direction she would not interrupt.

"One thing most people do not realize is the long-term damage caused by the loss of families; mothers and fathers raising their children. The caring and teaching that happens every day within a family is immense and its importance goes unnoticed and unappreciated by most people. Perhaps greatest among those losses is the teaching of values. Everything from the value of life to the value of love and sharing is denied to these children. By the time these children are ten or twelve years old, they have learned to survive on their own, often by ruthless means. It's easy to build monsters using material like this," Father Bertrand said.

Turning his wine glass by the stem and watching the rotation of the deeply red fluid, Hanley asked, "Is there any American aid coming into these countries, into Sudan?"

"Some, but much of that never reaches the people in need, or if it does, it goes to those nearest the point it enters the country. Supplies not taken through the major ports or airports are moved by truck to the remote areas. Thieves and groups like the SPLA take the rest before it can reach outposts and missions like those in Torit or Mapuordit. They use food as a weapon," the priest explained.

Michael Campbell said, "It's a logistics problem. Currently, the most common way of moving goods into Sudan's southern interior is by truck. Jean-Robert writes to Sophie and her father about the conditions there. He tells us that the truck routes are difficult even without the bandits. The roads are horrible, the trucks old. Breakdowns are a common occurrence. He says dust eventually stops anything mechanical and once the trucks stop, they are stripped of their cargo. There is an airstrip near Mapuordit, but few planes make the jump from the main cities or ports to the interior. A plane could at least bring in medical supplies and fly out those in need of serious medical attention, which many are, from what Jean-Robert says," Campbell said.

"The mission cannot afford to employ a pilot and plane on a full-time basis. Those that are there can make much more money flying for businesses or wealthy families. The dangers are many and life is hard. Although there is a true mission in Sudan, few people are inclined to be a part of it," Father Bertrand said.

Hanley had been listening intently as his friend and the priest talked about the need for a plane and a pilot. For a second, he thought of himself in Sudan, but then, recognizing how foolish that was, stopped.

Madame Paulinier set her wine glass down, the edge of the glass on her bread plate, the opposite edge on the table and then let go. The glass began its fall to the tabletop with the small amount of wine left in it. Hanley caught the glass at its mid-fall point and set it upright. While saving the glass, Hanley had not taken his eyes from Father Bertrand. Michael Campbell muttered, "Damned good," while the priest finished explaining why the Fathers of Notre Dame could not afford the services of a pilot and plane.

Sophie watched her grandmother's crystal begin its fall. When she realized Hanley Martin saved the crystal glass, she said, "*Merci*". Hanley heard her exhale, looked to see what he thought was an expression of relief on her face. He smiled and said, "You're welcome."

"Father, do the people served by the Mapuordit mission believe the missionaries are there to help or not?" Michael asked.

"Yes, I believe they still do.. When I was there, the people of the region saw the Catholic missionaries as religious, as representatives of the God the whites believed in. They had respect for the priests and nuns. Some of that has changed. The adults now fear they will be punished if they show support or any type of acceptance of the mission and its people. The children follow the adults and if there are none, they do whatever it takes to survive. Children are smart and they absorb everything around them. They learn quickly. Adults make the mistake of confusing intelligence and experience. Just because a child has little experience does not mean they cannot understand." He thanked Michael Campbell as he filled his wine glass. "The church and the mission of the Fathers of Notre Dame are committed to the southern Sudan. The needs of the orphans are many and the situation grows worse with each passing day. We will not leave until driven out. I fear this talk is difficult for our hosts; perhaps we should speak of other things."

Hanley said, "One last question, Father. Have any Americans ever worked in your mission?"

"No, they have not."

Madame Paulinier offered to complete her history of the Loire Valley and Normandy. Father Bertrand suggested she abbreviate the lesson as she still had three hundred years to go and the evening might not be long enough to accommodate her profound knowledge. She took this as a compliment and continued with the lesson.

The hosts and guest moved to the living room where the lesson was completed. Father Bertrand asked Hanley when he started his own businesses and what had been his motivation.

"Well, the idea came to me on the first date I had with my wife. We were at dinner in a little Italian restaurant in Kokomo and we were telling each other our plans for the future. I had been thinking about someday starting my own business, but my plans were not very well thought out. That conversation helped me begin to identify an idea, an idea for my first business. It also led to other things, as you may have guessed," he said. He had not thought about that dinner for some time. "Lately, I've begun to wonder what I might do now that I find myself alone, now that my daughter lives too far away for me to be involved in her life as much as I was before. The truth be known, I haven't been that involved for some time."

Turning in his chair, the priest asked Hanley, "Mr Martin, what will you do now, once you return to Indiana?"

Hanley said, "I'm not sure. It seems I'm at a crossroad in my life. I can't say for sure what got me to this point. It's hard to identify the combination of people and experiences that render a life, especially after all these years. I've always had this need to be useful and it's greater now than ever. For whatever reason, I also feel I should be doing something else, other than running my business. What is that, time running out on me? I don't want to grow old and realize I haven't done enough with my life. I'm not trying to minimize the importance of my family or my businesses. I do believe I need to do more. What that is, I don't know. Maybe I'll come and work for you in Africa."

"We can always use good people." The priest watched Hanley intently. "Have you ever thought of traveling to Africa?"

"No, I've barely been out of Indiana until now."

"Maybe you should consider it." He smiled at the American.

Father Bertrand and Madame Paulinier prepared to leave at half past ten o'clock. They said their goodbyes and were at the door when Father Bertrand turned to Hanley and said, "I think you will do something else with your life, something you may not have expected. When the tapestry that is a life unravels, it never looks the same once it's mended." He smiled and offered Madame Paulinier his arm as they walked to his car.

**

Hanley finished telling Sister Mary Claire the story of the dinner party. He smiled at her and said, "My decision to come here was not as impetuous as you may think. A series of events pushed me in a direction I had not anticipated. It seemed meant to be. I looked for answers, found some, still need some. I thought perhaps you had them. If all these events brought me here, why not believe it?" he asked.

She looked at the garden, took Hanley's hand, squeezed it and said, "I will think about my role in all of this. Maybe I am meant to do more than I thought. I will pray for guidance."

Placing his other hand over hers, Hanley said, "Thank you."

Near the edge of the clinic, some distance from the garden, Father Robineau watched the nun and the American, saw them standing close to each other, holding hands. Hanley looked up, saw the priest watching them, saw him frown.

18

A smoky filament, caught by the dry wind off the Savannah, twined around the American's head, sliding across his eyes, pulling moisture from the surface. Hanley rubbed his eyes, spreading new tears to sooth the dryness. The fire he built near the box porch next to his room was not for heat. It was July, the nights in southern Sudan were very warm. He just liked sitting by a fire.

His guilt lasted a second, as the small branch made the arced journey from his hand to the fire. Taking firewood away from others so he could relax was not a good idea. The fire, while small, still produced silky yellow flames. Occasionally ghosts of a blue hue appeared in their centers, backed by the red and orange coals beneath. His eyes now clearer, Hanley watched the flames shudder in the night wind, bending like dandelions, sometimes disappearing, only to pop back again, like 'flowers in hell', he said to himself. Sitting on the edge of the porch, he waited for Sister Marie Claire to arrive. Their plan was to continue a discussion that progressed from the original questions of his having been picked by fate for good fortune to one of a more general nature, of the events, in whatever sequence they may take, that influence a life. They talked of the subtle, often unnoticed influence of everyday living, the accumulated occurrences that make one man rich and another destitute. The butterfly effect, he thought was how statisticians referred to it; a person sneezes six times in a row before leaving his house in the morning and misses being struck by a person in an old black pick-up truck running a red light along his route to work. All very interesting, but he had plans to discuss another topic.

Hanley no longer felt trapped in Africa, seeing the people with a deepening understanding of their problems, saw the immensity of their need, understood the barbarity of their tormentors. Six months at the mission brought on a feeling of familiarity with the area and the people working and being treated at the mission. The shock of being in a new world, one so completely different from Indiana and America, had worn off, replaced with a feeling he was now part of the mechanism, knew the systems, the people and how things worked. That is, within the mission itself. There were activities outside the operation of the mission he still questioned. The questions were about the network he now believed existed, an organization with a noble mission, albeit, perhaps, a dangerous one. This network, he believed, was working to rescue children, children taken from their families and sold into slavery. Sister Marie Claire was in the middle of this network, near the center, perhaps the primary organizer herself. She'd certainly been here long enough, had amply demonstrated her impatience with government and church bureaucracies. In a community of officials and volunteers seemingly at a loss on how to protect a besieged people, on dealing with the task of bringing aid to thousands of displaced families, hurt, sick and hungry, a strong personality, someone with the courage and intelligence to confront the problem, would, by some disorganized, informal, natural selection, emerge as a leader. The nun was the one, was at least a part of the original effort, Hanley believed. Yes, he could see her in dark rooms and in the back booths of restaurants, scheming with others, talking to family members of children known to have been kidnapped or missing, identifying known or probable routes used by thugs trading in humans, recruiting people to watch for victims, arranging for rescues.

As he heard her approach, she asked, "A fire in the summer is wasteful, no?" Coming from the direction of the larger buildings in the compound, Sister Marie Claire came around the corner of the barracks building to his left. He had not seen her that day until now. Walking around to the other side of the box, she sat, scooping her skirt beneath her, this night wearing a dark blue kerchief, a white blouse and a skirt the color of the sky he saw that day. "Was your day productive?" she asked.

In his hand was a glass, the typical dirty glass from the mission dining hall, in it whiskey, the remains of the third bottle he tucked into the tail of the Beech, the world's most expensive rum runner, he thought. Noticing the whiskey did a good job cleaning the inside of the glass, he thought about the cost of washing dinner dishes with expensive Irish whiskey. He was not yet drunk, not close enough, had enough in the glass to get him part-way there, but he would not open the fourth bottle, unless the rest of the glass convinced him otherwise.

"My day was good, and yours?" he asked.

Her profile was still noticeable in the dusk, not a typical French profile, he thought, recalling every political cartoon he ever saw showing Charles de Gaulle's famous facial protuberance, the nose that France followed from war to peace, forever recognized by millions of Americans as what all Frenchmen looked like, until Bridget Bardot came along. The nun looked more Scandinavian, something her mother might find hard to explain. Hanley, beginning to feel more relaxed, could not recall which part of France she came from. "Which part of France do you come from?" he asked.

"What?"

"Where in France were you born; where are you from?"

Sister Marie Claire looked at him, straightening up, as if good posture were required to speak of France. Rubbing her cheek, she paused, cleared her throat with a mild cough-like sound, looked at him and said, "I'm from an area, Pays de Loire, southwest of Paris. It was once a part of Brittany, but that changed some years ago. My family has been there for many generations. We, my ancestors, were either farmers or public servants, with priests and nuns occasionally breaking the mold. Breaking the mold is what Americans say, *oui*? *Bien*." Hanley had nodded while staring at the flameless embers of his fire.

"You don't look French to me," he said. "You look Scandinavian." Sitting up more, he squinted into the smoke, which flowed over him, curling back as it hit the building, the air around him thick, burned his nose and throat. Standing to find clear air to breathe, he felt light-headed, a bit of worry coming to him, carried in with the smoke. Maybe a bit too much to drink, he thought.

Seeing her watching him, Hanley waved away the smoky air and said, "Tell me something, Sister. When you take Jumma and drive to Rumbek or Juba, you don't just go for supplies, do you? There's other business to conduct while you're there, isn't there? I watch Jumma after you return from these trips. He walks out to the camps and talks to the people. He takes notes, or reads to them from his notebook. Then he'll sit under a tree or against a truck and write. I doubt he's keeping a diary of his trips to Rumbek to buy supplies. What is he writing about? What is he telling the people in the camps?"

"Have you asked him?"

"Of course I've asked him. He says it's about the food they eat, you know, how much, what kind. He never looks at me when he answers. He's such a good kid. He doesn't want to look at me when he's lying," Hanley said. The glass in his hand was now empty. He tried taking a drink, found nothing there, thought about bottle number four, felt mildly guilty, but more annoyed. Setting the glass on the box porch, he looked at her and said, "I find what you're doing admirable, really, I do." He was guessing, pressing her to see if she would tell him what he suspected. She was looking away, as if he wasn't there as if she didn't see him, he thought. Her shoulders were hunched up, giving the impression she was cold. It was a warm night. The fire had burned down to dull embers pulsed by the warm night breeze, the thin sticks, wood chips and bark having made a weak fire to begin with.

"Tell me what you're up to," he said

"Up to? I do not understand. What is 'up to'?" Arms crossed, Sister Marie Claire used her hands to warm her upper arms, rubbing them.

"You can't be cold," he said. "It's a warm night."

"It is a habit, that is all." Standing up, she turned to him. "Let's walk," she said.

His steps felt uncertain, off-kilter, the drinking altering his balance, the ground now a tilting, moving surface, the tilts and moves subtle, shifting, not giving him a pattern he could work with, as if he could work with one. Summoning his concentration, trying to accumulate it somewhere between or behind his eyes, a pool of steadiness, like mercury in a sealed glass tube, countering the alcohol sloshing around in his head. He started feeling nauseous, a headache there for the taking, but he did not want it. Don't throw up, he told himself.

Concentrating on the nun walking before him only made matters worse. Seasick in Sudan, he thought. For a second, he noticed how trim she was, felt guilty, then remembered he was close to drunk. "You look like a dancer, you know? And, you sing well. Really well. Ever think of going into show business? I mean, did you ever think of going into show business before you married God?" he asked. He was gushing about a nun. He would not open another bottle.

Turning quickly, she said, "You have had too much to drink. It is shameful."

"Oh, come on. You're from France, for God's sake. You drink wine with your morning cereal. You let your kids drink wine at dinner. I think the word croissant means wine sponge or something like that, doesn't it?" he said. The American stopped, closed his eyes, almost toppled over, reached out and felt her hand take his, steadying him as he opened his eyes.

"Be quiet. I'm going to tell you something, I don't think you'll remember it tomorrow, which may be why I am telling you. I pray this will not be a mistake," she said, still holding his hand. Studying his face for a moment, Sister Marie Claire presented Hanley with a look of what he took for doubt, shook her head slightly and released his hand. Turning, she walked away, stopped, came back to him, looked in his eyes and frowned. Lips moving slightly, she past her hand over her face, as if wiping away moisture, as if someone had thrown water in her face, then looked away toward the bush, seeing something out there, something she worried about.

"I knew you would have questions. I watched as you watched Jumma and me, although I did not think you noticed me watching you. I heard you were asking questions of the doctors, questions about the children and the women, about the killings, the rapes, the abductions. After the girl was shot at the clinic, you began to wonder, I think. How could you not? It is understandable," she said.

"Dr, Dyzak said there is a network, a network of people helping the children. Your network. He said it was your network. Is it?" Hanley asked.

"No."

"Then whose is it?"

The lines around her mouth deepened with the frown that formed, the question bringing the response the American expected. He knew she was the driving force behind this network, how could she not be? The care and the commitment were there, he'd seen it, the tireless dedication, the years she'd given to this land and the people. Her faith was tempered by a pragmatism, a knowledge of what must be done, of how to get it done, who to trust, where to turn for favors, how to pay them back. The nun opened her mouth, then shut it. The air around them was chilling, not enough to be uncomfortable, but enough to notice. Standing together near the edge of the compound, there was still enough light to see each other's expression. Hers was uncertain, maybe wary; in the darkening evening, it was becoming hard to tell. "Tell me," he said.

"I am not certain there is any wisdom to telling something that may cause you problems, information you may not want to have in your possession. Does that make sense to you?" she asked. Hanley shook his head, the determination set hard in his face. Lowering her gaze to his chest, she sighed, saying, "No, I suppose that would make little sense to you now."

"Just tell me this, at least. Are you simply monitoring these children, determining they're alive so their families have hope, or are you actually trying to rescue them?" he asked.

"There have been a few rescues. Individual children taken from homes and from shops. Not many, as it is dangerous for the children rescued and unpleasant for those children left behind. Especially the girls left behind. We also are trying not to bring attention to ourselves, to protect the effort. If we are uncovered, the children will lose the only hope they have. Also, there are two of us from the church involved. Exposure would put the church and the bishop in a difficult position," she said. He thought she looked forlorn in the dim light, her face carrying the worry for the children as they talked. This is where her heart is, her center, this is why she has stayed in Sudan, probably fought to stay. The danger, the hardship, the heat and dust, her heart is steeled to it, armored for the children. Hers is a special kind of bravery, he thought; and I don't have it.

"Who else from the church is working in this network?"

"A teacher in a school in Wad Madani. She is not a nun. The risk she suffers is great, but she is dedicated, most fervently, almost fanatically. And she is kind, the kindest heart I have ever known. A woman of great and good spirit. I fear for her safety every day," she said.

Folding her arms over her chest, for comfort against the subject, he guessed, she frowned, her head down, her hips moving back and forth as she pushed a stone around on the ground, using one foot, then another. Speaking without looking up, she said, "I don't feel comfortable talking about this. Perhaps it is better you do not know, better for everyone. You have become a valuable member of our mission. Moving doctors and medicine as and when needed has made our clinic better, we can help the people more than we have in the past. I certainly do not want to jeopardize that. And the government probably watches the plane. The diocese tells me they are asking for copies of your schedule. The bishop believes they may want them in advance to monitor where you fly within Sudan at least. We are afraid they will try to stop you altogether if they suspect something, anything. If they send in soldiers to stop you, it will be dangerous."

"Do you think that's possible?"

"In Sudan, anything's possible. Can we walk back? I'm tired and starting to chill." Arms still folded, she started back, stopped before him, looked up, searching for something in his face, it seemed, then smiled. "What good there is in Sudan is found in the hope still alive in many of its people, mostly in the children. We can till the soil and grow crops, dig wells for water or oil, build new roads, build new buildings. All that is meaningless unless we are successful at raising the children to be good, to be kind and generous and loving adults. To be leaders. I see these things in the adults here still, loving and caring. I see it in you, in your eyes. What you are doing here makes a difference. To us, it makes a difference. If it makes any difference to you, well, that is up to you. The paying of a debt of any sort is a personal obligation. It means different things to the people involved. I believe you will recognize when you have met your obligations, the ones you feel in your heart, the ones that seem to haunt you. You are a good man, Monsieur, and good men always find their way," she said and then walked on.

The sounds of the night, the sounds he had not noticed as she talked, grew loud around him, the leaves of the trees, their paper noise as they brushed together, the crickets and frogs, the silence of the birds, the movement of the unknown. The clamor of the country, more subtle than a city but as insistent, pushed on him. Watching her walk away, he was struck with the feeling that she was, as he had suspected, the person he needed to find, the person that would tell him what he needed to know. But that was wrong too, for now he was beginning to think she wouldn't tell him what he needed to know; she would show him.

19

The fine dirt of the floor pressed into her nose, so she tried breathing through her mouth and choked. The man on top of her, smelling like a goat, was the third and she knew he would not be the last. Rifle bullets from the bandolier around his chest pressed against her spine, the pain as bad as the pain below. The helplessness was the worst. Nothing, no one would stop this.

Taught by older women not to scream or resist, Aisha felt the calloused hand pressing down on her neck as she was penetrated from behind. After the second man had finished, she was rolled onto her stomach as the third man hissed instructions and mounted her immediately. There were at least five men in what had been her family's *gottia*, keeping her after driving her mother and two aunts from the village.

She prayed to Allah to let her live, but she knew there was little chance of that. There was nothing left of her village in Northern Bahr El Ghazal but the scorched rings that were once the foundations of the one-room homes of her family and friends. Most of the people had fled the area and the Baggara militias as they advanced. The government gave support and protection to the Baggara and gave none to the people of western Sudan. She had returned to the village with her mother and two aunts, hoping to retrieve any family belongings they might find and search for food. A small group of militias came upon them and seized her when she attempted to flee. Ignoring the other women, the men immediately set about molesting her. They were practiced and efficient.

The man with the odor of a goat pushed down on her shoulders so hard, she thought they would separate as his pace increased. He finished inside her and used her back to push himself upright, spitting on the back of her head as he rose. As another prepared to mount her, gunfire stopped the assault, her assailants crouching around her. Shouting at each other, the men ran to find better cover in the brush nearby. She heard their guns boom as they shot toward the incoming gunfire. Aisha started to sit up, trying to push her *toab* down, but as she did, the pain in her groin and lower back gripped her, taking her breath and freezing her for an instant. Blowing the air from her lungs, she lowered herself slowly onto her side, working the cloth down over hips and to her knees where it stopped. Satisfied she was covered, she listened for sounds of the men who raped her. They were now some distance away, their shouts muted by the dry wind blowing across the floor and over her head. She began to weep. As she did, the ache rose in her body and stifled her sobs, a hand of pain over her mouth. Eyes squeezed closed with shame and fear, she failed to see the man who returned. When he said, "Get up, you will come with me," her sobs broke through the pain and she wept for where the world had left her.

***

In August, southern Sudan was hellish even if tranquil, which it was not. Work for the mission continued through the heat and havoc, the abominations and savagery of the militias and outlaws sending a relentless stream of torn and abused Sudanese into the compound to wait for what attention they might receive. The doctors and nurses did what they could to ease the suffering. Medical supplies were inadequate, as was food. A good deal of suffering stayed with the people despite the best efforts of the medical staff and clergy. It was never enough. The despair of the maimed and sick soon became the shared despair of the workers of the mission. Their faith became as the child waiting for the comforting touch of a distant and inattentive father, mistaken in his convenient estimate of the child's strength and willingness to endure. To endure, a person needs hope and the French nun knew hope was as scarce as sympathy in Sudan. Without a parent's love and interest, children suffer, left to find their way, deprived of the wisdom and protection that gives comfort and hope. She wondered where their God was; he was not in Sudan.

Thinking of the American, the nun knew he had flown over one hundred times in nine months for the Fathers of Notre Dame's mission in Sudan. Most of those flights had been into Ethiopia, Kenya and Northern Sudan. He shuttled medical supplies, patients and occasionally visitors to the compound at Mapuordit. At first, the flights went smoothly, with little problems with customs and inspections. Things had begun to change in the end of May, especially his flights within Sudan. Officials in Khartoum and Port Sudan were increasingly difficult, at first causing some delays, then confiscating cargo, specifically medicine that combated malaria and dysentery. Visitors were not bothered unless they traveled with targeted cargo. The church began segregating the flights carrying visitors and medical supplies. As the raids on villages in southern Sudan increased in number and lethality, visits by doctors slowed as the church and aid organizations adjusted to the increased risk and developed the strategies required to protect the lives of contributors and officials.

Sister Marie Claire knew the American struggled to maintain the plane. He expressed regret at not having learned more than basic maintenance, which he now practiced almost daily. As with everything else mechanical in southern Sudan, dust and grit and its management determined reliability in machinery. The plane was well-built and rugged enough to function well in difficult environments. She knew Hanley was taking no chances and monitored the engines and electronics as much as he could.

Compliant grasses and shrubs around the airstrip absorbed the mid-morning heat, as Sister Marie Claire found shelter in the tree-shade close to the plane. Perched on his aluminum ladder, the American inspected the left engine, knowing he would find more dust than the last time and that he would need to increase the frequency of his maintenance routine. Unnoticed by Hanley and the nun, Jumma approached the plane and called out his greeting, startling the American so much he lost his balance, kicking the ladder sideways. Moving quickly, Jumma caught Hanley, helping him right the ladder.

"Are you alright?" Jumma asked.

"Yes, thanks. If it weren't for these work gloves, I would have fried my hands on the cowling trying to stop my slide," Hanley said.

The young African studied the care with which the American removed dust from the cooling fins of the engine's cylinder housings. Brushing and blowing, Hanley worked meticulously to remove what dirt he could, periodically removing the dust that accumulated on the housing as well. Hanley checked the breeze to try to keep dust from blowing back on the engine.

"So, Sister, how were things at the clinic this morning?" the American asked.

"Busy. I wanted to visit with the doctors and inventory our supplies before leaving for Aluakluak with Father Robineau. That is a change of plans. We were to leave this early morning. I wanted to get some things done before we left. That is why I'm here. We need to talk. Jumma, would you mind leaving Mr Martin and I for a few moments while we discuss a matter? Please. I will hold the ladder."

"Yes, Sister," Jumma said, moving aside while the nun took the old ladder in each hand. She said to Hanley as Jumma walked away, "You work on the plane more and more. It is not breaking, is it? Without the plane you are of little value to us."

"I'm just trying to keep it operational. Dust get's into everything. It's hard to keep up with it. It's like shoveling sand against the tide," Hanley mumbled.

"I'm sorry, what was that?" she asked.

"Nothing. Hold that ladder steady while I get down. Hold it, there. Thanks." Hanley stepped into the dust beneath the engine and wiped his eyes on the shirt sleeve bunched around his elbow. "I'm thirsty," he said. "Just when I think I have a handle on managing this heat, managing my thirst, I find I haven't. It's still brutal, as far as I'm concerned, but controllable. Water and food; Americans have no clue as to their good fortune. None. The amount of food and clean, clear water wasted every day in America would keep thousands of these poor Sudanese bastards alive for a year."

"I'd prefer you not refer to these people that way," she said

"Sorry, I get cranky when I'm dying of thirst," he said. "It's hard not to think about it around here. I'm learning not to worry about it. But, I've not really died of thirst yet, have I?"

"Not yet."

"I understand that the Diocese of Rumbek is sending a new priest to replace Father Robineau next month. Are you upset ? How long has he been here?"

"A long time."

"Will the people be troubled by his leaving; I mean, will they see it as a bad sign?" Hanley turned and gathered the brushes, tools and rags he used to battle the dust as it tried to take over his airplane. Kamikaze Spores, he once called them when he and the nun were talking of the work it took to maintain the plane.

"No, they know we are here for only a set amount of time. We tell them so. They do not expect much of anything in their lives to last, I would guess," the nun responded.

Hanley said, "I wonder if this is a sign the church will become more active in the process of protecting its people. Between you and me, I've always thought it was bullshit to claim to be a shepherd guarding the flock, only to stand by while the wolves carry off the sheep. The Catholic Church does a great job at helping themselves, but not the people, not here."

The nun watched as the American folded the rags into squares, bundled the brushes and tools together and walked to the rear of the plane, climbing through the rear door, to store his cleaning tools. Sister Marie Claire took down the ladder and carried it to the old shack and put it inside.

Walking back, the nun found the American sitting in the doorway of the plane, staring off into the distance. when she turned to follow his gaze, she saw people moving across the land. They were walking toward the mission. There were perhaps eight or ten of them, a line that varied in height, both adults and children. There was now a steady flow of the refugees coming to the Lakes Province in Southern Darfur and Western Bar El Ghazal. The number was small compared to those who had been forced to migrate elsewhere to places like Chad or the Central African Republic. Driven from their farms by Nomadic Arab militias and the Sudanese government, refugees were appearing every day in the region, they were woman and children, as it was mostly the men of Darfur who were being killed. Those villages fortunate enough to receive prior warning sent their women and children out into the countryside to hide in the brush or behind rock formations, anywhere sparse country provided concealment. The men remained behind to face the militias who were often supported and protected by government troops. Outnumbered and barely armed, they became easy prey for the murderous raiding parties. The women caught were raped and sometimes murdered. Young girls were also raped. Sister Marie Claire said to Hanley, "A United Nations aid worker told me of a young woman who fought back and was killed and left dead and naked in the road as a message to other women not to resist when molested."

"How old was she?" Hanley asked.

"Just a child."

"This won't stop soon, will it?"

"I don't think so."

"Everyone I see here is young, very young. When people look at me, they appear to be dumbstruck. You once said it's because they seldom see someone my age and because I look older than I really am. You also said whites look older anyway.

You said I must look 'biblically old' to the Sudanese. You mangled the word biblically, by the way, but I kept my mouth shut."

"What is mangled?"

"Twisted, badly pronounced."

"Oh. Then, thank you." She smiled and said, "You think you are humorous, but you are not. It's not your fault. You are not French and, therefore, don't really understand humor."

The American wiped his eyes and forehead against his sleeve again and squinted into the distance. The line of refugees was gone. "Sister, do you think God has abandoned us here in Sudan?" he asked.

"I think he is busy elsewhere. It is a big universe, you know, and we are so small."

"Many an anxiously rationalizing theologian would disagree with you. I was raised to believe my soul was the focus of God's attention every second of every day. It appears he's lost interest. Kind of like my ex-wife, I suppose, and not just in my soul either. I hope to hell there is something really catastrophically bad happening on the other side of the universe that keeps God so busy, he or she or it has forgotten about us."

"She?"

Squinting in the sunlight, Hanley said, "When I was a kid, my grandmother said that I must believe there are more good people than bad in the world. She saw that particular bit of faith as necessary if we were all to carry on each day. Basically, I think she was right. She was one of those thin and fierce little Irish women that kept their families together through all manner of difficulties, who understood how fleeting the good times would be when they came. I know, and I don't know how I know, but I know there are thousands of women just like her in Sudan; different cultures, different experiences, different circumstances, but the same. They have the same dedication and commitment to their children and their loved ones. I keep thinking that maybe God is here in the women. He certainly isn't here in the men. That's what has always struck me as bullshit about God being a man, you know, a father figure. God can be found in the women and children if here on earth at all. Or in dogs."

A small wind so hot, it stung Sister Marie Claire's face blew for an instant and brought with it more khaki-colored dust. She closed her eyes to keep the dust out and said, "Think of how much faith it takes to overcome the horror all of these people see every day of their lives. God expects that from all people, not just those forced to live a life of abuse and fear. If God creates us, then allows us to live our lives without his help, then what becomes of our prayers and our faith. My God would not do that."

Hanley climbed down from the plane and walked toward the terminal shack. He stopped and said, "Maybe God has a telephone that tells him who is calling and when it rings, he won't answer when he sees it is Sudan."

The nun said, "When I return from Aluakluak this evening, I will bring with me some information that I will share with you. It is important that you understand the need to protect this information. You must not share it with anyone. Once I let you into this, you must protect whatever you learn. Always. Protecting the information is protecting the children. Do you understand? *Oui?*"

"Yes, I understand."

"*Bien,*" she said.

***

When Jumma had time to sit and think, his memories would visit him. To ward off his recollections, he wrote recipes, mostly. His recipes were what he imagined he could do with his native foods if they were plentiful. If he could add the herbs and spices, the garnishes he read about in books or those described to him by the doctors and others visiting the mission, the food would be wonderful. He thought his recipes were good. Hunger made him a creative writer of recipes.

Sometimes Jumma wrote of things other than food. He tried poetry, as he understood it to be, tried stories, but was never satisfied with the results. Now he had something else to write about.

Jumma had a new notebook, much larger, thicker than he normally used. The nun gave it to him. This one was not for recipes or stories. No one knew of the contents of this notebook, besides he and Sister Marie Claire. Jumma did not carry it with him unless he was with the nun or Azari, the man who drove the big truck. Even Azari did not know what was in it; Azari could not read. Azari barely spoke at all. Jumma would go with Azari to Rumbek, Yirol and other towns when picking up supplies or moving patients. Jumma rode along to help with the loading and unloading, but that wasn't all Jumma had to do on these trips.

For months now, Jumma had been visiting families in villages in southern Sudan, searching for the parents of abducted children, gathering names, physical descriptions, birth dates and any other information that may prove useful in finding and identifying those swept away by the war. The nun asked him to so this. It was his part of her plan, a plan to bring these children back to their families.

Jumma wrote a short story in his small notebook. The story was of a man who taught his children to survive in a world where days were always dangerous and tomorrows did not exist.

***

A pain in his lower back, on the right side, like pinched skin, only much deeper, moving back and forth like an electric current, was one of a half dozen things keeping him awake. Rolling over, Hanley grunted and the bed squeaked in response. Trying to find some comfort, enough to sleep if he could, was at least something he could do other than thinking about the nun and her network.

Sister Marie Claire's offer of information was not surprising; he had expected it, had been asking for it. Now he would get it and with it would come something else, another thing he was expecting; a request. He had the feeling this was all planned, well-planned, for some time. Her objection to his invitation from the church to bring his plane and fly for the mission was probably a ruse used to cover her excitement. When the nun learned he was coming she started planning. Sure she did, he thought. I bet it didn't take her long to find out what kind of plane it was and how many children it would hold; not long at all.

20

As they rode the rough road to Yirol, Jumma, who had been reading, gave up and now looked out the window at the passing countryside. Driving the Land Cruiser over the rutted road was difficult for Sister Marie Claire, but he knew she enjoyed the challenge. Raising her voice to be heard over the struggling machine, she said, "Jumma, when we get to Shama, we will stop to see a family where I will change the dressing of one of their daughters who we treated last week at the clinic. I want you to find a family there, a family who lost a son, a small boy. I have information that the boy is in a city in the North; Wad Madani is the name of the city. Find the family. Here is their name. I'm told they live on the east end of the village. They have been taken in by the wife's family. Put this paper in your pocket and don't lose it. As always, do not talk of what we are doing. Use the story that you are from a private agency, a relief group, and you need information about their boy. Learn what you can. Try to determine if they know where he is. Whatever they know will be useful even if it is wrong. We can compare their information to what we already have, perhaps verifying what we know or eliminating bad information if possible."

Nodding his understanding, Jumma noted the landscape beside the truck as blurred, but that in the distance was clear; the opposite of his memories. Turning to look at the nun,

Jumma saw the concentration on her face as she drove; fierce, he thought, as always. Sister Marie Claire was as determined as anyone he'd ever known. Jumma's father gave everything he did his complete attention and commitment. He no longer had his father nearby but he did have the nun; the nun and her plan. He was a part of it, willingly followed her as she laid it out, assembled the information and gathered the people she needed, which were few. Jumma was proud to be one of them, to be included and trusted. He was proud of what they were doing, of being part of something larger than himself. What he felt for the plan and the part that he played in it was what he had always hoped he would feel about Sudan. Their shared mission was something he could do to make his country better. It made him feel good.

"Yes, Sister, I know what to do, what to say. One thing though; when the people of the villages learn there is someone willing to help, they offer all the information they have. They understand they are not to speak about the visit. Having their children returned to them is too important; and so they don't talk of it to others, of this I am certain." Jumma looked at the road ahead and nodded to confirm his information.

"Do you think any of them doubt you; that you may really be from the government?" she asked.

"I don't know. No one has ever asked me that. There is too much fear. When I explain that I work for a nonprofit group, not affiliated with the government, they accept that. I also believe they know that the people of my tribe would not be of the government. They want to help."

Jumma knew the nun believed this. She believed making a difference, doing something about the children was what mattered most. Doing what the church and the government will not do, they must now do.

A bump and a jolt brought Jumma's attention back to their trip and to their mission that day. It was a warm morning, dry as always, the sun just above the horizon. A small herd of cattle stood off to the right of the track, all the color of browned butter, thin, all rib lines and pelvis bones, casting shadows on pale hides. As the Land Cruiser approached, the herd turned toward the rising sun. Jumma noted their condition with sadness. Sister Marie Claire's head turned to watch the herd as she passed it. She asked Jumma, "Have you ever talked to Monsieur Hanley about this?"

"No."

"No?"

"No. I would not without having your permission first." Jumma wished he was sitting in the cooling shade of a large tree, writing in his notebook.

"I'm thinking about telling him of our plan," she said.

"When?"

"Soon. We will need his help. His part will take some planning and preparation. It will be soon."

When, exactly, is soon, Jumma wondered.

***

Aisha's sleep was fitful, the floor under her sleeping mat hard and irregular. When awake, she concentrated on the soft rhythmic snore of the women asleep on the low cot beside her, hoping it would lull her to sleep again. One thin wool blanket was all she had to keep her warm. Even in September, the large house in Wad Madani was cold at night. Sold into slavery, she had been in the house almost a month.

The Baggara had taken Aisha to Nyala by truck where she was transferred to another truck with nine other women and two small boys and shipped to Wad Madani. There, she was taken to a home and put to work as a servant, cleaning and doing laundry on the weekend and working in an old cotton processing facility on a draw-frame during the week.

The lack of sleep was worsening her physical condition. Her fingers were constantly bandaged, her back and groin always ached. The muscles in her lower back had been badly pulled, also the product of the assault. Her period was late and she constantly prayed not to have been impregnated by one of the Baggara. Forced to sit for up to fourteen hours a day on a stool with nothing to support her, she found it impossible to remain upright after only a few hours. The result was a small man, Arabic she believed, who poked her in the back with a wooden rod while screaming threats and obscenities in her ear. The breath he bathed her in was horrible, from bad teeth, garlic and tobacco, among other things. With a face scarred by acne and a large, crooked nose, she thought the shop manager was as ugly on the outside as he must be in. When not praying to be rescued, she thought of how she might end her life. The idea of escaping on her own never entered her mind. She harbored no expectations of sympathy.

Almost daily, one woman would say Aisha should be glad she was not killed or kept for sex, to be passed around until someone, tiring of it, killed her. Another woman would occasionally stroke her head and say, "You must be strong". There was some caring in that, she thought, some feeling other than fear. That was all, a bit of advice, a stark assessment. There would be no love, nor someone to hold. None of that.

That night, lying on the cold floor, listening to the sounds of the building and the city, Aisha wondered if anyone heard her prayers. What hope she had she put in the words she muttered, praying through that night and into the day that followed.

***

Torn and creased, the note and its contents on Sister Marie Claire's lap had not changed with each reading over the past two weeks. It was the note that caused the nun to develop her plan.

The noted was from a man she knew, a Nur and a merchant in the town of Rumbek, where the archdiocese had offices. The man had a sister who was driven from her home by the Baggara, along with her husband, two sons and a small daughter. An older daughter vanished after the attack on their village. The merchant, Paul, believed the older girl had been taken captive and sold into slavery. For several weeks, he had been quietly making inquiries so as not to bring attention to himself.

The note also contained new and encouraging information. Word had come from relatives in Wad Madani that Paul's niece was working as a servant in a household in that town. She was taken there along with several other young women and forced to work in the home of a wealthy family with ties to a government official in Khartoum. The note did not identify the official or the relationship with the family in Wad Madani. Some of the girls were also working in the family's cotton processing factory. Two of the girls had been badly abused and may not have survived, the relatives were not sure. The note ended with Paul's plea for help, asking the nun to find a way of bringing his niece back to his family in Rumbek.

The story was not new to her or the people of the mission, nor was the plea. Kidnappings had become commonplace, serving as both punishment for the Sudanese and income for the Baggara, who seemed fond of the arrangement. She remembered this man, Paul. He was small and wiry with a thin mustache and smile. He owned and operated a popular restaurant near the diocese, specializing in a mix of traditional Sudanese dishes and a close approximation of western food. She knew it well. The restaurant was small with small round tables, their black paint chipped, showing yellow wood underneath, the tables crowded together, the smoke from the grill and the cigarettes of the customers creating a cloud over the room. Savory smells, onion and meat, overcame the smell of tobacco that greeted patrons who waited outside for tables. Church officials and guests dined there while discussing business. Visitors, especially from Europe and America, were warned not to discuss the conflict that surrounded them. All were careful not to discuss any politics in public places.

Khartoum would be a problem. Paranoia, like a thin mist, covered the capital, blinding it, perhaps willingly, to the troubles, the darkness of the people in Darfur and Southern Sudan. Harsh measures were now a standard policy. When suspicious, they moved quickly to quell that behavior, which was any they believed to be a threat to their government, using any means necessary, including the use of militias. Stopping threats was only a small factor in explaining their behavior. Other issues were involved. Many, including the doctors and others at the mission, questioned the church's determination in matters relating to its human rights record. She knew better, many times trying to convince them of the church's dedication to ending the conflict, working with the Sudan Council of Churches to bring peace. She wasn't always successful, but she kept trying. Hanley was the most skeptical. As an American, she expected him to be cynical; from what she saw and read, it was one of their most defining traits, she believed.

Low sunlight through the single window of her room shone as a quadrilateral on the bed cover. She laid the note in the center of the irregular sunshine and walked to her small writing desk. At times like this, when she was reminded of the random cruelty around her, of just how rare the true compassion of humans was or of her inadequacy, she turned to letters and her mother. Knowing that she was now at risk of never seeing her mother again, she missed the simple love and caring her mother had always given to her. A note to her mother, just to state her love and loneliness, was all she would do; perhaps it would be enough. After that, it would be time for the evening meal and a talk with the American.

21

As parties go, this wasn't much, he thought. He had little experience with parties, not having had any birthday celebrations he could remember. But for a party in southern Sudan, he thought it was probably okay. Hanley watched Father Robineau move around the dining room, saying good-bye to the doctors and nurses, the native staff and officials from the diocese, including the bishop, who had traveled from Rumbek. Shaking hands, exchanging embraces and pleasantries, the old priest seemed genuinely moved by the affection he was receiving. He'd earned it, Hanley thought. This many years in Sudan, serving the people here, he'd damned well earned it.

Sister Marie Claire crossed the room to stand beside Hanley. "I'm glad we had this farewell party. He has been a passionate champion for these people. To most, he seems kind, even timid, but he is not. He has stood up to government officials and even the diocese. Maybe not of late; he has grown tired, but for many years, he did. When I first came here, he was a lion, a quiet lion, but brave. I admired him for his bravery," she said, a look of genuine admiration on her face. Hanley reminded himself that she recently said Father Robineau did not stand up to the diocese for the children and the network.

"Will your network miss him?" he asked, testing her consistency or at least her memory.

"The network? No, it will not miss him. He has not been involved with the work we are doing, the recovery work, I will call it. He will be missed by many others," she said.

Hanley watched as a young nurse, talking to Father Robineau, wiped her eyes and then began to weep quietly. Holding the old priest's hand, she raised it, pressing it to her cheek, her eyes closed. The priest stroked her hair, then bent close, whispering in her ear. The nurse nodded, took the old man's hand from her cheek and kissed it. Hanley suddenly envied the old priest, not certain why. Maybe it was simply because he would soon leave Sudan.

***

Beans, again. These were yellow-green, ugly in a threatening, you-may-be-poisoned kind of way, with a spot here and there on their, shriveled skin. They were long, curved, like a string bean, only thinner, like the people they failed to nourish. In an oily broth, they appeared to have been a culinary afterthought. "We should let Jumma cook", he said aloud. No one heard. But it was something. As tired as he was of eating some type of bean almost every night for dinner, Hanley knew he was lucky to have anything to eat at all. Sudan had taken over fifteen pounds off him. Using his pocket knife, he added holes to his belts and lived with the bunched waistbands of his pants. Any joy he had from his new thinness was measured against the realization millions of Africans would have welcomed any body fat at all. Africa is crazy, he thought.

He arrived at the dining room early with a letter from Elizabeth. Her divorce was slow, with her husband, Gary, dragging his feet throughout the process. After an initial meeting with Hanley's attorneys who were representing Elizabeth, Gary agreed to everything. Hanley thought Gary might be hostile to the attorneys but wasn't, they reported. Elizabeth would share custodial rights of his daughter with her husband and agreed to the proposed visitation schedule. Hanley knew Gary's protestations were mostly a show for his own parents, demonstrating he could stand up to his wife and his father-in-law. But then Gary demanded more time to review the documents, asking for numerous adjustments and corrections. Now, the final date for the divorce decree was set. His daughter would be free of her husband by the first of November. She was already living in Hanley's house in Kokomo with Carrie and his old dog. Rocky's last letter said all seemed well, except that Carrie and Weed were not exactly pleased to be living together. Rocky told Hanley that she truly believed Elizabeth was more concerned for the dog's safety than that of his granddaughter. He supposed she was right. Rocky wrote every week, but the letters came to Hanley in clumps, sometimes up to a month late.

The letters were treasures to him now. Sudan proved their value, enhanced it, made him reassess, see and admit the mistake of his prior complacency. Even the fights with his ex-wife now had a nostalgia he would have laughed at a year ago. And Sudan changed flying for him and the change was saddening. The change brought a new depth to the feelings of doubt over his decision to come to Africa. Flying now had the feel that handling a gun always gave him. Guns were too unpredictable for him, too much to go wrong with too much ease. Friends of his who used guns were amused that he would consider a gun more hazardous than an old plane.

The letter had the news of his daughter's plans to redecorate his home. She also announced her plan to enlarge the garden areas in both the front and back yards. Rocky was acting as a consultant to her former gardening pupil. With the money at their disposal, Hanley knew the effort would someday be spectacular or as spectacular as ornamental plants could be. At the end of the letter, Elizabeth again implored her father to come home, to tell the church he must leave, that his daughter and granddaughter needed him in Indiana. Maybe I should, he thought.

Father Robineau came into the dining room, his white shirt stained brown in spots from his sweat and the African dust. With him was a new Slovakian doctor Hanley met two days before, a short and plump young man with a head of thick, black hair. His pale face was cradled by a heavy dark stubble. He had, Hanley thought, the palest eyes he had ever seen, like ice over blue water. Seeing Hanley, the priest said, "Ah, Hanley, the young doctor thinks we should find the land and build a new city to house those fleeing Darfur. He believes there are enough humanitarians to support such a project. What do you think?"

"All good ideas are proven wrong over time. In America, the land of the good idea, we allow our politicians to prove that theory over and over again, which they do. The same goes for humanitarians, but the ratio is much smaller. I think one politician cancels out hundreds of caring individuals." Hanley said.

"Are all Americans this cynical?" asked the doctor.

"No, most are just smart-asses. They're usually younger. In my country, cynics are just smart-asses with some age on them," Hanley explained. "How long before you leave us Father?"

"Maybe three more weeks; at my age it would seem to be a short time, but in Africa, it's perilously far off."

Through the window, Hanley saw Sister Marie Claire approaching the dining hall. Always a fast walker, her pace was almost furious and raised small dust clouds as she crossed the barren yard. With her head still down, she rushed through the door and to the table where the doctor, the priest and the American sat. Stopping next to the chair of the American, she said, "Forgive me for interrupting, but I need to speak to Monsieur Martin for a moment." The priest smiled and shrugged. The nun turned and walked away, heading for the door. Hanley rose and followed her out into the evening light, the air cooling, but still warm. Smoke and dust blew past as Hanley jogged a bit to catch up. The nun said, "I need to tell you something and then ask a question. I could not do this with Father Robineau there. It is better that we discuss this alone."

"I see. You need to give up this idea that someday, I'll run away to Paris with you. I believe the man you're married to would send me straight to Hell, although I probably shouldn't let that concern me as I'm on my way, no matter what I do.

However, I don't want you to throw away a perfectly good career over me."

She smiled at him and said, "If I would throw it away, it would not be for you. It would be for someone more handsome and more sophisticated, which means I would have many, many men to choose from."

"Yes, you would."

"There is something more serious than your infatuation with me to discuss. I have a note in my pocket from a man who has asked me to help him. He wants to bring back a niece who has been kidnapped and taken to a city north of here. Wad Madani. She is enslaved, working in the home and the factory of an Arab business owner. The Baggara killed her family or drove them off and abducted her. They probably raped her also, that is what they do. Women and children, including boys, are taken by truck and train to the cities of the North and sold into slavery. Muslims try to convert them. Some resist, many don't. Many die. He wants his niece returned."

"I assume he came to you because of the network. Am I right?" Hanley asked.

"Yes, he knows of the network. People who have loved ones that have been abducted search for information; are they alive, if so, where have they been taken. When word reaches the members of the network that someone is making inquiries, we watch that person, see who they meet, who they talk to. When we think it is safe, that they are safe, we approach them, offer our help. We stress to them the importance of discretion, of keeping secrets," the nun explained.

"You know that's crazy. People can't keep secrets. They're desperate. Some are stupid. It's dangerous. Or is that it? Is it the danger you like?" Hanley smiled the odd smile that sometimes unnerved Father Robineau.

"No, don't be a fool. I hate danger. There is such riskiness…"

"It's very risky."

"Yes, I'm sorry. Thank you. It's very risky. However, it is necessary. The church knows nothing of this, or at least they have said nothing to me about it. Someone must stand for the women and children here. Going through customary channels works if the channels work themselves, but they don't. How do you say it, the rules don't apply? I must do what I can do," she said.

"What exactly do you want to discuss with me?" he asked her.

"I want you to fly with me to an area southwest of Wad Madani–"

"Stop right there. You want me to fly you for what reason? If it's what I think it is, the answer is absolutely not. Sorry, but neither one of us is prepared to do what I think you're proposing."

When she spoke again, her voice was flat and unemotional, her eyes fixed on his. "I want you to fly to an airstrip outside the city of Kosti to meet the people I have been working with. There, we will pick up a group of children and young women and return them to the mission. Once here, we will reunite them with their families if we can; if not, at least they will be safe with us," she said.

"This man, this friend, his niece will be in this group?"

"Yes."

"No. I won't do it. Sorry, this is crazy. There are so many reasons not to, it's hard to know where to start. I know something about this airport, but not a lot. I know where it is because it's my job to know where I can put down if I need to, I know it's unpaved and does not have IFR. I know the runway is long enough. I know nothing about its security. God knows who or what will be there to greet us when we land. It's probably close to seven hundred hundred kilometers…"

"Eight hundred."

"…alright, eight hundred kilometers away. That's over five hundred miles to me and, to land, taxi, load, takeoff and return will take over two hours, probably closer to three. Do you know just how much Hell can be stirred up in three hours? What happens if your friends screw up? I suppose I can trot over to the terminal and say I stopped to use the can. That might work. No, sorry, Sister, I think I'll decline."

While he talked, she looked at her feet and began pacing back and forth in front of him. When he finished, she was facing him again, arms crossed over her chest, her gaze level and fixed on his eyes. "You must reconsider. Please. So much planning has gone into this. I have been in touch with those in Was Madani for the past few weeks. In another month, they are prepared to gather at least ten, but not more than a dozen children over several days and hide them until they can arrange transportation. They will move them by cars and a van to Sennar and then to Kosti. Changing the routes they travel will allow them to slip by." As she explained the plan, he sensed something familiar about what she was saying; he had heard it before or knew it was coming, what she said, this moment. He expected it. It scared him. There was an urgency in her voice. Where her hand touched her blouse, clutching the fabric, the blued cotton appeared between her fingers as scalloped edges, her knuckles stressed white and her slender, freckled arms shook slightly from the effort.

"No," he said.

Her mouth turned down just a bit and her eyes hardened. "We'll talk later. Please do not say anything about this to anyone. If you don't help, we will still bring them south another way. Please don't tell anyone."

"I won't," he snapped. "I wouldn't do that and you know it." He was sorry he could not control his anger.

As he turned away, the nun grabbed his wrist, saying, "I'm sorry. I didn't mean it; I'm upset, that is all. Please talk to me. No, don't walk away."

The evening was starting to chill. A small fire burned in the dust nearby, the heat warming a young man and a tiny child, a girl, huddling beside him. The man stared blankly into the rising smoke, as if looking for his dream. The smoke came and flowed over Hanley, nudged to him by the always shifting breeze. His eyes began to tear. With the back of his hand, he wiped the tear away and said, "There are things you probably haven't considered; using the mission's fuel for an unsanctioned purpose, space in the plane for a least a dozen people; not to mention just how easy it is to disable a plane like mine. Parked, it is a sitting duck. Anyone with any knowledge of a plane's construction and a rifle can do a lot of damage in a short time. Then there's the noise. You know that's true. How long can you hear that plane coming before you see it? We're not going to sneak up on the good folks of Kosti, now are we? That's right, shake your head," he said.

"Jumma and I have…"

"Jumma! Oh, for Christ's sake! Are you crazy? You can't involve him, he's just a kid." Hanley's reaction made the young man and the little girl turn from the fire to look at them.

"Don't yell," the nun said. "I think we should stop and talk again tomorrow. I'm tired and need to think more about this. Don't say anything to Jumma. He respects you so and if he sees a bad reaction from you, it will hurt him."

"Good. I hope it does. It's a bad decision by both of you." Hanley looked away from the nun and into the face of the small child beside the fire. She was watching him. Her eyes were large, too big in a face showing a hint of malnutrition. The eyes reflected the firelight, the only kind of light in the eyes of a child running from war, he thought. He felt his shame coming out, as if the girl took it and held it before him. He said, "We'll talk tomorrow," then walked away.

***

The chirps from within the grass were carried to him by the wind, as were the cries of the sick and smell of smoke. He read Elizabeth's latest letter again and then Rocky's last letter before turning to an old copy of the *International Herald Tribune*. After that, with an arm over his eyes, he tried to sleep. The evening's events, the request from Sister Marie Claire, their argument kept him awake. He did not know what to think or do about this. The struggles and challenges of Africa were so far from what he knew. He had not adapted, could not get used to it. All his experience failed him. But he knew one thing; it was time to make a decision, to test his theory about fate and its role in his life, to put up or shut up.

22

The first week in September, Hanley returned from Nairobi with medical supplies and bottled water, after delivering an American surgeon, an ophthalmologist, back to Kenya. The surgeon performed five cataract procedures while at the mission, and now was off to Zimbabwe to hunt lions. Sister Marie Claire was in the second seat, with Jumma strapped into a jump-seat behind the nun. The supplies took up little room in the rear of the hold, covered in a blue plastic tarp and strapped to the right side, across from the rear door. Wanting to spend some additional time with the doctors that Hanley shuttled from the larger airports to the mission, Sister Marie Claire had come along on four trips. Usually, she sat in the one of the two jump-seats attached to the bulkhead that separated the cockpit from the cargo area. Hanley removed a storage box and attached the second jump-seat, a folding seat with a three-point seatbelt, to hold the passenger securely. The first jump-seat was attached to the bulkhead on the other side of the cockpit door, where Jumma sat. The doctor being transported usually rode in the second seat in the cockpit, where the co-pilot would normally sit. When there were no passengers but she and Jumma, the nun occupied the second seat.

With the key to the intercom open, Hanley could talk freely with Sister Marie Claire, as there were no air traffic controllers to interrupt. Even with headsets, the noise of the C-45's engines intruded on their conversation. They were about forty-five minutes from Mapuordit, heading northwest, with the plane in a slight sideslip due to a north by northwest head wind. Hanley checked the manifold pressure and rpm's, gave his gauges a quick visual sweep and said, "It won't be long. The weather is clear all the way in. If you look just off the nose of the plane to the right, you'll see Torit."

Hanley pushed the nose of the plane down slightly as the nun rose in her seat to peer into the haze below. Torit looked to her more like a rough patch scratched in the dust than a major city in southern Sudan.

"It doesn't look like much from either the ground or the air," she said.

Hanley said, "You're right, it doesn't look like much from up here, but really, what does? The larger cities, I guess. I've only seen them from commercial aircraft. I don't fly near big cities myself, unless I can help it. They can be dazzling at night, the really large ones. I didn't see Paris at night but I suppose it's spectacular. You've been in Sudan for seven years, isn't that right? How much longer will you be here?"

"I do not know. For as long as the church wants me here. It's not a decision I have to make, it's made for me. I don't worry about it; there are too many other worries here for me."

Squinting into the sunlight coming from the West, through the window beside Hanley's head, the nun said, "When I was younger, I tried to be completely in control of my life, to be what I wanted. As a child, I struggled against my parents, against my school and even against the church. After the university, I entered the order and, as a novitiate, the urge to control stayed with me. I found that control was a tricky game; the harder you play, the more difficult it becomes. The skill, no, the effort, it takes to play well, and maybe the skill also, grows with the amount of control you desire. So, no matter how much skill or effort you apply, it is never enough; never. So, I decided to concentrate on doing what I do well and allowed God to control my life, which is what I should have known to do all along. Still, I find that I try to push for what I believe to be right or just, but I will yield to those circumstances I believe to be created by God, no matter what the outcome. Sometimes I try another avenue when one is closed to me. Controlling all aspects of my life is no longer a concern for me; has not been for many years."

"Okay. So, does the church limit the length of the stay at missions like Mapuordit or will they leave you there until you're too old to do your job? If so, what happens then?" Hanley asked. He turned the yoke, depressed the left pedal slightly and changed the plane's direction to put its nose in line with the mission, still some three-hundred miles away.

As the plane moved, so did the sun, blinding the nun, who raised her hand to block it. Deep creases formed at the corners of her eyes as she squinted to see the pilot. Her browned face, paled by the hard light, showed a slight smile of amusement and she said, "When I'm too old to work, I will no longer be useful to anyone and I will lie down and die. If we cannot make a difference, we do not deserve to hold a place on this earth. It will be time to give my place to someone who can. I think I have a few more good years left. How many good years left do you have?" she asked.

"Oh, I think my good years ended some time ago. And, being fundamentally selfish, I refuse to concede my spot to anyone. Anyway, I have found my calling, which is being a target for your abuse. What more Christian-like service can I offer than to sacrifice myself to protect others from your scorn?" he said, smiling.

"What scorn? I have nothing but complete admiration and respect for you and everyone. I suppose there are times when my earnestness, my focus to help others, causes me to push hard on the people I work with, but that is only because there is so much to do. Time and resources are scared–"

"Scarce."

"–scarce, that I feel we all must make a greater effort to succeed. If my tactics are hard–"

"Harsh."

"Stop it! I meant 'hard'," she said.

The American smiled again.

"Anyway, what else can we do but fight against what is happening here. The government is supporting all this, the abuse of the people. Who will help them if we don't?" she asked.

"Yep, you're right, the government isn't very supportive. The Janjaweed are more powerful than they should be, from what I can tell; too precise and well-equipped. I'm no military expert by any stretch of the imagination, but these guys seem to be too coordinated. They never seem to be short of bullets. From what I've been told, they spray bullets around like water from a garden hose. Someone is supplying them. It has to be a government, either Khartoum or elsewhere. I doubt it's the US. So, who is it? Who stands to gain the most from pushing the people from Darfur? And, why Darfur? Why not the people in the south?" he asked.

Turbulence shook the plane, making it suddenly rise and fall. "The plane shaking is making me nauseous," she said. "I have not eaten since thus morning. That is not helping.This headset is not helping either. It has all given me a headache." Resting her head against the back of the seat, her eyes closed against the sunlight. Opening her eyes, she said, "It's complicated. Nomadic Arabs want to graze on the land of the Darfur farmers as they move about and the farmers resist the intrusion. Retaliation and theft were factors initially. Then there are religious differences. But they always settled their differences peacefully. The government changed and supported the nomadic Arabs. Add to that the possibility that Darfur may have oil beneath it and then who knows who may be involved. With oil comes money and money changes men."

"Just men? I don't think so. Ask my ex-wife. If Darfur has oil, then things start to make more sense. I mean, the extent of the government's involvement starts to make more sense to me. I've always wondered if the influence of other Arab states is present in Sudan. Perhaps it is. If there is ethnic cleansing, it may be only part of a long-range plan to control what may one day become a money-making area of the country."

"That is such an ugly phrase, 'ex-wife'".

"It was ugly, trust me. If the Janjaweed and the Baggara are supported by Khartoum, then the people of Darfur stand no chance of surviving this, do they?"

"No," she said. "They will have little chance of remaining where they are. They will be swept away by the troops and thugs employed by the government, much like dust on a bare floor. Watching this happen is maddening. As we watch, these people are driven from their lands, many raped and murdered. It has happened so many times before and we still have not learned to care, learned how and when to become involved. I can only ponder. It is heartbreaking. My head hurts and I must stop talking about this before it gets much worse," she told Hanley.

"Well, we'd better do something," he said.

Sister Marie Claire opened her eyes. "So, have you thought about what I asked you to do?" she asked.

"Yes, I have. I've thought about little else these past few days. I've been remembering my conversations with my uncle, those conversations that have haunted me for years. Confronting ghosts, you could say. And, I remembered something he said that I had forgotten. He said, 'Sometimes letting it happen is the same as making it happen.' He was right. You're right. So, I will do it, fly you to Kosit if you agree to my conditions. First, you must tell me everything, all of it. Who's involved, how long has this been going on, who planned the rescue, all of it. I need to be comfortable with the situation. If something bothers me, I mean, beyond the obvious, then we will resolve it to my satisfaction or we will not go. The second condition is simply this; for the four hours or so this mission takes, I will be in charge. If I see something I do not like in route or on approach, I will stop the mission. I have built several successful businesses from scratch. I'm a very capable person. I can and will evaluate the situation and make what I believe will be prudent decisions based upon that information. If you will agree to my demands, then I will fly you there."

The nun looked at the American for a moment, then said, "I agree."

"Okay," Hanley said.

23

The plane had begun to show signs of neglect it had not experienced in the many years since Hanley restored it. Now, standing at the nose of the aircraft, Hanley saw signs of wear and use that caused him to grimace, as if he had a strong case of heartburn, which, he thought he might develop. The aluminum skin was dulled from the dust of Sudan and the lack of a good washing, reminding him yet again of the scarcity of water.

He came out in the first light of the day to inspect his airplane and to think, to be alone while he reviewed his thoughts, his fears about this rescue mission. As he stood before the old Beech, he saw some small dents and a burnish to the leading edge of each wing made by the ever-present sand and dust. Mechanically, the plane was sound, but would need some attention soon. December would make a year since the Beech's last annual and it was already the end of September. Finding someone to do the inspection and tune the engines will most probably mean a flight to Nairobi, which may be where he will be anyway, he thought. Hanley committed to the rescue flight without, he knew, having thought everything through. What was left to decide was where he would go after the return flight, if they made it back at all.

Hanley believed he knew how a man must feel after having jumped from a bridge. He felt as if he was no longer in control of his future, could not turn back. Even when he knew it would be better not to go through with this, he knew he would. What would his uncle say? His uncle barely set foot outside of Indiana his whole life. If children needed to be rescued in Indianapolis, he would have done that, Hanley thought. I should get in my plane and fly home and ask Rocky for a drink and then take the dog for a walk. It's early fall in Indiana and I'm here without a tree worth looking at. Why am I doing this anyway?

He knew what he was doing, at least what he was doing here. Even with his doubts, he knew this was it. Not right, or at least it wouldn't necessarily turn out right but this was it, what he searched for, the way to justify his luck, to make a difference in a meaningful way. What bullshit, he thought, what an ego. But, it was what it was. He was here, where he thought it would happen and it was happening. Time to put it up. "You asked for it," he said aloud.

Placing his hand on the nose of the Beech, Hanley closed his eyes and thought of how he would prepare for the flight to Kosit. He would need to think of everything that could go wrong. He would need help, perhaps a guardian angel, he thought. He feared an angel would not be enough, that whatever God there was forgot how much help Sudan needed. "Send more angels, for Christ's sake!" he said aloud.

"I believe he already has."

Hanley turned to see a man in his thirties, of medium height and reed-thin, with skin so pale, he appeared translucent, with jet black hair and dark eyes accentuating his complexion. "I'm sorry; I didn't hear you approach. How did you get here?" Hanley asked.

"Yes, I'm sorry. Jumma drove me but we stopped some distance away so I could walk. I have a slight back problem and the ride was rough. I thought walking would help and it did. As we approached, I thought about not interrupting, especially as it appeared you and the airplane were trying to communicate, but I could not help it after your plea. Not many people try speaking to God through the nose of an airplane. How has that worked for you?" the young man asked.

"Not well, I'm afraid. I'm Hanley Martin. You must be Father Laslo?" Hanley offered his hand to the priest. The young man nodded.

Hanley smiled and said, "How are you? You weren't expected until Friday."

"Yes, I've been with the bishop for a few days. I flew into Rumbek from Khartoum and rode over with your men bringing back supplies," the priest explained.

"Sorry about the plane, but lately, talking to it has become a habit," Hanley said.

"Don't apologize. I have a statue of a cat in my apartment in Budapest that I tell jokes to. She never finds them humorous. Metal cats are especially humorless, even more than real ones, I expect. By the way, please call me Jon. It's really Janos but I like Jon." He smiled and Hanley was struck by the ease with which the young priest made him feel comfortable, like old friends.

"Sister Marie Claire has been excited about your arrival for weeks; she's even more intense than usual, which I didn't believe possible. Do you really think God's sent us as many angels as we need? It's an optimistic thought, even for a priest, isn't it?" Father Robineau had been gone exactly one week and the young priest from Hungary was here already. Well, the church certainly doesn't waste time, Hanley thought.

"I was told you were at the airstrip. Jumma was good enough to bring me. This is a beautiful old airplane you have. I was told you flew it here all the way from America. How amazing. Was the trip difficult?"

"The food in Iceland was a bit tricky and the customs people on Port Sudan never write anymore, but no, other than the length of the trip, it was not a problem. This model Beech has been flying safely for over sixty years. It's a workhorse and, modified, has some length to its range. The ocean crossings were better than I expected, particularly the weather. I was lucky. Until I arrived in Sudan, it was a good experience, if you like to fly." Hanley smiled slightly and turned to the plane. He put his hand on the nose again and said, "When I was a kid, I saw one of these fly over my uncle's farm at a very low altitude. I heard it coming long before it cleared the trees over a low hill. It was painted a sky-blue with white trim. It was one of those clear, dry, warm summer days that seem like a dream even when you're living it. The sky was a dark blue and everything seemed to glow with an unnatural clarity, you know? My uncle's dog went crazy, barking and chased it after it flew overhead, running across the field as if it was a migrating monster bird flying north. Two of his cows trotted the other way, to get away from the noise, I suppose. Anyway, I fell in love instantly and bought this one when I could afford it. I spent several years restoring it. It handled the trip well."

The young priest said, "Sometimes God sends us messages in ways we never recognize. It is something even the most gifted of us cannot fathom. The time and signs we are given by God never stop, not even in Sudan. Einstein thought he found the right way by looking at time and space. I believe time and thought are more interesting, perhaps a more correct combination. I have just read that scientists are looking at 'dark matter', an invisible element which they believe makes up most of the universe. I have an interest in this. What if dark matter is God's thought or God's spirit enveloping us? Instead of time and space, maybe it is really time and spirit. It would explain much that physicists can't. They are looking for physical rather than spiritual proof. That may also explain why physicists have, of late, become such creative speculators, would it not?"

"You are way past me at this point, Father. I can't program a clock radio properly. That's how well I manage time. Programming the clock of the universe is up to God, not me. Right now, I'm worried about how I'll manage getting this plane a tune-up before the end of the year."

"Don't worry; I believe you will find a way. You seem to have found your way very well so far, isn't that true, Jumma?" Jumma walked up behind Hanley from the back of the plane. He smiled and said, "I'm sorry, Father, I did not hear what you said."

"I said I believe God has helped Mr Martin find his way to us and to Sudan."

"Yes, we have been blessed to have Mr Martin and his plane here with us. Sister Marie Claire says he is an answer to a prayer she has been saying for a long time. He is her winged angel, she said."

"She's full of ... sorry, she overstates things at times. She can't help it, she's French," Hanley said. He felt his face go red. He knew what Jumma was really referencing. Sister Marie Claire seemed to know he would fly the rescue mission before he did and he resented it. She obviously confided her belief to Jumma and Hanley wished she hadn't. He didn't believe she would tell anyone else; still, he wished they talked before she had spoken with Jumma.

Father Laslo smiled. He began to examine the plane, walking slowly around, starting at the nose and moving to the left wing. On the way past, he touched the propeller for a second, his finger running along the edge and then trailing across the plane of the dull, black blade. He continued around, occasionally touching metal as he passed, as if he was blind and getting to know an object by feeling it. Watching him, Hanley had the impression the priest was trying to learn something from the plane, some history, perhaps something Hanley didn't know. Maybe a flight that had some particular meaning or event attached to it, something. Who knew, Hanley thought.

When he reached the tail section, the priest stopped and bowed his head. After a brief moment, he resumed his inspection of the plane. The brief stop at the tail spooked Hanley for some reason. When the priest rounded the right wing, Hanley asked, "Does everything look all right to you?"

Father Laslo stopped, looked at the airplane for another moment and said, "Yes, yes, it will do just fine." He turned and walked back toward the Land Rover, parked out of sight. Jumma ran after him.

Hanley, watching them go, blinked hard twice and said, "Well, shit."

24

"Have I heard what? I've heard nothing. Has my schedule changed?" Hanley asked.

"I was in Rumbek this morning. There was a news report on the radio in the cafe. I stopped for coffee and a roll. Something happened in America. Terrorists. Apparently, they hijacked airplanes, passenger planes and flew them into buildings in New York and maybe Washington. I am not clear about all this; the reports were a bit confusing. I do not think the reporters had good information," the young French doctor said. He was new, had replaced Dr O'Connell, who returned to Ireland, much to the relief of his family, Hanley supposed. The new doctor's name was Courtier.

"Just New York and Washington? Are you sure?" Hanley pushed himself up from the old lawn chair, thinking terrorists would not be interested in Kokomo, Indiana. His fear made his mind race; would Elizabeth have a reason to be in New York? Rocky's twin sons lived in New York. She must be frantic. What was the best way to reach his family?

"Excuse me, will you? I need to use a phone," Hanley said, walking off toward the mission office.

***

Making s-shapes and their reverse, a centipede-like bug swam fiercely through the warm broth to the inside wall of the white bowl, wedged two of its tarsi into small spider-web cracks in the glazing and hoisted itself out of the soup and headed for the rim, unnoticed by the nun, whose soup the bug had just dog-paddled through. Once over the rim, it made an inverted beeline down the side of the bowl for the tabletop, hit the wood at a dead run, scurried for the edge of the table and was smashed flat only one inch from its goal by Jumma. A bug's existence in Sudan was only marginally better than a human's, Hanley thought as he watched all this.

Jumma scraped the bug's guts from his hand on the table's edge. Hanley checked his soup for swimmers while listening to the nun as she discussed the proposed flight to Kosti. Hanley asked many questions over the last half hour, none of them pleasant.

"Have you heard from your family?" Sister Marie Claire asked Hanley, momentarily changing the subject.

Hanley, his head cupped in his left hand, elbow on the table, pushed a spoon around the rim of an old white bowl, making a rough hum as it bumped along the uneven, cracked edge, said, "Yes, I spoke to my daughter and my, her neighbor. Everyone's fine. Rocky, the neighbor, has twin sons living in New York. They're also fine. The entire country's shaken, mad, you know. This must be like what my parents felt when Pearl Harbor was attacked. I'm afraid all hell will soon break loose. Someone will pay, it's just a matter of who. I wouldn't want to be a Mid-Eastern country right now. Thanks for asking."

Beneath the shade of a trellis attached to the mission's dining hall and kitchen, the three sat at a picnic table. They sacrificed what comfort the inside provided from the heat of the day and the bugs for some privacy. As they talked, hushed tones rose in intensity as the discussion grew heated. The nun stood up to Hanley's persistent questioning of the plan's details, his concerns about the reliability of her co-conspirators and the safety of everyone involved, especially the children to be rescued. Finally, he wanted to know what the nun expected would be the Catholic Church's reaction to the mission, should they return safely or not.

"I expect the church will deny any knowledge or involvement in the plan and its execution. They will be telling the truth, as they are not aware of it. At least I do not know that they are aware of the plan," she said.

Hanley stared at her, his mouth open slightly, a black fly buzzing, interested in his ear. "Yeah, well, ask Father Laslo what he knows. What will they do to you when they find out? How bad will the repercussions be?" he asked.

"I believe the church will transfer me immediately, probably back to France. After that, I expect I will be asked to leave the order. Hopefully, I will be allowed to stay here to continue to help, but I expect that will not happen. Khartoum will want to punish someone and will pressure the church. If I'm out of the country, the church can more easily refuse to cooperate. I am putting the church in a difficult position, but they have been there before," she explained.

"What's the chance they don't hear of this, they don't find out?"

"Very little, I am afraid," she said.

"Yeah, I understand the church has been there before, but not with Muslim extremists. The rules don't apply to them. Their rules are no rules at all. If we didn't believe that before, we should now. We will be putting the church and others in a bad position."

"Is not the church already in a bad position?" Jumma asked. "I'm sorry for interrupting Sister, but the persecution of my people will continue, no matter, will it not? We are at least doing something," he said.

Hanley looked at Jumma for a moment. His expression softened a bit and he smiled slightly. He said, "You aren't interrupting. This is your life and your country. If anyone has the right to speak, it's you. God, what would ever make you think you can't? You have more at stake here than anyone. We need to know what we will do if we make it back. This is your home, you will have to stay and accept the consequences."

Jumma's expression demanded an explanation.

Hanley said, "It means if you stay, and your involvement is suspected by the government, you may be the one they will try to punish. The sister will probably be made to leave Sudan and I, I will probably be forced to leave also, immediately, I expect. If I have enough fuel, I will fly to Nairobi as soon as I deliver the children and the two of you. You see, I have virtually no standing here. I have obtained a work permit through the church as a contract employee. The church can offer me no protection and won't. Under the circumstances, I wouldn't. Once back on the ground, the plane is vulnerable, a sitting aluminum duck. If I lose the plane, I'm already a prisoner. An old white American is easily spotted in Sudan. Probably as easily hated, I expect. That fact, and the fact that I have little resources available to me mean that I would not make it out of the country. I'd eventually be caught maybe killed. The plane is my salvation. If I lose the plane, I lose my freedom. We must know what we will be facing and have a plan ready for what is to come, if we get back at all." Hanley looked at the nun and then off into the bush, staring at nothing, feeling again that he was in a dream, unable to control what was happening to him, helpless and stupid, hating the feeling. Hanley's head snapped up and he said, "Unless you come with me. Jumma, you could wait it out in Kenya, wait until the uproar dies down, then return. You could do that. Think about it," Hanley suggested.

"Things will never die down in Sudan," the young African said.

Dust swirled across the Savannah, its swirl broken only as it passed behind a bush or one of the sparse trees that dotted the barren earth around them. It was the dry season, and an especially dry one it was. Hanley wondered for an instant if the dust meant more than just the wind moving the parched earth or was it the dust kicked up by the feet of people fleeing the madness that was what was left of their lives. At that moment, an image of Carrie came to him, bundled in her pink winter coat and pants. She was wearing her Belinda Hanley expression, the same mixture of exasperation and impatience she shared with her grandmother when both were tired of having to deal with him. He loved his granddaughter so. Now, all he wanted was to see Elizabeth and Carrie again.

"Will you have enough fuel to fly to Kenya?" Sister Marie Claire asked him. The question brought Hanley back to the picnic table.

"That depends on how much time we spend on the ground at Kosit. We will fly in at dawn, with the sun just above the horizon and behind us. We want it to be in the eyes of anyone looking our way. We will fly out into the morning sun," Hanley explained.

Jumma looked up and smiled. "God comes with the morning sun, does he not? He will be with us that morning. He will come out of the morning sun to help us rescue these children."

Hanley looked at Jumma and smiled, saying, "I'll keep the engines running as we load the children. I will stay in my seat while you and Jumma get them onboard. Just before we land, you will switch from the second seat to the open jump-seat next to Jumma. When I tell you, both of you will move to the rear hatch, drop the door and load the children. When they are onboard, I will move out and take off. You will need to make certain all the children are sitting down once they are onboard. Put their backs against the wall of the plane, trying to balance them by number along each side. Two things are absolutely essential, I believe. First, the children must be waiting as near to where I will stop the plane as possible. Second, there can be no hesitation when it comes to the loading. Once that door drops, the children must board as fast as possible. The Beech makes an awfully easy target. If there are soldiers nearby, we will have more trouble than we can handle."

"I will speak with my contact about this when I can. Maybe in a day or two," she said.

"Good. Okay. I have thought about when the best time will be to do this. All things considered, I believe that early morning, just after daybreak, will be the best. Moving the children through the night will provide some cover for the truck, especially if it can travel sparsely traveled routes. The children can sleep while traveling and be awake when the plane lands. Tell your people to have something sweet for them to eat when they wake up. We want them up and moving fast when they need to be."

"What about guns? Should we take them?" Jumma asked.

"Do you have guns?" Hanley asked in return, a bit startled by the question.

"No, but I think we can find them if we need them. I know a man in Rumbek who may help us. He knows many people, including people who help the rebels," Jumma said; he seemed forlorn to Hanley.

Hanley looked at the nun and said, "No guns. I know enough about them to be afraid of using them. I can fly a plane, but I can't hit the broadside of a barn with a gun; no guns, okay?"

Sister Marie Claire nodded. A smile spread across her face as she watched Father Laslo leaving the dining hall door and walk toward them. She rose as he neared the table, but sat back down when he motioned her to remain seated. The young priest stopped behind Hanley, placed a hand upon the American's left shoulder and said, "I see we are enjoying the fresh air of Sudan, is that right, Jumma?"

Jumma smiled and nodded, saying, "Yes, Father, we thought we would take our meal outside today."

The hand squeezed Hanley's shoulder a little. "Mr Martin, were you a pilot in the US military?" Father Laslo asked.

"No, I was never in the military. I was in college when Viet Nam ended and not required to serve. My draft number was a little above one hundred and I was not called. I was licensed pilot when I left school and went right to work," he explained.

"I'm sure your experience will serve God's purpose well. Sister Marie Claire believes you can fly your silver plane to the moon if you wished to, isn't that true, sister?"

The nun blushed a bit and turned to Hanley. "You would think the seminary would have removed all the evils from a man before making him a priest, but as you can see, some small amount still hides inside them. The seminaries should do a better job of cleansing these undeserving young priests before turning them out into the world. I must write the bishop and suggest they examine their methods before we are all taken down by these small devils they leave inside them." Hanley saw her blush even more, as she watched the priest's delight in what she said.

"Perhaps you are right. I will leave you to pray and ask God to remove the small devils I still shelter. They are well hidden and only appear when provoked by nuns who believe it is their duty to search out all the evil in men and bring it to God's attention. Nuns are God's detectives, did you know that, Mr Martin?"

"Yes, Father, I have learned just what ecclesiastical sleuthing really is after meeting the good sister and her friend Sister O'Brien back in Indiana. They are God's CIA."

"Who?" Jumma asked.

Hanley laughed, instantly realizing the rarity of the act, then surprised by it, by both the laughter and the realization. He said, "Jumma, you are why Sudan will someday be a great nation."

25

October 5th

Dear Elizabeth,

It is Wednesday and it has been a slow day for me. On Monday, I flew a doctor in from Khartoum to perform surgery on a woman who had a difficult birth Saturday night. Had the doctor not been here, this woman would certainly have died from complications. I flew the doctor back to Khartoum yesterday. I'm tired, as I have been flying every week to Khartoum, Ethiopia or Nairobi. Supplies are now always short. The number of refugees has tripled in Mapuordit in the past six months. The raids on the villages in Darfur have increased substantially and the people are fleeing with what they can gather as they are forced from their lands, the lucky ones, that is. Most are going to Chad or the ROC, but some come here on their way to Ethiopia or Kenya. So many are killed, many are raped and brutalized. It's insane here.

The Sudanese government is more of a hindrance than a help. The church does what it can, but it's in a bad spot. They have little protection and they know it. Muslim extremists are more involved in the politics of the country, at least that is what I'm told, although this is not a region of great importance to them, like Gaza or the Balkans. I suppose we are in as safe a region of Sudan as any, but we see the results of the persecution and it's very ugly. I know this is an unpleasant subject, so let's change it.

So, how are you and Carrie? I'm still sorry about the marriage, but I believe it was the best thing you could have done. Time will tell whether Gary is a good father, but I think Carrie will be fine. She has too much of your mother in her to let this get on top of her. Don't give up on instilling some compassion in her; it's in there, it just needs some coaxing to come to the surface.

The house is certainly big enough for the two of you and having Rocky next door is a great help, I'm sure. I know she's happy. Her letters almost sing, she's so happy. Weed can stay with her and visit you whenever you and he decide it's okay.

Rocky also told me about your mother showing up at her door and outlining what she believed was Rocky's role in your life and Carrie's in particular. I was mad at first, but if there is anyone on this earth that can handle your mother, it's Rocky. She said Weed actually hid behind her couch in the den when he heard your mother's voice.

Next week, I'm going north with Sister Marie Claire to visit some displaced children. They're everywhere in Sudan. Homeless and orphaned, they can be found in every refugee camp and group of people fleeing Darfur. Many have been taken in by relatives, aunts and uncles and older siblings, but too many are alone. The sister wants to help or at least try. So, we travel north to see what we can do.

I want you to know how very much I love you and love Carrie; saying it is never enough. Words are so inadequate, you know. I love you and I'm proud of you, of the person you are and will be. Squeeze Carrie for me, do it every night. Tell her I love her too.

When I see how bleak the future is for the people of Sudan and how they continue to strive, to try to live their lives somehow, every day, no matter what happens to them, it makes me realize how damned lucky I have been and how fortunate you and Carrie are. We take our futures for granted most of the time, like it comes with a guarantee. It doesn't, you know. Anyway, I love you.

I'll write in a week or so and tell you about our trip. I miss you both.

Love,
Dad

26

Hanley had been rubbing the same spot on the side of the Beech for five minutes when Jumma said, "If I may, I believe the metal under your cloth cannot possibly shine more than it does now. Your beautiful airplane shows most of our country along its side. I think it is the biggest mirror in all Sudan."

"What? Oh, sorry, I was dreaming a bit, I guess, thinking of something and lost track of what I was doing." He looked at his plane and said, "I know it's as clean as can be, but I take some comfort in polishing this old metal. I've been doing it for years and it's been therapeutic. Right now, I need as much therapy as I can get."

The morning had been spent cleaning the plane, wiping down its wings and tail, inspecting the controls surfaces, checking for problems. The day before, Hanley and Jumma worked the inside of the plane, Hanley in the cockpit and Jumma in the cargo area and the space behind the rear bulkhead. Hanley finished the day making a list of items he believed they would need to help secure the women and children they would be bringing to the mission; blankets, water and juice, bags for anyone experiencing airsickness and some toys if they could find any, which he doubted. The first-aid kit Hanley kept on the plane was sitting on the ground outside, waiting to be taken to the mission once they were through with today's work. Hanley had a list of items he wanted added to the kit, a list Sister Marie Claire would be filling from the mission's supplies. Fully aware the nun would change the list, if not discard it altogether and use one of her own, he made one anyway.

Bending over to pick up the first-aid kit, Hanley wondered why he didn't walk away from Sister Marie Claire and her plan to save these people. His doubts now seemed limitless. This is the definition of real recklessness, he told himself over and over. He was now afraid, really afraid. He now believed it was out of control. He carried apprehension and the feeling of not being in charge of his life as he would carry a fever. Hell, he had only known her for a little over nine months. Why had he committed to do something so stupid to someone he barely knew? Had she been waiting for someone to come along, someone like him, someone gullible or dumb enough to be manipulated as she had manipulated him? How long had she been waiting?

Hanley picked up the first-aid kit and called to Jumma to gather his things, telling him they were going back to the mission. As Jumma retrieved his clipboard, pen and his water bottle, Hanley locked the plane's rear door and strode to the Land Cruiser. He was now mad and wanted some answers. Jumma barely made it into the old vehicle before Hanley gunned the engine and drove off toward the mission, leaving a cloud of dust, which the wind carried to cover the nose of the plane Hanley had so patiently polished ten minutes earlier.

The truck slid to a halt near the clinic, Hanley leaping from the truck before it was completely stopped. Seeing Sister Marie Claire reading something on a clipboard, he crossed the room and asked, "How did you know I would do what you wanted, to agree to fly to Kosti? Did you know? Well, did you?"

Hanley was standing, close to the nun who turned her back to him as he questioned her. They were alone inside the clinic. The late afternoon sun was shining on the counter where a box of gauze sat warming in the sunlight, waiting to be placed in the first-aid kit from Hanley's plane.

"Yes, I knew. I had been praying that someone would come to help me. Before you came, the church relied on the UN and others to bring us supplies and doctors. Then word came that someone had volunteered to bring his plane to help us. I knew then that God had heard me. I knew then that I had a chance to do what no one else seemed willing to do. So, when you came, I started making plans. I was confident you would agree. Why else would God deliver you to me? God would not send you here and then tell you to refuse. I did not use you, God used you. God will use you to help these people."

Hanley's anger was growing. He felt used and stupid. "Wasn't it lucky that God sent you someone dumb enough to be led around by the nose?"

"Luck was not involved. I do not believe in luck. There is only the will of God, nothing else. You are an instrument of the Lord's will and plan. Accept your fate for it is a good one and a good cause. You are an angel with wings, only your wings are metal. They shine in the sun as well as any wings in heaven. Do not question the will of God. Remember, this has all happened for a reason. Be glad you have been chosen to be a part of it." The nun turned toward the door and walked away. She stopped in the doorway, turned toward the American. Her right hand gripped the door frame and she swayed a bit as she looked at him. Her expression was a mix of weariness and determination. She said, "We have only a few days left before we go to Wad Madani. Please believe in this. It is important that you do. God will not let us fail; he would not do that."

"It's not God I'm worried about," Hanley said

***

Two days after her talk with Hanley alone in the clinic, Sister Marie Claire rode in one of the mission's large trucks to Rumbek. Driving was one of the doctors, a large Yugoslavian with dark red hair, a crooked nose and a large droopy mustache. Hanley said the doctor looked like an American cartoon character named Yosemite Sam. She did not know who that was.

The truck cab was hot and the doctor was talking about football, a game the nun loved, but did not want to think about now. Trying to ignore the doctor, she suddenly thought about Sister O'Brien and her love of American football, a completely different game. What was the name of the team she loved so? She could not remember. Her mind was focused on the conversation she would be having after they arrived at the diocese to pick up mail and supplies for the mission's church. She was scheduled to meet with the archbishop to brief him on the needs of the mission and then she scheduled some personal time, telling the diocese she would be visiting another nun who worked at the diocese and lived in Rumbek. In fact, she would be seeing the nun, but only briefly. The restaurant of Paul, the uncle of one of the young women she hoped would meet the plane in Kosti, was in between her friend's apartment and the diocese. Stopping there would not be out of her way and, if seen, would not seem out of the ordinary-just a quick meal before returning to Mapuordit.

As the truck pulled into the drive of the offices of the Catholic diocese in Rumbek, Sister Marie Claire saw a young woman walking behind two men as they moved along the sidewalk near the building. She carried two large, overstuffed briefcases and a large white plastic cylinder under her right arm. The men carried nothing, puffing cigars and talking loud enough to be heard from inside the truck. The girl was small and dark, with a long dress and sandals. She looked exhausted, more than exhausted, she looked as sad as any person the nun had ever seen, as if she was a witness to the tragedy that was her life. Now Sister Marie Claire was also a witness to it. She became short of breath and snatched some air. Turning his head sharply at the sound, the doctor asked, "Is something the matter?" Sister Marie Claire cleared her throat and said, "Nothing is wrong, I just thought of something I meant to bring with me today and forgot."

The doctor smiled and said he had done the same thing many times. He pulled on the door handle and when it opened, he rolled out and onto the graveled surface of the parking lot. Sister Marie Claire did not move. Watching the young woman struggle up the street, the nun's jaw muscles bunched as she clenched her teeth and hissed, "Pigs" at the men walking and laughing before the girl, then said, "Forgive me Father."

***

Paul Abimaje brought two cups of coffee to the round table next to the door in the back of his small restaurant. Servers, Paul's own children, passed close by as they moved in and out of the kitchen door next to the nun's shoulder. A name had been carved into the wood of the table where she sat; the carving was poorly done. Sister Marie Claire tried to read the name as she waited for her friend to return. When he did, she smiled and took in the smell of the coffee. It was strong, its warm richness reminding her of the coffee her father made each morning, a smell from her childhood. She wished for a return of the feelings she had then; contentment, comfort, an excitement for what the day would bring. Now her days were filled with fear and misgivings, a longing for peace and safety, for comfort. She missed her father and his hugs. Phillip Audebourg would have been proud of his daughter and her plan. Claire had always made him proud, even when she failed, he would commend her for her efforts, no matter how small or great. He only cared that she always tried.

Sister Marie Claire sipped the coffee while she looked around the restaurant. The room had only two other customers, old men sitting near the window to watch the street and its entertainment. They would grunt as something caught their attention, the loudest coming when young women would pass. Frowning as she watched, she said, "Hanley Martin gives this plan a real chance at succeeding. Without the plane, our ability to move that many children at once that distance would have been limited, if not impossible. If we can load them and depart in a small amount of time, the smallest possible, then we will be back to the mission before anyone can pursue us. Once there,

I have arranged to disperse the children immediately, to scatter them across the countryside. Finding them will be difficult. Jumma has spent months locating relatives and devised a system for contacting them when we return. The relatives do not know of the plan. You are the only one."

The man looked up and raised a palm to the nun to silence her. "You have not told the other relatives? How can that be? What if they will not accept the child? What happens then?" As he began to speak, coffee spilled from his lower lip and onto the table, where it pooled in a small hole that had been drilled by countless diners over the years. He wiped it up with the side of his hand and looked back to the nun for an answer.

"They will not refuse their own. Even if they do, the mission orphanage will take them, which is much better than the life they are living now, no? It was my decision not to tell the relatives. If only one told someone else and that person told someone else, in a week, too many people would know and the plan would have been compromised. No, it was the right thing to do. Jumma has worked to make certain we can contact these people quickly and move the children to safety. Some will be placed with people in the surrounding villages until they can be delivered to their families. We know that the plane will be recognized if seen. The American and I know the risks. We will deny that anyone else was involved. Jumma is to stay in the plane so he will not be seen. It is to be hoped that since we will arrive in Wad Madani just after dawn, there will not be anyone at the landing strip."

A child began crying somewhere outside the restaurant, a high-pitched scream that wound down to a long, pleading cry. The nun took a spoon from the saucer of her drink and began tapping the table, slowly but steadily. The man facing her turned to look out the storefront windows of his business to see the child. He turned back to the nun. "I have spoken to my contact in Wad Madani. He assures me all will be ready and he will meet you at the airstrip at dawn. The process will be more elaborate, more complicated than first thought. He believes the children can be acquired and moved safely as planned. One child is now sick and may be left behind. Unfortunate, but necessary. Too much is at stake. My niece will be of much help in this process. She is good with children, can comfort them. Her value in this matter will be obvious. I pray this will work."

Chairs scraping the floor interrupted the conversation. The two old men were leaving, making a loud production to signal their departure. One tossed a small coin to the tabletop while struggling to get into his jacket. The other watched and then, with a new grunt showing his exasperation, grabbed the elusive sleeve of the coat to assist. For another thirty seconds, they wrestled against each other and the sleeve of the jacket until both stopped. They left the restaurant with the arm of the man pinned to his side by the twisted coat. Once outside, they began again, both turning in a tight circle, pulling on the fabric, finally getting the arm through and the jacket on straight. Leaning against a light pole, they rested before ambling down the street, cursing each other and the coat.

Normally, the nun would have found the scene amusing, but this afternoon, it only irritated her. She was not amused by men anymore, at least not now, not while she planned to save some children from enslavement by other men. These thoughts pained her. No matter how careful she was not to label all men as bad, she struggled with the urge. Too much misery came at the hands of men. She must be careful. Other men were helping her save these children.

"It will work. Tell your friend the plane will stop at the end of the landing strip, turn and stop again. Have the children nearby and ready to board when the door opens. We want to have the children on the plane and take off in five minutes. The engines will be running and so there will be dust and noise. If the children know this ahead of time, they may not be as frightened and the loading will go smoothly. Do you understand? As I have said, I want Jumma to remain in the plane. I will be the one outside helping board the children. Your niece and the others must help with the loading. With only

twelve children, we can load them quickly, don't you think?"
The man nodded. Paul Abimaje said, "I have told the man not
to have any of the children wrapped in blankets so that they
can walk if needed. The morning will be cold this time of year.
Perhaps you can have blankets on the plane for the children."

"We will try," the nun said.

Pulling on his earlobe, the man said, "We risk much to do
this. I am doing it for my brother and his wife, as they cannot.
I understand why you do this; you are an instrument of God. It
is your duty. But the American, I don't understand. Why would
he do this? I don't trust him. I think he might change his mind
and fly off with you and the boy and leave my niece and the
others there. If they are caught, things will be worse for them
than they are now. It is a risk, don't you agree?"

"No, I don't agree. He will not change his mind. We will be
there, this I know. We will be there, I promise."

27

The small boy was shaken awake by a large rough hand that smelled of cigarettes and apples. The hand shook him by the shoulder and a man's voice told him to wake up and stay quiet. The child had been dreaming of his mother as he always did. He ached for her. By now, he could not remember her face, exactly. He started to cry, but the man hushed him and he stopped. He often cried when he was first put to work in the shop where he pushed the cart with the linens on top and the broken wheel on the bottom. He learned to stop after the owner beat him when he cried. Now he could stop whenever he was told.

It was still dark and the room where he woke was full of movement. In the darkness, he could just see other children sitting up on the hard floor, wide-eyed and shaky as he was. He had fallen asleep in the back room of the house with the girl. A man and woman he did not know, the same man and woman who took them from the shop, whispered to the others. He was hungry, but then he was always hungry. A scrape on his knee seeped a smelly liquid and hurt.

The man returned, knelt beside him and whispered in his ear. "Stand up, child, and be silent. We are leaving. Make no noise whatsoever and you will be safe. If you speak or make a noise, everyone will suffer. Do you understand? Good."

All the children were now standing, the adults forming them into a line before the door. Scared, he still hoped his parents would come for him as he closed his eyes and waited to be told what to do. The door opened, the woman said, "Follow us," and led them into the cold night. They all climbed into a van and the van drove away from the building. Now he was to take a trip with the others, but he did not know where. He wanted all of this to stop; he wanted everything to be as it once was. He wanted to go home.

***

Instead of little sleep, Hanley had no sleep this night. Now, it was time to get ready and leave for the mission's landing strip and the flight to Kosti. He was anxious, but no longer afraid. If all went well, they would be back by 9:00 a.m. Allowing for two hours' flight time each way and one half hour on the ground, nine o'clock was a reasonable expectation. Going to the foot locker, Hanley opened the lid, slid his hand down along the right inner wall of the metal box and under some shirts, folded and resting on the bottom. There, he felt the hard metal case of a pocket watch Rocky had given him. Surrounding it with his fingers, he pulled the watch from the locker, examined it for a moment and put it into his pants pocket. Not interested in its marking of time, Hanley took it to have a part of Rocky with him on the flight. He considered taking her photo, but thought the watch to be more meaningful; he had not asked for the watch, it was a gift.

Jumma would be waiting with the Land Cruiser near the edge of the mission, where, at three-fifteen, Hanley would meet the boy and the nun. The plane was ready, what supplies they assembled stowed onboard two days earlier. The weather would not pose a problem.

For the hundredth time in the past week, he reassured himself this was a simple task. Fly the plane, land, load twelve children and depart. He figured the window for problems to develop was approximately twenty minutes at the most. It would be maybe five minutes before landing for anyone on the ground that might hear the plane's approach to get to the landing strip by the time it touched down. Assuming there was no one at the strip to begin with. Five minutes out, ten minutes on the ground from touchdown to taxing, turning and to a full stop; fifteen minutes at most to load the children; another five to secure the plane and depart-maybe twenty to twenty-five minutes on the ground. Okay, twenty-five to thirty minutes total time, from hearing the plane approach to rotation and departure; a simple plan. Nothing was ever simple, not even in the best of circumstances. Sudan was not the best of circumstances and he knew it.

Hanley sat on the edge of his cot, staring at the floor and his bare feet. He wished he'd slept, but knew that adrenaline would take over once he was flying. Bending over, he reached underneath the stand beside his cot and pulled a shallow white porcelain bowl to sit on the floor near his feet. In the bowl sat a damp cloth, white and rough, resting in a half inch of water. Squeezing the water from the cloth, he used it to wipe his face and neck, then his arms. This will have to do, he reminded himself again. Bathing was never a regular practice in Sudan as water had more essential uses. He should shave, but that was not possible either. When he returned to Kokomo, he would take a shower twice a day for the first week, he promised himself.

Hanley passed through the door of his room into the dark hallway. His eyes had adjusted to the darkness, allowing him to find the doorknob and slip outside with just a few squeaking floor boards to announce his movements.

The night was very still and cool, the buzz of insects the only noise he could hear. Smoke from the evening fires drifted away while the light from the still smoldering coals dotted the landscape, marking the spots where people were sleeping on the mission's grounds. Taking a moment to orient himself, Hanley noted the location of the fires and the direction he needed to go to reach the Land Rover. Hoping to avoid stepping on someone and waking the whole complex, he headed toward his meeting with the nun and Jumma.

***

Jumma knelt beside the vehicle and shivered as he waited. He was cold. Even though the morning was unusually chilly, he had worn khaki shorts and a white shirt, his usual uniform when he worked at the mission.

The last two months had been the most stressful he had known for some time. His life at the mission settled into a routine and flow that suited him. He was working and being useful, caring for those less fortunate and assisting both the nun and the pilot. He liked both, though he would prefer they not argue as much as they did. For the past eight weeks or so, he had been working to contact the families of the children they hoped to rescue, telling them only that their child or relative had been located and he would provide additional information as it became available. Hoping to avoid any undue attention and contact from the relatives, he explained that he worked for a private organization that specialized in finding missing children from the Darfur and southern Sudanese regions. He provided no contact information only saying he would be in touch when he had more to tell them. Most of the families were so glad to have any information, they did not ask questions, but only thanked him for his efforts. Some did ask who he was and the name of his organization but he immediately asked them for the specifics of when and where the child had been taken. This always deflected their curiosity. The work had been difficult and exhausting at times. He shivered again and waited.

***

Hanley was the first to arrive. He saw the form of the truck and steered toward it in the darkness. He did not see Jumma or the nun. As he approached, the form before him changed shape slightly at one corner and he realized that someone was now standing near one of the front fenders. His heart raced a bit until he realized it must be the young Sudanese. "Jumma?" Hanley's whisper sounded like it came from a thirteen-year-old with a voice in transition.

Jumma smiled and said, "It's me, Mr Martin."

Hanley reached for the truck and followed the side with his hand as he approached the young man. "No Sister Marie Claire?" he asked.

"No, she is not here," Jumma answered in a low voice. The American remembered the nun's repeated reminders to be as quiet as he could. She insisted he demonstrate his whisper for her, which she reviewed and suggested he modify. There was nothing she did not try to control, he thought.

Leaning against the hood, Hanley tried to relax, but became more restless as the time crawled past. Once he was in the air, he would be all right. Noticing Jumma's head turning, Hanley heard the sound of someone approaching. A woman's voice hummed a melody softly as she walked toward them. When close, Sister Marie Claire said, "Hello, my heroes. Let us leave now before anyone wakens."

"Don't say that. We're not heroes," Hanley snapped back at her.

"Not yet, but I have faith," she replied.

"You'd better have enough for both of us," he said.

She opened the door of the Land Rover, flipped the front passenger seat forward and climbed into the back. Jumma started the truck and immediately drove off toward the airstrip. Having picked the spot where he parked the truck days before, Hanley made certain Jumma walked the route out of the compound several times, noting bushes, depressions in the ground and any large rocks to avoid. Now reasonably certain he knew what was ahead, Hanley strained to watch for problems as Jumma drove until they were away from the compound. After what Hanley estimated to be two hundred yards or so, Jumma turned on the headlights and increased the truck's speed a bit. Hanley knew they would be airborne before anyone else could follow them to the plane. He relaxed some, turned in his seat and said to the nun, "Well, now would be the right time to announce any surprises. You may as well, because if you wait until we're in the air, I can easily turn around and land. You cannot stop me, so let's get everything on the table right now. Okay?"

Smiling, the nun said, "There are no surprises, at least not that I'm aware of. When we land, the children will be waiting. When my people hear the plane approach, they will bring the truck with the children to the end of the runway and we will take them on board and leave. I believe everything will work very well."

"My people? You sound like the Mafia," Hanley said. The nun smiled again and began to hum the same melody she was humming when she approached the truck. As she hummed, she reached into a pocket of her dress and pulled out a rosary. Fingering the beads, she moved from one to another. Hanley watched for a moment and then turned to watch the road in the wash of the old headlights.

The plane first appeared as a small reflection of the truck's lights. A large amount of time was spent on the plane's preparation and while he knew it hadn't made much sense, Hanley still checked and double-checked everything on the Beech that could be a potential problem. He knew this airplane as well as anyone possibly could, but he didn't take anything for granted. He was still worried, even after adjusting to his decision to assist the nun with her plan. If he was to make a mistake, it wouldn't be with the plane.

Jumma stopped the truck near the terminal shack and killed the engine. The truck creaked and popped as they stepped into the darkness. The sounds of the African night surrounded them as they made their way to the plane. Hanley unlocked and lowered the heavy door, warning the nun to step back. He paused to turn on the small flashlight he carried. When Jumma approached, Sister Marie Claire took him by the arm and said, "Jumma, before you get on the plane, I want you to know how much your help has meant to me. I know that I don't say thank you enough for all that you do, but this is too important and

I could not have done this without your help. You have always been special to us at the mission, but what you have done to make this happen is extraordinary. Thank you. I know God is pleased with you."

"And I am pleased with him," Jumma said, then turned and entered the plane. This made Hanley smile.

The nun busied herself with the task of making certain everything they put onboard for the trip was secured. Jumma also began an inspection of things in the cargo hold, but knew things were ready that afternoon. Hanley entered the cargo bay and told the nun and the young Sudanese he was going out to unlock the chain from the iron ring and the large flat stone and they would depart. He told them to buckle themselves in. Hanley turned on the interior lights of the plane. Outside, he unlocked the padlock and slid the chain through the wheel housing, slipped the lock through a chain link and snapped it shut. Even though the night had a bit of a chill to it, he was starting to sweat, his shirt clinging to the small of his back, cold and sticky. Pulling the rear door closed behind him, he locked it and turned to see Jumma sitting in the seat in the cargo hold. He doesn't look nervous at all, Hanley noticed. As he passed, Hanley put his hand on Jumma's shoulder and gently squeezed it, but said nothing.

Once seated, Hanley began the startup procedure, checking his fuel and battery levels, his magneto, ignition and electric boost pumps. As always, he started the right engine first. He used a rich mixture, cracking the throttle, but with no pumping, primed for about eight seconds and, waited twenty seconds for the fuel to vaporize, turned a couple of revolutions and then hit the mags and ignition boost. The big Pratt and Whitney engine turned over as it always did. Hanley started the left engine, turned on the running lights and landing lights and began to taxi to the airstrip. As the Beech rolled to its left, Hanley saw two people standing in the wash of the plane's lights. Two men in traditional Atuot dress stood near a bush next to the airstrip. The natives watched the plane as it moved into position. Hanley said to the nun, "Watch those men and tell me if they move toward the plane or the airstrip. If they move, tell me immediately." When he reached the end of the airstrip, Hanley quickly looked for any cattle or wild animals standing in the path of the plane. When he was aligned with the center of the airstrip, he advanced the throttles and the Beech moved forward smoothly. Two days before, Hanley chained an old set of mattress springs to the Land Rover, weighted it down with cement blocks and pulled it over the airstrip, grading the strip's remaining gravel to an acceptable smoothness. The plane rolled along, gathering speed until the tail rose and then the nose of the Beech rose as well. It was a smooth rotation, just like all the other times Hanley and the Beech departed. The landing gear came up and Hanley switched off the lights of the old plane as it gained altitude. He would climb to twenty-five hundred feet, which he would maintain until he was almost to Kosti, hoping to keep from appearing on any air traffic controller's screen. Hanley also believed a quick descent to the airport would minimize his exposure to anything that might be used to prevent his landing, although he had no clue what that might be or what he would do if anyone tried to stop him. Having thought of a plan, no matter how ill-conceived it might be, made him feel better, more in control. Pretty childish, he now told himself.

"I hope your people have only twelve children when we get there. We can perhaps take one or two more if they are small, but not more than that. Any more, if they are bigger, will be a problem. I do not want to turn away a child, period. That's a memory I do not want to live with," Hanley said through the headphones. He was tuned to the Khartoum air traffic control frequency, listening for any mention of his aircraft.

Hanley looked over to see the nun still working her beads. Her head shook slightly from side to side. That was all the response he got from Sister Marie Claire.

28

The sky was beginning to lighten in the East, to the right of the plane. Hanley checked his watch; it was 5:36. He had been navigating by compass and time. Soon, he would begin his visual search for the White Nile River, which he would follow to Kosti and into the airport.

After almost an hour in the air, a voice came over the radio, attempting to reach Hanley and his flight. "Flight A806D this is Mapuordit mission, do you hear me? Mr Martin, please respond." It was Father Laslo. Hanley did not respond. The attempt was repeated several times and then stopped.

Sister Marie Claire was asleep, her head resting against the side window, the headphone a pillow of sorts. When he noticed her sleeping, Hanley unplugged her headphones. He wondered if Jumma was awake. Now Hanley plugged her headphones in, keyed the mic and said, "Sister, it's time to wake up." She did not stir. Hanley pushed her shoulder with his finger.

The nun swatted his hand away. "I'm not asleep. You should watch where we are going and leave me alone."

Hanley took his headset off and, shouting over the noise of the engines, asked, "Jumma, are you awake?"

"Yes, Mr Martin, I am awake. When will we be there?"

"In about one-half hour. I want you and Sister Marie Claire to be fully awake when we land. We all know what we are to do, so let's be prepared. I want to land and depart in under twenty minutes if possible. Okay?"

***

The desk top was hard, but it was better than sleeping on the floor. Assad lay curled up on his side so all of him fit on the desk. His head rested on his left arm and he was cold, or at least he was until he drifted off to sleep. Guarding the small group of storage buildings at the airport had been his job every night for over six months. He did not mind, he slept most of the night and, during the day, he helped his older brother. It was important when you are seventeen and a man going places. He had things to do. This was not his only job, as he was assisting his brother with his business, storing electronics and other items, such as watches here in Kosti for movement to Khartoum to be sold on the streets. Why they had to be stored here, he did not understand. His job was to drive his brother's van to meet other vans on the edge to the city, bring the merchandise back to these storage units and then guard them through the night. It was a good job and he and his brother were doing well. Anyway, no one ever bothered him out here. If they did, he was ready for them, so let them try.

Lying on the floor next to the desk was an AK-47, a fully automatic 7.62 mm rifle, one Assad knew was the most prolifically made and used weapons on earth. Assad thought himself a capable shot, but it did not matter if he or the gun were accurate; it was capable of spewing a large number of bullets effectively and reliably at close range. Assad fired the rifle once, destroying an old yellow oil drum, the noise ringing in his ears for the rest of that day. He was confident he could kill someone, if need be. Yes, he felt good about it.

He turned slightly in his sleep, dreaming about driving down a dirt road backward in his brother's van.

***

Ten minutes after Hanley tried to wake the nun, he spotted the White Nile and followed it north. He estimated he was about twenty minutes from the airport at Kosti. The airport was just west of the river. Hanley would fly up the river and then turn east. The Kosti airstrip ran almost directly east-west. He wanted to land with the rising sun behind him and in the eyes of anyone watching the plane. There were several large buildings on the south side of the airstrip. There was also a terminal building to the left at that end of the strip, which he hoped would not be open when they landed. Hanley learned what little commercial traffic traveled in and out of Kosti did so at mid to late morning. The truck with the children would be parked to the west of the terminal behind a smaller storage building. He felt certain he could land and take off without incident, once the children were on board.

As the sun rose, the sky turned from a deep red to a pink haze with no clouds. The river moved in gentle curves, flowing north through a land that barely noticed, having been arid too long to care much anymore. Having flown this route several times on his way north to Khartoum, Hanley now recognized the landmarks he established. They were close and Hanley began his descent, banking slightly while turning east.

"We're just about there, so let's get ready," Hanley told the nun and the young African.

"Yes, Mr Martin," Jumma said. Hanley could hear the exhilaration and perhaps some fear in Jumma's voice. He was reading a book on hiking in Europe which he placed in his wornout backpack and then secured between his seat and the plane's outer wall.

Turning to look at Jumma, Hanley was satisfied that all was ready and there was enough room for him and the children. How scared they must be right now, he thought; how scared, but how hopeful. He wished *he* was.

***

He was sitting up before he realized he was awake. Shaking his head, Assad tried to reconstruct his dream to explain what just happened, but couldn't. A noise in his head sounded like the drone of a bug, a dragonfly maybe, but no, it wasn't. In seconds, it registered that a plane was approaching in the distance. Another sound also came to him, voices from men talking nearby.

Shaky, Assad slipped off the desk and went to the door of the office to listen. The men were talking about finding somewhere to eat breakfast. He had to piss, but was afraid to step outside. Damn these men, he thought. Their conversation stopped suddenly and one man said, "Listen!" to the others. He said he believed the plane was landing. Assad knew this was unusual as flights to and from the airport happened in late morning at the earliest. Maybe it's an emergency. He opened the door and stepped outside to see members of the Sudanese army nearby. They were smoking beside a UAZ-469, an old Russian military jeep. Its gray-green paint was faded and there were two small holes in the rear quarter panel that he could see. Someone shot the thing in the ass, Assad thought.

Turning, Assad went around the corner and began to urinate on the building and in the dust next to it. Once done, he looked around the corner at the soldiers while struggling to zip up his pants. The men were looking south toward the river. The sound of the plane was getting closer. Hoping to not draw attention to himself, Assad stayed behind the corner where he looked south for the plane. In the haze, just above the large gray warehouse near the east end of the airstrip, he saw a plane flying east, but with its left wing dipped, turning toward them. "Where are you going?" he asked the plane.

***

As he banked and began his turn, the new sun passed across the bottom of the plane's windshield, like a bright ball rolling along a table's edge, and then disappeared behind the nun's head. Completing the arc, from the river to about two miles east of the airstrip, Hanley was now heading west at a bearing of 260°. At an altitude of sixteen hunderd feet, he began his final approach to the small airport, the unpaved runway looking more like a service road in an industrial park, which, in fact, it was. He added a bit of right rudder and lowered his flaps incrementally, cutting his airspeed to one hundred and twenty miles per hour for his final approach. The Beech was never an easy plane to land and his procedure was to be at near stall speed when he reached the runway. The sun was now above the horizon behind him and the area was well lit, with the white and pale gray buildings glowing slightly in the morning sunlight. Hanley brought the nose of the Beech up as the buildings beneath him blurred a bit and the ground rose quickly to meet the airplane. Just before the wheels touched the surface, the tail of the plane twitched, causing Sister Marie Claire's head to shake, as if she disagreed with the whole affair. There was a bump and the Beech hopped once and then settled on the runway, the large warehouses on Hanley's left coming up quickly. He was now applying the brakes as hard as he could, hoping to control the roll enough to stop just at the end of the last large warehouse and turn the plane to depart when the children were on board.

***

Two vans sat in the shadow of a small warehouse that was empty. The man behind the wheel of the white van knew this building was not being used, his father's friend assured him of this. Behind him, his wife and five of the children were sitting on the floor, the women singing softly to the children who were quiet, thanks be to God, the man thought. Behind his van was a second truck, with two women and six children in it. There were to have been twelve children but one had been moved and he did not know to where. He regretted that, but at least these would be going back to their families. Taking children from their enslavement was what he did to make things better in a world that had gone mad. He was afraid, but glad to be doing something. He hated this war. It brought shame to his country and to him. People were not to be slaves, especially children. Suddenly, his stomach began to rumble, loud enough that his wife stopped singing and listened. His stomach rolled again and then he heard something else, in the distance; a droning, an engine; the plane. It must be! As quietly as he could, the man pulled on the door handle, pushed on the door and slid out, next to the building. Inching toward the corner, he looked east and into the rising sun. Blocking the light with his left hand, he managed to see a small object as it disappeared into the sun, its sound now unmistakable. It was the American and the French nun, it must be. He felt tightness in his chest. He turned and walked quickly to the second van. As the window on the driver's side came down, he said to the young woman behind the wheel, "They are coming. We must do this right. Remember, stay behind me, park directly behind the plane, the children will run along the side and into the door. If a child hesitates, I will deal with it, you keep the others moving." The woman's eyes showed a bit of panic and she blinked constantly. She nodded and watched as the man returned to his van. She is terrified, he thought as he walked away.

As he climbed in the truck, the man said to his wife, "This is it."

29

Hanley unlocked the tail wheel and, using his throttle and pedals, turned the plane around at the end of the dirt runway, near the corner of a long one-story warehouse now to the right of the plane. He reduced the throttle, to idle the engines and set the brakes. "Let's go," he said.

Jumma was already up and at the rear door. Having released her seatbelts, Sister Marie Claire clambered out of the second seat and into the cargo hold. Hanley waited at the controls. The cargo door release lever snapped under Jumma's weight, the door went down quickly and Jumma jumped to the ground. The nun said, "Jumma, don't," to keep him for leaving the plane, but it was too late. As Jumma turned, two vans came out from behind a building toward him.   "Keep your eyes open!" Hanley shouted to the nun. She stood in the plane's doorway, looking for anything moving near the plane. Just as Hanley noticed movement near a building along the runway, Sister Marie Claire called to the American, "Hanley, there are soldiers here!"

Hanley saw them as they emerged from behind a building halfway down the airstrip. He did not notice them while landing. "I see them. They've stopped. Don't stop, no matter what happens," he yelled back to her.

With his head turned to the approaching vans, Jumma did not see the soldiers. Hanley watched the soldiers for any sign of aggression. He calculated how long it would take to get airborne, should they begin moving toward the plane.

Twisting in his seat, Hanley shouted, "Let's move, Sister. Let's get this done!"

***

Assad saw the plane flash by the opening between the buildings and watched the soldiers climb into the vehicle, turn and drive off toward the runway. Turning, he tripped, one foot over the other, landed on his hands and sprang to his feet. Running through the office door, he scooped the rifle from the floor and ran back outside. Following the soldiers seemed too risky, so he turned and ran to the back of the building and along the rear of the warehouse. When he reached the end, he turned right, ran the length of the building, crossed the space between it and the next warehouse and squatted at the corner. Peering around the sheet metal capping, he saw the plane sitting approximately two hundred meters to his left, its propellers still spinning. Its nose was pointed to him, the plane at an angle so he could see its tail. From where he squatted, he saw a native African, young, in a white shirt, standing near the end of the plane, the rear door of the plane was open and a woman was standing in the doorway. A man was sitting in the plane, where a pilot would sit. He must be the one that flies the plane, Assad thought. Where were the soldiers? Turning, he saw the soldiers sitting in their vehicle, near the end of the building next to him. They had stopped almost immediately after turning on the runway. They just watched the plane. Why don't they do something, Assad wondered. As he watched the soldiers, the sound of the vans turned his head back around. He watched as people began climbing from the van and moved toward the plane. They were mostly children, with some adults leading them.

A voice shouted to his right. A soldier was now out of the vehicle and shouting to the people to stop. The other soldiers did not move. Now more soldiers climbed from the old UAZ and began shouting at the plane. Children entered the plane, helped by the adults and the African. The soldiers became more agitated, their voices rising as they watched. No one at the plane stopped. Why weren't they listening? Why didn't the soldiers go and stop them? Assad didn't understand. Turning to the plane, Assad raised the rifle to his shoulder and fired at the people near the plane. At first, nothing happened, but then a woman and a child fell to the ground, then the African. A man picked up a small boy and flung him into the plane and then did the same with a small girl. A man appeared in the plane's door. Assad began shooting again, this time at the plane itself. As he did, something hit his arm, then his neck and jaw. Then he was on his back, looking up at the morning sky. Time slowed down while a great pain enveloped him. He began swallowing liquid to keep from choking. It was warm, thick and bitter. A man appeared above him and, just before he died, Assad heard the deafening sound of large engines streaking by and saw the man above him turning as the plane passed.

***

Hanley was turned in his seat when sound of the gun firing began. Sister Marie Claire screamed, "No!" and Hanley was out of his seat. He saw the nun on her knees, pulling children in on top of her. A small boy came through the door as if thrown by someone and landed on the nun, then a small girl on top of those already heaped near the door. Hanley reached the opening in time to see three people getting into a yellow van. On the ground near the door lay three bodies, a woman and a child, their bodies twisted and blood-soaked. Near them lay Jumma, face down in the dust, the top rear portion of his head was missing, an ugly wound in its place. As Hanley stood there, sickened, he felt a punch to his right side, just below his ribcage. He spun around and grabbed the doorframe, his knees wobbled and he righted himself. Instinctively, he grabbed the cable and yanked as hard as he could, bringing the door up. Sister Marie Claire was up and helped pull the door closed, while Hanley secured the latch. Hanley reached down, put his hand on his side and felt the wetness. He wobbled again and told himself to move. Using his hands against the plane's interior walls for balance, he moved toward the cockpit. Children were screaming and crying all around him. He became nauseated and his vision blurred as he climbed into the seat. A searing pain grew in his back and down his right leg. "God, please make my legs work," he pleaded silently, "don't let me be paralyzed."

Despite his fear, his legs and feet moved automatically as he shook his head. The Beech was rolling now; too much movement in the rear. He had forgotten to lock the tail wheel. Twisting the knob, he froze the wheel and applied the power, sending the Beech hurtling down the runway. As the tail came up, Hanley pulled back on the yoke, the pain in his legs now almost enough to make him pass out. Bile rose in his throat and he spit up in his lap. He strained to clear his vision and searched his gauges for the information he needed. He saw the altimeter, now showing he was at five hundred feet. "We need more altitude," he said aloud. At two thousand feet, he put the top of the plane's instrument panel on the horizon, reduced the engines to cruising speed and trimmed the plane. Leaning forward, he rested his head on the yoke and closed his eyes. "Don't pass out," he told himself, "stay awake."

30

The children were all crying, some sitting, and some standing while a few were lying on the floor of the plane. As it lurched forward, Sister Marie Claire began pushing the children down while telling them they must sit. She spoke to them in both Atuot and Dinka dialects, hoping she was being understood, asking them to be calm and sit on the floor. Shoving them against the outside wall, she moved between the children, giving them each a blanket and an old stuffed toy or a book. She was not crying, but she wanted to. Praying, she asked God to help her through this. "Hanley, are you all right?" she shouted to the American. She saw a round blood stain on his shirt just above his belt as he swayed among the children, trying to reach the cockpit. There was no response. "Please, God, help us," she prayed.

When the plane left the ground, the children were all sitting down, most with their backs to the wall of the cargo hold. Two were curled up on the floor; she left them there. Aisha, the young niece of her friend, comforted the younger children, watching the nun as she moved among them. As the plane climbed from the Kosti airstrip, Sister Marie Claire moved to the door and looked at the American. Hanley was hunched over, his left hand gripping the yoke, while he fumbled with the large levers on top of the plane's center console. His shirt was soaked in sweat and the bloodstain on his back was now the size of a bread plate.

"I need to look at your wound," she said.

"You can after I get the plane stabilized," he said, his voice just above a whisper.

"Can you fly?" she asked.

"Yes, but I've never flown after having been shot, so we'll just have to see how it goes." He was breathing hard, his words strained and thin to her ear. Her heart sank and tears covered her cheeks. She wiped them away quickly. "Are the children okay?" he asked.

"Yes. They are very frightened, but they are good."

"Then sit down in that seat and help me or we may not make it very far," he told her.

The nun watched Hanley try reading the fuel and oil pressure gauges. He said, "I'm looking for signs the plane had been hit by the gunfire, but I'm having trouble focusing." He tried turning to look at the left engine, but he grimaced and stopped turning. "Look for smoke coming from the engines, will you?" he asked.

Sister Marie Claire looked at the right engine and saw nothing out of the ordinary. She climbed from her seat and peered out the left window, her hand braced against the top of the instrument panel, her body pressed against the American's. He moaned from the pressure. "There is a small line of smoke, a wisp, coming from the engine, from the side I can't see," she told him.

After she moved back to the seat, she again saw Hanley leaning close to the instrument panel. She saw him close his eyes and open them, wait a second, then squint, trying again to see the gauges.

"I still can't see them clearly," he told her. She watched him struggle, tears welling in her eyes, seeing him blink rapidly, clearing his vision. "I can see it. Shit, we're losing pressure," he said from between gritted teeth.

"I think our heading is correct and our altitude was near two thousand feet, which is good enough," Hanley said, "but I'm worried less about the plane's stability and more about flying on one engine. I've never had to do that. The Beech can do it, but it changes everything and I'm not certain I could manage the changes. I don't think I can last much longer and keep you and the children safe."

"Here, let me look at you." The nun pulled at Hanley's shirt as he shifted to his right to give her more room to maneuver. She tugged until the shirttail came out of his pants. Just below his ribs was a small hole with blood seeping from it. Pushing his shoulder forward, she saw a slightly larger hole in the middle of his back near his spine. Blood was also leaking from the exit wound, but faster, his lower back a smear of red. Turning, she went to the cargo hold where she retrieved some cotton, gauze and antiseptic cream. Back in the cockpit, she wiped the areas as best she could, smeared on antiseptic and stuffed cotton, covered in the cream, into the wounds. Hanley grunted hard when she did, but stayed awake. "That is all I can do for now," she declared.

***

The pain was overtaking him and he had to concentrate. Hanley was scared, hopelessly scared, death-row inmate scared, he thought. He wanted to see Elizabeth again, to hold his granddaughter, to have a drink with Rocky.

"You've jumped off the fucking building," he said to himself. The pain in his back was turning to numbness in his hips and legs. He could still move them, but for how long?

They'd been in the air for twenty minutes. He was running close to one-hundred-and ninety-five miles per hour airspeed, the limit for flying without excessive vibration. With the engine damage and the children, Hanley didn't want to risk any additional speed. They were approximately seventy miles southwest of Kosti. That left roughly four-hundred-and-thirty-five miles to the airstrip near Mapuordit. He knew he wouldn't make it. He would have to put the plane down somewhere. The trick would be in judging his own condition and he knew that was a big risk.

"Listen, this won't work for much longer. We need to get to a place where I can land and you can get help. I want to fly for as long as I can, but I'm afraid I won't be the best judge of how long that will be. You have to help me. We need to identify a place near a town or village where we can land. You'll have to help me think of where, watch my condition and then help me land. Not asking a lot, is it?" Hanley wanted to smile, but couldn't. He coughed and the pain made him twist and sit up straight, then coughed again. The nun caught him under his right arm to support him.

Suddenly, Hanley's vision cleared a bit and the pain subsided. Shaking his head, he checked his gauges and saw the oil pressure in the left engine was still falling, but slowly. He said, "For some reason I'm feeling a bit better." He looked at the nun, seeing her clearly for the first time since leaving Kosti. Her face was drawn and white. She looked grief-stricken. He said, "This was not your fault. When I looked at the soldiers, I didn't see any of them shooting at the plane. I saw the blast from one of the big buildings on our right, but I couldn't see who was firing. I don't think it was the soldiers. Maybe it was a security guard-who knows."

As he said this, she began to weep uncontrollably, burying her face in her arm against the plane's window. "For the rest of my life, I will be haunted by this day. I will never forgive myself for Jumma," she said.

Hanley said, "I knew what I was getting myself into, but Jumma, Jumma was a mistake. I should have insisted that Jumma stay behind. You were too close to the deal. I should have intervened." He shifted in his seat and his right foot began to go numb. He tried to move his toes, but couldn't tell if they moved or not. "It was bad luck, that's all," he said. "Stupid, never fair, wish it hadn't happened bad luck. Whoever fired that gun could have been in the bathroom when we landed, heard the plane, ran out and started shooting."

He saw her wipe her eyes with her skirt. "I need to take your pulse," she said. Taking his wrist, she felt for his pulse and said,

"It's rapid but stronger than I would have guessed. Shock may be coming on, your eyes look glassy," she told him. "We need to be careful."

"I'm hurting a bit. My foot is going numb again, but the leg still works. Anyway, we must find a place to land and soon."

Following Hanley's instructions, the nun pulled a section map of southern Sudan from a webbed pocket on the side wall, opened and spread it over her lap. He asked her to find Kosit and then Mapuordit, which he had marked on the map. She drew an imaginary line between the two with her finger, reading off the names of the village and mentioning roads her finger crossed. Hanley listened for a name that was familiar to him, but found listening difficult.

"Did you mention Shambe?" the American asked.

"Yes, it is along the line. I know Shambe. It is about an hour from Yirol. I know a merchant there. There is a road that has a long stretch which is straight. It is close to the village. There is a telephone in the village. Hanley, can you make it to Shambe? We need to get you medical attention right away."

"I don't know. I don't … we don't have much choice, do we? It will take about an hour and fifteen minutes to get to Shambe. I can radio ahead to the mission and get them started to meet us there. When I do, there will be much less control of what happens to the children. We will not be near the mission and able to move the children ourselves. You must have considered that."

"Yes, we will face that later. We must get you medical help. We must get to Shambe," she said. As she did, the right engine coughed, a heavier, darker line of smoke now trailed behind the plane. Hanley watched the oil gauge, hoping the rate of loss to be about the same as before the engine stuttered. It wasn't.

31

Feeling as tired as he could ever remember and shivering with chills, Hanley tried to ignore the pain in his back and the numbness in his right leg. Things were getting worse and he knew it wouldn't be long before his ability to manage a landing would be a problem. He couldn't think of what would happen if he lost consciousness. They had been in the air for about one hour and fifteen minutes. Hanley needed to stay focused, but was now struggling with the pain and the weakness that was enveloping him. The desire to sleep was suddenly overwhelming. "Talk to me," he said.

The nun leaned forward to examine his face. "Can you still move your legs?" she asked.

"Yes, but my foot has lost most of its feeling. I'm so tired. I'm very weak."

Aisha made her way to the door of the cockpit and listened as the nun and the American spoke. "Sister, will we be all right? He is hurt, he flies this plane. Will we be all right?" Aisha asked.

"Yes, he is hurt, but we will be landing soon. The people from the mission will come for us, for you and the children. We will be all right," Sister Marie Claire told her, her gaze never leaving Hanley's face as she answered the girl's question.

As they spoke, Hanley's head fell forward as if he had fallen asleep. Grabbing his shirt collar, Sister Marie Claire shook him and yelled, "Stay awake."

Hanley's head came up and he said, "Sorry, I just wanted to close my eyes for a minute, that's all. I can do this, you know."

"I know you can," the nun said.

Aisha looked at the pilot and said, "You can do it."

There was never any doubt, once she realized she was being rescued, once she was taken from the factory by the two women, placed in the van and driven into hiding, once she knew hope had been given to her as a gift wrapped in the bravery and determination of strangers, she was never going back to slavery. When the young man in the bright white shirt took her hand to guide her into the plane, when she saw his smile despite the swirling deafening chaos of the rescue, after seeing him dead on the ground, she understood it was her duty to take his place in the rescue of the other children. How could she not?

Keeping the pilot awake until he could put the plane back on the ground was all she could do. Gathering the children around her, Aisha said, "Listen to me. I want you to say 'You can do it', 'You can do it'. Please say it with me." She repeated the phase several times. A first the children hesitated but as some began, the others soon joined in the chant. It was in Masalit. As its was repeated, the chorus grew louder, guided by Aisha, determined the pilot would hear them above the Beech's engines.

Hanley heard the voices of the children behind him. . He could hear them as if their voices were coming through his headphones, a chorus of children chanting to him. The voices took on a strange quality, like children, but stronger, the voices otherworldly, eerily harmonic, changing to sounds he didn't want to hear, he didn't want to know. He shook his head to clear his mind; he must be hallucinating. "What are they saying?" he asked the nun.

"It's in Masalit," she said. "I think they are saying, 'You can do it'.

Soaked with sweat, gripping the yoke as hard as he could, Hanley sat up straight, the pain in his back as great a pain as he had ever known. The numbness in his foot continued to grow and his legs were slow to move. "Let's see if we can raise someone at the mission," he whispered to Sister Marie Claire. "You'll have to do it for me."

Tuning to the frequency for the mission radio, Hanley and Sister Marie Claire immediately heard the voice of the young priest, Father Laslo. "This is Mapuordit mission calling Beech Aircraft T806D. Hanley, come in, Hanley. This is Father Laslo. Can you hear me? Over."

Following Hanley's instructions, the nun keyed the microphone on the right-side yoke and said, "Father Laslo, this is Sister Marie Claire. We are in an emergency and need help. Did you hear me? Over."

There was a brief pause and then he answered, "Yes, I understand. We received a call at the mission just some moments ago from the diocese in Rumbek. The authorities called the bishop, claiming that a plane like the one being used at our mission had landed at Kosti and departed with several children. That was you, was it not, Sister? Are the children safe?"

"Yes, Father, they are. Soldiers fired on us and Jumma was killed along with others…"

"What? Jumma! What?"

"…Monsieur Martin has been shot also. That is why we are calling. We must land soon, near Shambe. Can you meet us there, on the road between Shambe and Yirol? Over."

"We, uh, yes, uh, most certainly, I will, uh, get the doctors and some supplies and we will leave immediately."

"Father, please listen carefully so you can tell the doctors about Mr Martin. Have you a pencil and paper? Over."

"Yes."

"Monsieur Hanley has a bullet wound that passed through his right side below his liver and exited his back just left of his spine. It has done damage to him internally. He is weakening quickly and his legs and feet are losing feeling. I believe he is hemorrhaging internally and has nerve damage. We must land soon. Do you understand? Over."

"My dear God. Yes, I have it. I will gather everyone and leave immediately. I will pray for you and for the lives and souls still in your care and for those who were once in your care."

The microphone clicked off, leaving only an irritating static in her ears. She looked at Hanley who sat straight in his seat, gripping the yoke to keep himself upright. His face was drawn, his lips stretched tight over his teeth, a bubble of spit growing from the corner of his mouth. "They are on their way," she told him.

"Yes, I heard him. Let's start making preparations. Make certain the children are seated with their backs to the walls and that they stay that way. Have the young woman help you and make her understand how important..." Hanley gasped and went rigid and pain struck him in the lower back and hips. The bubble on his lip turned to pink foam and he groaned with his teeth clenched as if he was trying to lift a piano by himself. After a moment, he blew out breath like a woman in labor would as the pain subsided. "Sorry," he managed to say. "It's important that the children be seated against the wall when the plane touches down. Have them link their arms and grab their clothes. That may help keep them in place. Then come back here so we can go over the landing procedure. You will have to help land this thing if we are to have any chance at all."

Aisha nodded in understanding as the nun explained the procedure Hanley outlined. When she was finished, Sister Marie Claire hugged the girl and kissed her forehead. "You will see your family again soon. This is my promise and God's will," she said to the girl. Aisha's eyes were wide with a single crooked tear line rolling over her dark cheek. She smiled and turned to the children.

Hanley, his eyes reading the instrument panel as best he could, trying to interpret the information he would need to safely hand the plane, said, "You will need to be my legs and feet, I'm afraid. Put your feet on the pedals. Now, as I turn the yoke, you will press the pedal in the direction I'm turning. If I turn left, you press the left pedal very slowly without a great deal of pressure. I will say, 'harder' or 'not so hard', depending upon what I feel is needed. Do you understand?"

"Yes."

"After we touch down, you will need to apply the brakes to help stop the plane. You do this by applying good pressure to the top of the pedal. I mean good pressure. Are we okay with this?"

"I'm so sorry. I didn't want anyone to—"

"Stop it! We need to focus on this or you will never be sorry again, about anything. I can't imagine how foolish this all will have been if we fail to give these children back to their families. Can you help me fly this airplane?"

"*Oui.*"

"Okay. Okay then. Let's check our distance to Shambe." Hanley's breathing was labored, like a severe asthmatic might sound. Both corners of his mouth showed pink foam. His face was drawn and angular, every muscle bunched, a sign of the pain he was experiencing. He was still focused, trying to keep himself and the plane under control.

The nun looked at the map and began calculating the distance. Trying to concentrate, she looked at the distances she marked, applying the airspeed calculations she and Hanley had devised. "I believe we are about twenty minutes from Shambe."

"We have been flying for almost one hour and fifty minutes. That leaves us about seventy miles until we are there," she said.

"Good. We're only at three thousand feet and so getting to the ground won't take long. I will start down slowly, so that when we are there, we will be low enough to search for a spot to land. Can you get me some water? I need some water badly. My mouth is so dry, it hurts to talk."

"Yes, Hanley, I will get you some water," she said.

32

Watching his cattle, the man sat beneath his favorite tree, an old tree, the best shade tree on this side of the village. The morning was quiet, the cattle grazing on what little grass was left, especially after so dry a season. His cattle were thinner this year than most. He wondered when it would rain again. His wife had cried over their poor crops and how desperate their lives had become. He was hungry, but there was nothing to eat and if there was, he would give it to his children.

The heads of the cows started to come up, a sign that something disturbed their grazing. A lion? Standing, he surveyed the plains with his hand shading his eyes. The brow of his dark face was burrowed. Lions were not common, but possible. He knew he could not afford to lose any cattle and might not be capable of scaring a lion off by himself. Then he heard it; an airplane. He had seen them before, miraculous things, carrying men into the air. What it must be like, he could not imagine. Searching the sky, he saw the plane coming toward him from the northeast, just above the horizon. This thing makes much noise; it is too loud; how could anyone stand to be in it for even a little bit of time? All the cows' heads were up now, some were moving about as the sound of the plane drove them away.. It was then the herdsman saw the smoke. Do they have ovens on these things, he wondered. It must be a small oven for the smoke was thin.

***

The plane came in low over the plain, at seven hundred feet, low enough to see the road and anything near it. Hanley was following the road from Shambe southwest toward Yirol, the village now a mile from where they were. Sister Marie Claire was describing the area and the road as they passed over, a herd of cattle moving near the old, rough track they would use as a landing strip.

"This will do," Hanley said.

"Yes, I believe it will too. Anyway, it is all we have," she said.

"I will swing around and land going toward the village to reduce the distance you will need to walk. The girl will have to help you with the door, but you can do it." He coughed and stiffened, his chest against the yoke, which brought the nose of the plane down slightly. Sensing the change, Hanley leaned back and brought the nose of the plane up. His voice was a wheezing whisper. "When the plane touches down, I want you to push the tops of both pedals forward as hard as you can. That will apply the brakes. If I've told you this before, I'm sorry. We will have plenty of room to land, but I want to get the plane stopped and the children off. Sit them in the shade and leave them with the girl. Tell her, if someone approaches, tell her to get the children back on the plane and shut the door and lock it. Show her how before you leave. Do you understand?"

Sister Marie Claire said she understood.

Continuing southwest, Hanley climbed to fifteen hundred feet and swung the nose of the Beech a few degrees to the right and started a semicircle that would bring him around to a northeast heading following the road back to Shambe. When he asked, the nun pushed the left pedal and helped ease the plane through the maneuver. As the plane completed the arc, Hanley set the flaps and reduced his speed, easing the plane down toward the road. He strained to see, focusing as best he could on the picture developing before him, watching the roadway, which appeared as a line of a slightly different shade of beige across the arid ground. As he pushed the controls forward, he said, "Watch my rate of descent on the altimeter here," pointing to the dial on the panel between them. "Count the seconds between the longer marks and tell me if there are less than three seconds between them."

She watched the altimeter needle fall, her lips moving slightly as she counted off the rate of descent. The Beech was losing altitude at a rate of just over one hundred feet every three seconds.

The plane passed over the herdsman and his cattle, all of whom by now were alarmed and heading in the opposite direction of the plane. At five hundred feet, Hanley dropped the landing gear and began pulling the nose of the plane up slightly. The ground seemed to be coming up faster than he expected, causing Hanley to pull back on the yoke. The stall-warning signal came on and Hanley dropped the nose, adding a bit more throttle. The warning went off just as the plane touched down hard on the road. The force of the contact caused the Beech to bounce back into the air and come down hard again. The children began to scream and cry as they bounced along with the plane. After two hard bounces, the Beech settled onto the roadway, running and bouncing toward Shambe. Each bounce caused large waves of pain to run from Hanley's lower back, down his legs where it vanished into the numbness of his feet. Dizziness overtook Hanley where he leaned against the side of the cockpit for support; he would not let go of the controls.

Her prayer was answered, but the language of answered prayers is God's language. The nun had failed to understand God's message. Much had been gained, but much had been lost.

The plane, the tool she had hoped God would send, shook relentlessly, the children screamed and cried as the nun's shoes slide off the pedals. Sister Marie Claire brought them back to the worn metal once more. Pushing as hard as she could, the nun applied the brakes while Hanley kept the plane on the roadway. Thirty seconds after touchdown the plane rolled to a stop. Hanley cut the ignition, silencing the roar and thrum of the big engines and slumped over, his wounded body failing faster now. Struggling out of her seat, the nun slowly pulled him upright. Taking water from a bottle, she splashed his face and patted it while saying, "Hanley, wake up. I'm going to check on the children and go for help." She called out, "Aisha, are the children safe? Aisha?"

Appearing behind the nun, carrying the smallest child in her arms. Aisha told her the children were frightened, but alright. Leaving Hanley, the nun turned and led Aisha and the children from the plane, sitting all of them on the ground beneath the Beech. The morning air was now warm and the shade comfortable.

"I will go to the village for help. You will stay with the children right here. Do not leave or let any of the children leave. If someone comes near you, put the children back on the plane and close the door. Wait here until I return. Do you understand?"

Aisha nodded and the nun immediately turned toward the village and started off at a trot.

***

The girl watched the nun until she was perhaps three hundred yards down the road. She turned, counted the children, told them to stay where they were and entered the plane.

Moving toward the cockpit, she looked at Hanley, who was still unconscious, his head resting against the window frame. His mouth was open, his breathing a shallow wheeze. A thin line of blood ran from his lip and onto his shirt. Turning, she took a blanket from the floor of the cargo hold, placed it over the American, tucking it around his shoulders and arms. Putting her lips to his ear, Aisha whispered in Masalit, "You did it," then turned and went back to the children.

33

Too much sugar; Elizabeth looked at the teaspoon and shook some back into the sugar jar. Putting sugar in tea was frowned upon by her friends or former friends, that is, but she didn't care. She liked hot, sweetened tea, especially on cool fall mornings. From the kitchen window, she could see Weed lying in the sun, where she had chained him next to the garage, the flagstones of the patio freezing beneath her feet as she ran back to the warmth of the kitchen.

Just as she was about to stir her drink, the doorbell rang. I'm not expecting anyone, she thought. Maybe it's Rocky. No, Rocky comes to the back door, taps and then comes in. Laying the spoon next to the cup, she turned and went to the front door. Carrie was sleeping over at her grandmother's, which had allowed Elizabeth to sleep in on this Saturday morning. It was already ten o'clock and she was still in her underwear and a robe.

When she peeked through the side glass, Elizabeth was startled to see a nun standing on her front porch. She was puzzled for perhaps two seconds and then fear seized her and she slumped against the door. What else could it be?

Opening the door, she heard, "I'm Sister Mary Kathleen, a friend of your father and a friend of a nun serving in Sudan with your father. I'm sorry to have come here unannounced but I need to speak with you. May I come in?" Elizabeth tried to say yes, come in but could only manage a nod and waved her inside.

"What's happened to him? Is he dead? Is he?" Elizabeth was close to crying, trying to control her panic as she asked the questions. Standing in the foyer, the morning sun through the side windows warmed Elizabeth's feet.

"Is there somewhere we can sit?" the nun asked. Hanley's daughter pointed to the living room then followed the nun as she walked to a wing-backed chair and sat. Elizabeth sat on a large sofa covered in a floral print fabric. The room was large, bright and airy. Elizabeth noticed the nun looking about the room, approval seemingly on her face.

"My friend is Sister Marie Claire. I believe you may know who she is. She has been working with your father for the past eight months at the clinic in Mapuordit. Yesterday, she and your father attempted the rescue of some children. These children had been taken into slavery in the cities of central and northern Sudan. Some people, a network or underground, committed to freeing the children, took them to a city called Kosit where your father, my friend and a young African man named Jumma flew to meet them and return the children to their families in the South. Soldiers fired on the plane as it sat on the runway. Jumma, the young African was killed. A member of the network and a young girl being rescued were also killed. Your father was wounded and taken to a clinic in Shambe, a small town between Kosit and Yirol. Your father's plane was damaged by the gunfire and he was forced to land on a roadway near there. Sister Marie Claire walked to the town and received aid from people she knew in the town. People from the mission arrived and carried your father and the children to the town and then took the children on to Mapuordit. Sister Marie Claire stayed with you father and the doctors from the clinic."

"Elizabeth, your father's wounds are severe. He was shot through the side and the bullet damaged a kidney and a fragment lodged in his spine, nicking the spinal cord they believe. The doctors believe, but they're not certain. It is infection and the loss of blood that is causing the most problem. He has been flown to Juba and will be evacuated to Nairobi and then to France." As the nun explained what had happened at Kosti, Elizabeth covered her face and wept hard into her hands. She heard little of what the nun said after hearing her father was wounded. Her head swam as she thought of what to do, about Carrie and Rocky and the goddamned dog. Would her mother even care? How could this be happening? Why didn't he stay in America? She wanted Rocky here.

***

Hanging up the phone, Rocky returned to her den to sit across from Elizabeth, still curled up on the sofa, Weed lying beside her. She held a ball of tissue against her mouth; her eyes were red and swollen. She held the dog's ear in her hand, rubbing and stroking it for comfort.

"We are on a flight to New York at 6:10 in the morning. From there we fly to Rome. I know you won't sleep but you must try. Everything is packed and the hotel has a reservation for us near the airport. If we leave now, we can be there by eleven and get some rest before we get up. I have some pills that will help you sleep." Rocky was exhausted, having dealt with the news about Hanley while providing support to Elizabeth and arranging their travel. She was thankful she was able to call on Beverly, Hanley's office manager to help her. She wanted to lie down and sleep but knew it was impossible. The worst had been dealing with Belinda, who was astonishingly uncaring. She did, however agree to keep Carrie while her daughter traveled to Africa. Elizabeth had refused to speak with her mother, leaving it to Rocky.

Having been a doctor's wife gave Rocky an unfortunate ability to guess at the severity of Hanley's condition, if the information the nun had delivered was anywhere near accurate. Who knew? Hanley's survival would depend on how soon he had received medical treatment and how good that treatment was. Rocky knew that southern Sudan would not offer Hanley much hope, or her.

***

The red light on his answering machine was blinking in the dark as Michael Campbell walked past his den on the way to the kitchen. He was thirsty and needed a drink. Sophie had insisted they attend a small party thrown by their neighbors, even though he had resisted. Now, just home, he wanted a Scotch and water before bed. Stopping, he took two steps backward, walked to the phone in the den and punched the button. The voice was that of Sophie's uncle Jean-Robert. The message made the Englishman sit heavily in the arm chair next to the phone. Hanley Martin had been shot during an attempt to rescue some children in a town in Sudan with a name Michael had never heard before now. "What the bloody fuck had he been thinking?" Campbell said aloud. It did not seem like something his friend would do. How did he get pulled into that, he wondered? Maybe it was the French nun; must have been. The message said that Hanley was in bad shape. Sophie's uncle was back in France, near Paris. Jean-Robert said he had received a call from the diocese in Rumbek and called his niece when he had received the news. "Michael, are you in the kitchen?" Sophie called from the stairs. "If you are, will you bring me some water?" she asked.

He did not answer right away, thinking about the news and what he should do. "Michael, did you hear me?" his wife called to him.

"Yes, I heard you," he yelled to her. "Come into the den, will you?"

As she entered the den, Sophie saw her husband slumped in the chair, his right hand cradling his forehead. "Michael, what is it?"

"It's Hanley. He's been caught up in some sort of botched rescue attempt and hurt, badly. Maybe fatally, who knows. The message is from you uncle. Listen to it while I get a drink."

Sophie listened to her uncle's voice, trying to picture what might have happened. Michael came back to the den saying, "There were no real details in the message. The nun, Sister

Marie Claire, must have been involved. Your uncle was right, what he said in his letters. Hanley and the nun had grown close. Remember, he said she was not happy with the church's lack of involvement in the conflict in Sudan. From his description of her, she would be very capable of trying something like a rescue and drawing Hanley into it." He took a long sip from his drink before sitting in another wing back chair in the den. "Do you think I should go to Sudan?" he asked.

"No, I don't want you going there. It is bad enough that Hanley has been hurt; I don't want you hurt too. No, you won't be going to Sudan," she said emphatically. Sophie's voice was tight and her tone irritable. She seemed mad and Michael suspected a bit shocked as well. For years Sophie had expected news of this sort to come to them about her uncle.

"I can be there as fast as anyone, especially if the head of the order helps arrange my transportation from Khartoum to wherever Hanley is being treated. Hanley will need someone with connections outside the church and his family will need someone with resources who can help them with the government if that is an issue. Airbus and the church together with the US government may be capable of getting Hanley out of the country and to decent medical care. Anyway, I will just be a friend coming to help with no affiliation to the church or America. I will call Alexandre Ganier right away and explain the situation. I'll get his opinion and then we'll talk."

"There will be no talk. I don't want you to go. That's all I have to say and it should be enough." She looked at the glass in his hand, rose and left the room. Michael picked up the phone and punched in the number for the president of Airbus. "I can at least get his opinion," he told himself.

34

Waving her blue handkerchief about, Rocky tried to chase away the flies tormenting her. They were after the tears on her face. Damn you, she thought, get away from me. The wooden bench she sat on pinched the back of her legs. Wiping her tears, she stood and straightened her blouse. The evening was cool but not chilly, not in Kenya she thought. Since arriving that morning, she and Elizabeth had remained with Hanley until late afternoon when Elizabeth had given out. The young priest, Father Laslo took Elizabeth out for some food and perhaps some wine.

Sister Marie Claire had met them at the hospital, which was a mistake, Rocky now realized. The nun accompanied Hanley on the flight from Juba to Nairobi. She tried to explain to Rocky and Elizabeth why Hanley was involved and what happened but Elizabeth exploded the instant they were introduced. What little of her mother Elizabeth had in her came roaring out, blasting the nun and the mission, Sudan and anyone else Hanley's daughter could think to include. Father Laslo intervened, allowing one of the doctors to take the nun from harm's way. Sister Marie Claire, who had so desperately wanted to stay with Hanley, left to fly back to Sudan on Father Laslo's orders, accompanied by the same doctor. The priest said the nun would only remain in Sudan a short time.

Hanley was semiconscious. He had been that way since landing his plane almost five days ago. Two doctors from the clinic in Mapuordit found Hanley in the plane thirty minutes after he had landed and ten minutes before the nun and a friend made it back from Shambe. By then, the doctors had Hanley on a canvas stretcher beneath the plane, intravenous bottles and antibiotics already administered. Hanley was taken to a small, ancient clinic in the village where he was placed on a wooden platform with a thin, tick mattress covered in graying linens. There he had lain, his condition worsening. The doctors found the bullet had shattered a lower rib, fragmented into pieces that had cut into his right kidney and nicked his spinal column. The bleeding had stopped and he was stabilized. Despite his condition, the Sudanese government demanded his arrest, then removal from the country, but after the Catholic Church interceded, he was flown to Juba and then Nairobi.

After his daughter had left, Rocky told Hanley that the children had all been taken to Mapuordit. A search of Jumma's room had yielded his notebooks, one of which contained contact information with the families of the rescued. The mission would attempt to reunite them, Father Laslo had told her. She hoped Hanley had heard her.

Spots covered the front of her linen skirt, the stains left by the tears she had wept for Hanley. Not one for prayer, Rocky had been pleading with God since Elizabeth had called her on Saturday. No one had listened, certainly not a caring God, she thought. She feared he would die in a corner of the world that time and other men chose to ignore.

***

Wherever he was smelled sickly sweet, like rotting flowers in a vase. He tried to speak, to call out for Elizabeth but could not.

He saw milky light and vague shapes, then things went back to complete darkness, and this went on back and forth for some time and then there was only light and shapes. The light he saw was weak but steady. Steady was good. The darkness was gone, at least for a while.

He thought of the streetlight at the entrance to his uncle's farm, obscured by the morning mist which brought a dampness to his skin. He wished to feel it again, the mist, chilling, raising his flesh wherever it touched, but he couldn't. At least for now he had this steady light. There was something else he felt, something new.

It was odd, this new feeling; this lightness, strange after having lost the feeling in his feet and legs.

***

Pushing through the door, Rocky made her way to the corner bed. Sick and dying people lay scattered about. A woman cried, softly pleading for help to no one and everyone. Hanley looked bad, only the slight movement of the sheet covering his chest telling her he was still alive. Taking up his hand, she noticed how dry and stiff his fingers were. There was as much to hate about life as to love she thought. She sat by the bed to wait. For what?

Rocky began to cry. How had it all come to this, how could he have thrown his life away so carelessly? She was alone on a bench far from the new start with Hanley she had hoped for. Her exhaustion pushed her down, hunched her over. Now a sudden constricting pressure in her chest made her afraid to breathe. It must be the stress she told herself, a dusting of fear covering her heart. The pressure eased; the crying helped.

The wall behind her was rough and hard but warm. She slumped over, too tired not to. Her head hung over her knees, her hands on rough, dry wood, arms locked in support, tears wetting the closely woven linen stretched over her legs. The bench trembled beneath her as she wept and prayed prayers full of anger even while pleading for mercy. Doubting the effect, she rose and left the room.

Evening had darkened the hallway. The hospital and everything in it smelled of death. As she walked the halls, she remembered her grandmother at night on her knees beside her bed, praying for a consideration or a gift or guidance. Rocky could not remember any proof of those prayers being answered. The wind blew through the open windows of the hallway, carrying her prayers away, pushing them to where they would never be heard. Her eyes burned, her nose ran. She felt sorry for herself and then ashamed.

Rocky returned to the room and the corner bed. Straightening the covers with some care, she pulled the sheet to Hanley's unshaven chin. The coarse weave of the cloth against his face did not make him stir; the coarse weave or the smell. The old bed linen had the sweet stink of something washed in sulfur water. These rough touches did not rouse him.

They said he would live but not walk again. He would remain in Kenya for weeks before he could be moved, first to Europe, probably France and then to America. Rocky hoped Hanley's dog Weed lived long enough to see Hanley again. It would be good for both of them.

35

Thin brown dust swirled around his feet and across the hard-packed dirt parking lot onto the gravel road. A small boy of five years sat on an overturned bucket staring at the new running shoes on his feet. They felt good to him. His new shoes and new clothes were clean and smelled good. His hunger was gone, but he was still scared; he was always scared. Locked in his arms was an old stuffed toy, a bear, its fur now matted and discolored in spots, one plastic eye cracked, a left ear soaked from the boys constant biting and sucking. The noise of the plane that had carried him to safety was still in his ears. He could not quit listening.

Standing beside him was Sister Marie Claire, dressed in a dull blue uniform, her head covered in a white kerchief. At the back of the parking lot, a man in a truck watched the nun and the boy from behind the steering wheel. He brought them to this spot near Rumbek.

The nun talked low and steadily to the boy as he sat in the cool of this late autumn morning. Her words were in French; he could not understand her. The nun and the boy were shaded from the sun by the building next to which they waited. He shivered at times, but was not uncomfortable.

***

As the nun watched the small boy, she heard the sound of an approaching vehicle. Looking up, she turned around, but could not see, the old building blocking her view. Sister Marie Claire turned toward the boy and said, "I know you cannot understand me, but the surprise I have been telling you about is here. I think you will be very happy and I hope and pray that God continues to bless you. You have been brave and now your prayers have been answered. Please remember the people that helped you for they gave much for this moment to happen. Two of these people were people I love. I hope that, in some way, God will help you to know this."

A car, an old gray Peugeot with a red front fender, rolled to a stop at the edge of the parking lot, the dust swirling about so thickly that the boy could not see it for a moment. The boy turned at the sound of the car door opening. A woman's sandaled foot touched the ground. The woman stood by the car and said his name. The nun watched his face, saw his face contort and the tears begin to flow. He uttered something, the word indiscernible, the bear clutched to his chest, an arm outstretched, he ran from the bucket and into her arms. The nun began to weep. The woman held the boy tightly to her chest and whispered something in his ear. The nun heard him saying one word over and over. Her head fell to her chest, tears trailing down her thin face. Sitting behind the wheel of the Peugeot was the young priest from the mission. The nun looked up to see the smile on his face.

With his face buried in her shoulder, the small boy clung to his mother as she carried him to the car, his arms wrapped around her neck. The bear hung by its paw from the boy's hand. The nun hoped his fears were over and he was no longer afraid.

***

The building housing the Catholic diocese in Rumbek was built with a dark wood, somber in the afternoon's overcast light. It sat along a narrow-paved road, the asphalt bordered by two broad bands of fine, light dirt, while other buildings, painted white and beige, bravely faced its dark authority Michael Campbell met the bishop on the front steps. "Thank you for seeing me this morning," he said, a hand extended to be shaken by the prelate.

The corridor leading to the bishop's office was as dark as the outside, a long narrow hall, clad in a wood Michael did not recognize, stained almost black, light from the open, screened main door reflected on raised parts of the panel's grain, shiny ragged ribbons along the walls. The office, also dark, with a small wooden desk, scarlet curtains and carpeting the only hint of the church in his office.

"Mr Campbell, how is your friend, Mr Martin?" the bishop asked.

"He's doing all right, considering. He is paralyzed from the waist down. But, other than that, the doctors expect him to recover. Thank you for asking."

"You know, I admire what he and the good Sister Marie Claire did. I am completely saddened, however, that a fine young man lost his life in the process. Your friend and the nun have to bear that responsibility forever, I am afraid. We can offer them our forgiveness, but it is not our forgiveness that is important, but that of God," the bishop said. Michael noted a weariness in the bishop's voice. Pouring some tea into a cup on his desk, the cleric asked, "Would you like some?"

"No, thank you. Father, I need your help. Hanley's plane still sits near Shambe. I spent two days there, repairing some damaged oil lines and straightening some cooling fins around cylinders. I also moved it off the road. Some residents of Shambe have been watching it, keeping it from being vandalized. I want to fly it from Sudan to Morocco. I will make a stop in Niger and Algeria. Maybe two in Algeria. I want to leave tomorrow. I do not want any problems. Can you and the church help me?" Michael asked. The bishop busied himself with adding sugar and some milk to his tea.

"You do not need our help. If you have enough fuel to cross the border into Chad or the CAR, then I would say you should leave whenever you want. I'm told the government is not interested in the plane, not yet, at least. I would leave here and take the plane as soon as I could, if I were you. Good luck, Mr Campbell. And I hope God blesses your friend," the Bishop said.

***

A half-dozen boys and men stood beneath the tree, near the road leading to Shambe. Some shaded their eyes while others, mostly the boys, covered their ears, keeping out the noise of the Beech's engine, their dark faces gathered, bunched around their noses, expressions ranging from fear to fascination. Michael Campbell occasionally glanced their way, but watched the cattle more carefully, looking for any movement toward the roadway. A member of the Mapuordit mission staff asked the oldest of the men to move the cattle further away from the road, but the cattle remained where they were when Michael and the others arrived.

Earlier, on the way to Shambe with a doctor and two of the men who worked around the mission, Michael explained he was to fly the plane to France, to an airport near his home in Saint-Nazaire. There, it would stay and undergo further repairs and maintenance before being flown back to America, a difficult flight. The flight to France would not be easy, but he hoped to be there before the week's end. He would file a flight plan for Morocco from an airport in Chad. He could not chance a flight plan before leaving Sudan.

A call from the mission to a friend in England, the owner of a Beech 18, helped Michael with the start-up procedures. Hanley was in no shape to talk about the Beech. Michael watched Hanley do it before, once in Indiana and when Hanley left France for Sudan. The procedures went well and he was about to lift off. With any luck, he would be home for dinner in three days.

36

October 30, 2001

Dear Hanley,

This letter must be brief for I have many things to do and they must be completed soon.

I hear you have been moved to a private room from the intensive care area. That is the best news I have had since we landed in Shambe. I hope and pray for your recovery every day. I believe God brought you here and your purpose was to give hope back to the children. The prayers I say are for the children also.

The church has decided to work to reunite the children with their families. What else can they do, no? The kidnappings were illegal and the church will help, this I have been told. I stay with the children every day, helping them wait, using Jumma's journal to identify their families. You would be proud of how Jumma did this. The information he gathered about the families and the children was written as questions each child could be asked, the answer the information that would identify the child as belonging to that family. Even the youngest, who might not remember, could be helped this way. Jumma was so very bright. I am proud of him. His life was important and continues to be so.

I am leaving Sudan tomorrow, flying to Cairo from Juba and then to Paris. The church has instructed me to take a leave of absence, a month, to consider my future, but that requires no thought. I know what I will do. I will not be returning to Sudan, at least not as part of the church.

I spoke with Michael Campbell yesterday before he left for Shambe. He is taking your plane to Morocco and then to Saint-Nazaire, saying the entire trip would take less than seven days. He said the plane would be returned to America. I think that is wonderful. He is a good friend, one who cares for you, cares deeply.

I will write to you when I am back in France at my mother's home. I wanted to return to Kenya to see you, but could not. I hope you understand. Give your daughter and Ms. Vincenti my warmest wishes.

Adieu,
Sister Marie Claire

***

Elizabeth folded the letter, placed it on the bedside table, handling it as if it were a soiled diaper. "That takes nerve, I'll say that. I thought about tossing the damned thing in the trash, but Rocky said you should read it, or hear it. Same thing. I'm glad they're sending her back to Europe. She should never have left there. They could have sent her ass to Iran or somewhere like that," she said, looking out the window. Hanley did not respond, was not listening. The letter depressed him. Certainly, he was glad the children were safe and maybe would be reunited with their families, but the mere mention of Jumma's name brought on more guilt. Hanley was suffering from enough already.

Rocky was back at the hotel. Hanley was glad. Much of his guilt was for what he believed he had done to Elizabeth and Rocky. Jumma was simply more. The irony was in the fact that his search for clarity, to find the answer, did he owe a debt for his good fortune, had not produced an answer, only the knowledge he no longer owed anyone anything other than an apology. The knowledge was an empty one.

***

December 2, 2001

   Dear Hanley,

   Today I spoke with Sophie and Michael Campbell. I was surprised to hear you were flown to Rome and then America without a stop. My information was not good information, I fear. I was hoping for a chance to see you before you went on to Indiana. They were kind enough to invite me to visit them in Saint-Nazaire. Next week, I will drive to see them. My new apartment near Limoges is not that far. I will see the plane. Michael said the damage has been repaired. He hopes to return it to you in the spring.

   After I returned to France, I was here a week, I was summoned to Paris to the office of Father Bertrand's successor, Father Ranson, a truly colorless man. Father Bertrand is quite ill and will not return to serve the church. Father Ranson was polite, but blunt. My actions, he said, placed the church is a precarious place. My decisions were flawed. I was responsible for placing many people in danger and hurting you. He did not mention Jumma. I do not know why, but I am glad he did not. He told me I would be assigned to a parish near Dijon. But I will not go. I have other plans. Tomorrow, I meet with the diocese to arrange my retirement, such as it will be. Dijon will be like being put in a drawer, out of the way, a convenience. That will not be. I am afraid I have become a difficult person, perhaps more than I was before. I am certain Father Robineau would not agree.

   My mind is certain of this. I have spoken with a group that works to bring aid to those in need in Africa. I hope to join them and return to Sudan to carry on the work, unencumbered by the constraints of the church. We will see.

   I try not to think of Jumma. That is cowardly, I know, but when I do, I cry. I would cry all day if I did not keep him out of my head. It is hard. I want to remember him. He was the hope of his country, he and the other young men and women. There is such a waste of hope in Sudan and I was part of that process, at least for Jumma.

   When Jumma came to the mission, he followed the doctors and nurses, all day, every day. Jumma ignored his fear and sadness, his loneliness, missing his family, he set all of that aside to watch and learn. The doctors did not understand and scolded him at times. Jumma never stopped, was not discouraged by the doctors' rudeness. He never stopped learning, never stopped wanting to help. It was why I allowed him to be part of the plan to rescue the children. He so wanted to and I so wanted him to. I knew it would make him feel he was helping. Jumma was grateful for the care he received at Mapuordit. He wanted to return the gift of care and hope. Just like you. That was what you sought in coming to Africa, to Sudan. You wanted to know how to give back what you had received, for a lifetime of good fortune. But you already knew. When you stepped into your plane to fly to Sudan, you knew. The flight was simply the beginning, the down payment. The debt you owed was one of your own making. We all do this, we all wonder why we were chosen for good fortune while others suffer. But until the end, until our lives are complete, we will never know if we were fortunate or unfortunate. I think it is always a matter of balance, in the end. If our lives are good and we have helped others, given to those in need, then we have been fortunate. In a way, Jumma was fortunate. The children he saved are a testament to that. He was given a chance to sacrifice for the lives of others and he succeeded. His story will be remembered.

I will write again soon. I hope your recovery goes well.

Adieu,

Sister Marie Claire

***

Rain fell in a drumroll pattern on the roof of Michael Campbell's Mercedes, sitting outside the white metal hanger at the Saint-Nazaire/Montoir Airport. The wide door at the front of the building was open. Inside, Claire could see the Beech sitting in the darkened space, the gleam of the dull light of the rain-blurred sky a gray glow hovering above the cement floor.

"I have an umbrella, Sister, would you like to go in?" Michael asked, looking between the space between the front seat, making certain of his promise.

"It is no longer Sister Marie Claire. It is only Claire," she said, looking at the plane, feeling as if she had just discovered a memento in a drawer, once owned by someone whose friendship she lost. "Yes, I would like to see the plane, perhaps look inside, if that is permitted."

"Certainly. Let me come around before you get out."

Inside the hangar, the Beech looked bigger than she remembered. It was polished, brilliant even in the gloom. Standing before it, she raised her hand, to touch its nose, her long fingers just brushing the surface. A small sob broke, barely noticeable. Michael Campbell turned at the sound, but said nothing. Bringing her hand down to her chest, she clenched it into a fist, her head bowed. Swaying, her eyes closed, a tear rolled down her cheek. Lifting her head, she turned to her left, walking around the plane, looking, but not touching. As she came to the rear cargo door, she said, "May I look inside?" Michael strode to the door, turned the handle and lowered it, then extended his hand. Claire took his hand, stepped up and in. The interior was almost too dark to see, the general shape apparent, a slight shine from the wood flooring, the cargo net, spider-webbed across a window. The images of the children came to her, their backs against the wall, their arms linked, so small and frightened. There was something else, not an image, but more a feeling, perhaps an aura of sorts. They were resolute, especially when they chanted their belief in Hanley, that he could do it, he could rescue them. That memory, the idea it brought, undid her and she wept, both hands covering her face. This plane would haunt her the rest of her life. She knew this and welcomed it.

37

April 3, 2002

Dear Hanley,

It is late afternoon. I am in my apartment with the sunlight from the window covering the table where I sit, warming my hands as I write. I did not attend mass again this day. My mother will be unhappy. That I cannot help. There is a bitterness in me I am trying to push out, but I have not done that yet. I know what we did was the right thing to do. My regrets are many, considering. But the children were returned and that matters most.

From my window, I can see a park, a small park, with some mature trees and a fountain, the water from the fountain's spray turning blue and red in the sunlight, maybe green as well.
There are children there, small children with the mothers and grandparents. They seem happy, are safe, I think. I think about Sudan, dream about Sudan, always. I believe children are the reason we stay civilized. The park is pleasant. Watching it helps.

I may be leaving for Africa in June. The organization is still considering my request. I fear the events in Kosti are a problem. This has not been said to me, but I think they are hesitating. I have spoken to Sister Mary Kathleen. She has contacts who tell her the organization has received pressure from the Sudanese government to keep me out of the country.

Michael Campbell tells me the Beech has been returned to

Kokomo. I was surprised to hear that Sophie flew with him. He said the trip took nine days, that the weather was good, the trip a pleasant one. Michael also said you are doing well, your health is good, but you are not involving yourself in your rehabilitation. This worries me. It worries everyone, he said. Your daughter asked him to intervene. He said he tried, but did not believe it was effective. I know this will not mean much, but please help yourself. You did so much to help others, do the same for yourself.

Not hearing from you worries me. I hope you are receiving these letters and reading them. Mary Kathleen said she has not spoken with you since the Christmas holiday. I will keep writing. I want to speak with you someday, maybe visit you in America. I want to see you again.

I will continue to write. Please be well.
Adieu,
Claire

***

The room was darkening as the sun sank below the tree line, settling into the cradle formed by the tree tops and the roof of his garage. Keeping the house dark suited him now. Weed, already asleep on the couch, snored and shook, dreamt of whatever old dogs dream. Rocky had just left, the cup of coffee she'd set before him still steaming, the too large white cup used so he would not struggle trying to get himself another, the cup dwarfing the small glass of neat whiskey, another chore done to prevent him any unnecessary movement. She left, after dinner, after cleaning up, after preparing him for the evening, the coffee, the whiskey, the remote, the dog walked, the kiss on the forehead. He thought he might be losing her, that she might already be gone. He couldn't blame her if she was. She just hadn't physically left him yet. That would come, he thought.

Elizabeth had finally moved out, not without a fight. Her new home, two miles away, on the edge of a beautiful old neighborhood, was within walking distance of a good elementary school. It was a smaller house than his, with a large back yard, big enough for an ever-scrambling four-year old and a large garden. Rocky helped Elizabeth lay out the plans, a plan similar to Rocky's own.

It took him two months of constant arguing and insistence to wear Elizabeth down. It was the best decision for everyone. Hanley could not stand the idea of Elizabeth spending her life caring for him. The ground floor of his house was now his world. A former sitting room was now his bedroom, the bed low enough to allow him to roll from the chair to the bed. Two curved bars, inverted U's, were bolted to the floor, allowing Hanley to pull himself up and into his chair. He hated all of it, every bit of it.

He would never get used to it, the confinement, the struggle. It took him no time to realize that ninety-nine percent of the people in wheelchairs were significantly tougher than he was. His days were now spent scheming his own demise and getting up the nerve to do it. It might happen. He wanted it to be as painless and mess-free as possible. If he did it, he would use pills and booze.

He didn't regret Sudan. Focusing on the children was key, it made it all somewhat acceptable. Then there was Jumma. Nothing would ever help with that. He would never forget seeing the young African, face down in the dirt of the runway. He tried to forget Jumma, tried hard. Jumma would always be there and he did not want to live with that. Then there was the nun. But she was no longer a nun. She was again Claire Audebourg.

She sent four letters, he read only one, the first. After the third, he called Sister Mary Kathleen and implored her to intervene. The last letter came before she could stop it. It was still on the coffee table in the den, unopened. He couldn't read it; wouldn't.

He felt his hand nuzzled, the old dog demanding, in his insistent tired way, a late-night walk. Hanley wanted to walk too. There would be no more walks. Not anymore. But he no longer owed anyone anything, no more indebtedness. He owed himself one last thing.

***

The morning sunlight flickered in his eyes, strobed by the tree branches lining the road to the Russiaville Airport, still bare in the early spring, buds now appearing. Hanley raised his hand to shade his face from the blinding flash, trying to avoid a headache. Sitting in the front seat of Rocky's Lexus, his legs were tied together with strips of cloth, wrangled to make it easier getting him in and out. As the car bumped along, Hanley heard the rattle and clang of his wheelchair in the trunk, an ultra-lightweight model, something that Rocky or Elizabeth could handle. That he needed a device light enough for a woman to carry angered him to the core of his handicapped being. Once in it, he felt like it would collapse any moment. It was a good thing he lost weight, he thought. Being impaled on an errant part of a toppled wheelchair was not how he envisioned ending his life.

"I spoke with T.S. last night. He will have the plane out of the hanger and the rear door of the Beech open when we get there. I told him not to tell anyone we were coming, that you didn't want others around, but, you know T.S., so if people are there, try to be nice. They all think you're a hero," Rocky said.

Hanley said nothing. He didn't talk much anymore, some days more than others, some less. He was getting a headache. There seemed no avoiding it. Beyond the trees lining the road, the fields were a mixture of dull brown cornfields, strewn with the detritus of the last harvest, shards of corn stalks and tattered leaves covered the ground in shades of yellows and gold, and bright green, the weeds and grasses, vying for space and life. He saw nothing that interested him.

There was some excitement to this trip, a feeling he tried to suppress; he wasn't up for enthusiasm, didn't trust it, knew it wouldn't last. No matter how he felt about seeing the Beech, he couldn't climb in and fly off to somewhere else. All he had to do was look down at the wheelchair and he was slammed right back to earth, to his shriveling legs, his constant shoulder pain, his frustration and embarrassment. Back to the shitty life he made for himself.

The arrival of the plane in mid-March was a bitter experience for him. Greeting the Campbells from a wheelchair, seeing the look on their faces, concern and discomfort, the bottomless cup of pity he sipped from each minute they spent together. When he did speak, he apologized, hating the necessity. Even though the Campbells said they loved the trip, the time spent together, the adventure, as Sophie called it, he still felt they were the victims of his whim, unwilling players in the story of his stupidity, his tale of startling self-absorption.

Nearing the airport, Rocky said to him, "I thought we'd go to lunch after we see the plane. There is a new cafe in town. Good, I hear. Not just for the quiche-eaters. What do you think?"

"I don't know. Let's see how it goes," he said. "Listen, you don't need to do this, chauffeur me around. You have other things to do, I know that. It's not that I don't appreciate what you do, I do, but we both know this is not changing. I won't get better, I'll probably only get worse. It was me, my need, and you shouldn't be punished for it. It was my stupidity, my mistake, my problem." While saying this, Hanley stared at his dead legs, couldn't bring himself to look at Rocky, afraid of her face and the expression on it. Nothing was said for a few moments, Hanley relieved there was no response, silence from others his preferred interaction.

"I suppose you're right," she said.

Seeing the airport tripped open his trapped emotions. With short breaths, he tried controlling his racing heart. A growing pressure behind his eyes brought tears. This could be the last time I'll come here, he thought, no matter what happens. Turning to the window, he tried to mask the emotion, scratching an ear and then wiping his eyes at the same time, not fooling her, he knew. Turning in the main gate, Rocky followed an access road leading to the private hangers. Hanley's was at the end, the largest in the row, well-maintained, white metal siding, trimmed in a teal green, the roof a shallow pitch, enough to hold the snows of northern Indiana.

"I'll be the one that decides if I stay with you, not you," she said, turning in her seat. "You made the decision to fly to Africa, ignored me and your family. Well, it's my turn. When I'm ready to leave, trust me, you'll be the first to know."

"All right," he said.

He saw the Beech the moment the Lexus made the turn north onto the road fronting the hangers. It shone brightly in the sunshine, polished, perfect. T.S made certain of that, he knew. Rocky slowed the car, giving him more time to look at it, he thought. She's forcing me to look at it, in case I ask her to turn around and leave. Hangars faced the road from each side, some of the doors were open, the snouts of planes facing the air, metal dogs in their metal dog houses, chained to the ground, wanting out, wanting to run through the air, chasing time, engines barking at the sun, the moon at night if they could find it, but not with him, not again.

T.S. was there and no one else. He was sitting on a folding camp chair, the normal dark green color, a cup of coffee on the ground beside him, steaming into the morning air, disappearing before it reached his elbow jutting out over the cement. A magazine lay open in his lap, part of it hanging over his leg, something red, a block, perhaps with an ad printed across it visible to Hanley as they neared the hanger. T.S. looked up when he heard the car approach, a smile spread across his face as he struggled, wiggling, face turning red, from the chair.

"He's alone," she said.

"Yeah, good," Hanley said, shifting his dead legs to the right, feeling like he was pushing thin sacks of sand tied in an unwieldy bundle. Moving his legs this way was and would forever be odd, thinking of his useless legs as something apart from himself, getting them out of the way, as he would a box in the trunk of his car, blocking access to something he really wanted. He thought about having them amputated, but put that thought aside. He would carry them around, dead weight. Dead weight. It was all dead weight. He was dead weight.

Rocky's window dropped and T.S., leaning in to speak,

said, "Hey, thought you'd like the plane out in the sunshine. It's chilly in the hanger anyway. Planes, like dogs, should be outside, don't you think?"

"Funny you should say that," Hanley said. He was surprised at how good seeing his friend made him feel at that moment. Feeling good was rare anymore. Maybe it was the lack of expectation between them, old friends who passed beyond that, well beyond that a long time ago. Criticism was taken for exactly what it was, nothing more, a laugh was appreciated for what it was, nothing more. Trust was genuine, respect expected, love, whatever it was between friends was there, given, received, delivered free of charge, taken without guilt. He hoped he had given it back to T.S., enough to have made a difference. He's such a good friend, it wouldn't matter to him, Hanley thought.

"Why, what's funny about that? How much have you had to drink this morning? Rocky, it's a shame you still resort to liquor to get him under control. A woman as beautiful as you should just have to wiggle something. I know it would work on me," T.S. said, smiling.

"Charming, as always," Rocky said, showing a bit of a smile.

Hanley said to T.S., "I hadn't thought about a drink today until this very moment. Just seeing you makes me want to down a few. Jack Daniels would pay you a fortune if they only knew the effect you have on people. Come around here and help me out."

"Rocky, I promise I'll only drop him twice; once getting him out and then getting him in. It will almost be as good as doing it yourself, but you won't have to endure all the bitching on the way home," T.S. said, then laughed, a high bray that made Rocky laugh too.

Getting out and into the chair was not difficult. Hanley and Rocky practiced it so much that he only needed someone to bring him the chair. T.S. hovered until Hanley suggested he not, then held the chair while Hanley lifted his legs out and onto the ground, grabbed the right armrest of the chair, the top of the door jamb and lifted himself into the chair, grunting noticeably as he did.

"You sound like a female tennis player," T.S. said.

"Fuck you," Hanley responded as he strapped himself into the chair.

"Like you never left."

Fingering the end of the strip of cloth which held his legs together, Hanley thought of untying them, then didn't, thinking they would be more manageable, as if they were a bundle of sticks. Rocky closed the car door as Hanley wheeled himself away toward the Beech. He rolled only a few feet and stopped, looking up at the plane, searching for the two bullet holes in the engine cowling. He asked Michael Campbell to leave them, the scars, earned, reminders that the plane played a role, maybe even the greatest role, in what had been done for the children. As he rolled forward, Rocky and T.S. stayed by the car, Hanley turned slightly to see them staying behind, thinking perhaps they did not want to violate the space forming around he and the plane. The aluminum skin was again polished to a brilliance, the mirror skin turning everything around it into distorted reflections, dumb interpretations of those that looked at it and all that didn't. Hanley thought it was beautiful and realized how proud he was of the plane and what it had done. He wasn't proud of what he did, knowing his search for an answer came at a cost too dear to so many others. The rescued children did not make up for the people he loved or for Jumma, but they helped.

Rolling beneath the nose of the Beech, Hanley reached up, touched the cowling, felt the rough edge of the hole made by the same gun that killed Jumma, the gun that left his own legs dangling useless beneath him. Placing his hand over the hole, he felt connected to the plane, connected in a way he wasn't certain he understood, but knew he felt. "We did make it back, didn't we?" he asked the Beech.

Wheeling around, he pushed himself past the big engine, his left hand sliding over the propeller blade, feeling the cool smoothness across his palm, then around the wing and to the rear, where the cargo door stood open. Rolling up beside the steps leading up to the darkness inside, Hanley felt for an instant he could stand and enter the plane, but only for a second. In the presence of the plane, he seemed to gain strength.

His aching heart longed to fly this plane again. Wondering if any other plane but this one would have saved the children, the nun and himself, Hanley wheeled the chair forward and placed his hand on its cold, shining skin. He stared into the interior's darkness and thought of the children. He thought that, perhaps, now, the return of the children to their families was payment enough.

THE END